Shoulder Bags and Shootings

Books by Dorothy Howell

HANDBAGS AND HOMICIDE

PURSES AND POISON

SHOULDER BAGS AND SHOOTINGS

Published by Kensington Publishing Corporation

Shoulder Bags
and
Shootings

DOROTHY HOWELL

KENSINGTON BOOKS
http://www.kensingtonbooks.com

KENSINGTON BOOKS are published by

Kensington Publishing Corp.
119 West 40th Street
New York, NY 10018

All Kensington titles, imprints, and distributed lines are available at special quantity discounts for bulk purchases for sales promotion, premiums, fund-raising, educational, or institutional use.

Special book excerpts or customized printings can also be created to fit specific needs. For details, write or phone the office of the Kensington Special Sales Manager: Attn. Special Sales Department. Kensington Publishing Corp., 119 West 40th Street, New York, NY 10018. Phone: 1-800-221-2647.

Library of Congress Card Catalogue Number: 2010923998

Kensington and the K logo Reg. U.S. Pat. & TM Off.

ISBN-13: 978-0-7582-2378-4
ISBN-10: 0-7582-2378-1

First Hardcover Printing: July 2010

10 9 8 7 6 5 4 3 2 1

Printed in the United States of America

With love to David, Stacy, Seth, Judy and Brian

Acknowledgments

The author is eternally grateful for the support and assistance of many people. Some of them are: David Howell, Stacy Howell, Judith Howell, Seth Branstetter, Brian Branstetter, Martha Cooper, Debbie Caldwell, Candace Craven, Diana Killian, Elaine Fogel Schneider, Ph.D., Bonnie Stone, Tanya Stowe, and William F. Wu, Ph.D. Many thanks to Evan Marshall of the Evan Marshall Agency, and to John Scognamiglio and the hardworking team at Kensington Publishing for all their efforts and support.

CHAPTER 1

Good thing I had on a seatbelt. Otherwise, I might have launched myself out of my seat—not good, cruising at thirty thousand feet.

I was on an airplane and I'd just spotted the new Sinful handbag in *Elle* magazine. Oh my God, it was fabulous. And believe me, I know a fabulous purse when I see one.

I perked up in my seat, beyond excited, way past thrilled, bordering on crazed, and desperate to share my discovery with someone. The cabin was dark—first class passengers are so boring—and I was the only one still awake.

I hate it when that happens.

Where was my best friend, Marcie Hanover, when I needed her?

I'd call her as soon as we landed in Los Angeles. Yeah, okay, it would be after midnight by then, but she'd want to know.

Months ago Marcie and I acknowledged our true feelings about purses. We'd moved beyond being simply compulsive, obsessive, crazed designer bag lovers to being full-fledged handbag whores. Then, we'd taken it to the next level by starting our own purse party business.

My life had taken a lot of turns in the past six months. Right now I was pretty much penniless and a sort-of college student with a crappy part-time job. Not exactly the dream life for someone who's twenty-four years old.

But I, Haley Randolph, with my dark hair worthy of a salon-shampoo print-ad in *Vogue,* my long pageant legs, and my beauty-queen genes—even though they're mostly recessive—had scored a trip to Europe, thanks to Ty Cameron. Ty was officially my boyfriend now because, after several months of sort-of dating, we'd finally slept together.

Ty was way hot, totally gorgeous. He was the fifth generation of his family to run the Holt's Department Store chain, the fifth generation of his family to be consumed beyond all reason with business. Ty had also just opened Wallace, Inc., an upscale clothing store, and was now in negotiations for the new Holt's International.

He'd made all sorts of promises if I'd agree to come to Europe with him. Most of those promises had been kept— but not by Ty.

"Are we there yet?" Ada asked.

Ada Cameron, Ty's grandmother, was seated next to me. We were making the trip home from London together. She was in her seventies with gray hair. She dressed magnificently and acted really young. Ada was a hoot. I loved her.

Yeah, okay, I'd once mistaken her for a caterer and another time I'd suspected her of murder, but that was all behind us now. She was my new BFF.

I glanced at what I call the "plane channel" featured on the video screen in front of me. The tiny airplane that tracked the progress of our flight—it felt like we'd circled both poles by way of Siberia—was superimposed over Idaho. Or maybe it was Iowa. I don't know. My geography class wasn't until next semester.

"A few more hours," I said. "Want to see an awesome purse?"

"You bet," Ada said, and leaned toward me.

I showed her the Sinful bag in *Elle* and her eyes widened. "Gorgeous," she said.

How could you not like a grandmother who loved designer handbags?

"Do you know what I think would make this flight go quicker?" Ada posed. "A good wine."

"I don't think they have good wine on airplanes," I told her. "Just the cheap stuff."

"Even better," Ada declared, and rang for the attendant.

Ada was right. The wine helped. Long before we'd finished talking about clothes, handbags, shoes, and all the places we'd shopped in Europe, the plane landed at LAX. We were herded through customs by TSA agents—being a direct descendant of exiled Gestapo officers was a requirement for the job, apparently—and finally left the terminal. We'd FedEx'd everything we'd bought in Europe so, luckily, we only had a carry-on each.

"Need a ride home?" Ada asked as we stood on the curb.

Even at this late hour, airport traffic was heavy. Cars, busses, and shuttles drove the loop, picking up and letting off passengers, fouling the cool March air with exhaust fumes and noise.

I'd ridden to the airport with Ty so I didn't have my car here. Since it was so late, I didn't want to call Marcie to pick me up, even though I knew she wouldn't mind—that's just what best friends do.

"I'll rent a car," I said.

"Nonsense," Ada declared. "I'll take you."

The Cameron family was wealthy—way wealthy—so I expected a chauffeur driven Bentley to pull up to the curb and whisk us away. Instead, Ada led the way to one of the park-and-ride shuttle stops and we took a van to their off-site facility on Century Boulevard. The attendant brought us Ada's Mercedes, which lifted my spirits considerably.

Ada seemed to be dragging, though. I offered again to rent a car so she could go straight home.

"My place is almost an hour past your house," I said. "If you drop me off, you'll be really late getting to bed."

Ada thought about it for a moment. "Well, maybe you're right. Tell you what, you drop me off and take my car home with you. I'll pick it up from you in the morning."

"I'll just bring it back to you," I said.

Ada shook her head. "I have to pick up some clothing that didn't sell from the store that's near you. A donation to the women's shelter. I'll do that in the morning."

I drove the Mercedes—which was way cool—to Ada's house in Bel Air—which was also way cool—and helped get her things inside.

"See you around eleven," Ada called as I drove away.

I figured I'd still be sleeping at eleven in the morning, but I came wide awake at eight o'clock. Guess it was the time change.

I'd been gone for about two weeks. I was glad to be home, back in my own apartment again. I loved my apartment. It was in a great upscale complex in Santa Clarita, more or less a half hour from L.A.—depending on traffic—and I'd fixed it up just the way I wanted it, thanks to a really awesome run of luck with credit cards.

There were probably a thousand things I should do first thing this morning, I thought, as I scrounged through my cabinets for something to eat—such as call my mom. But no way was I doing that. Not yet, anyway.

I'd never really gotten around to telling Mom that Ty—the hottest bachelor among the descendants of Mom's social circle—was my sort-of boyfriend. When I'd left for Europe with him, I'd sent her a quick e-mail explaining that I would be out of town for a while. No mention of Europe or Ty.

I found a package of Oreos in my kitchen cabinet and ripped them open.

Mom was an ex-beauty queen—really—with a network of informants that would rival the FBI and CIA combined. Somebody was bound to have told her about Ty and me. I wasn't up to being grilled by her yet.

I spun the top off an Oreo cookie and licked the icing.

I desperately needed to talk to Marcie. She'd want all—and I do mean *all*—of the details of my trip with Ty, but she was at work. So what could I do but go shopping? Maybe I'd—

Oh my God! The Sinful handbag!

The image of the purse zapped me like a cattle prod. I had to find one. What was I doing sitting around my apartment when I could be out shopping?

I popped the rest of the Oreo into my mouth, then shoved in two more—just for the energy boost, of course—and dashed into my bedroom. I pulled on khaki capris, a red top, and sandals—not great walking shoes, but what did that matter when they looked great on me—and selected a red Coach satchel. I was almost out the door when I remembered Ada.

"Damn . . . ," I muttered, standing in my living room.

She was supposed to be here at eleven o'clock to pick up her car, and it was only nine now. No way could I sit around for two hours.

What if the department store shelves were picked clean of Sinful bags while I sat here? The scene played in my head, one gorgeous handbag after another disappearing until there were none left.

I had to do something.

Then it came to me: I'd pick up the clothes from Holt's that Ada wanted to donate to the women's shelter myself. The store was only seven minutes away—six if I ran the light at the corner—and it would save her the trouble. Then I'd bring her the keys to the Mercedes and she could pick it up whenever she pleased. And I could zip to the malls to find the Sinful bag.

Cool.

I rushed to the parking lot of my apartment complex and another brilliant thought struck me. Maybe I'd take the Mercedes to Holt's to pick up the clothing, then drive it back to my apartment. That way I wouldn't have to spend time transferring the stuff from my Honda to her Mercedes, plus the Mercedes was really cool to drive. And everyone at Holt's would see me in it and be jealous.

The Holt's store—yes, it's the Holt's store Ty's family has owned for generations which, you'd think, would get me a little more than my seven lousy dollars per hour—wasn't open yet, so I drove around back.

All the choice spots near the building were already taken, so I had to settle for a parking slot a ways out. So many cars in the lot at this hour meant the early morning replenishment team, who restock the store daily, was inside. A truck was backed up to one of the two loading dock bays, so the truck team was there, too. A garbage truck pulled into the lot, heading for the Dumpster. A couple of guys were having a smoke. A few stragglers, late for work, were just getting out of their cars.

Nobody paid much attention when I parked the Mercedes and got out—I looked around just to be sure—which was kind of disappointing.

Never mind, though, I was on a mission. I had to pick up Ada's clothes, drive back to my apartment, swap cars, get to Ada's house with the keys, then get to the mall and be the first in line when the stores opened.

I hurried up the loading dock steps into the stock room. It was pretty busy in there with boxes being unloaded from the truck, the replenishment team pulling stock and loading it onto U-boats and Z-rails, the janitor getting equipment out of the cabinets, and the display team hauling mannequins around.

Sometimes, merchandise doesn't sell. It might be damaged and unrepairable, or out of season. Or in the case of Holt's women's clothing, it might be just so damn ugly no one who'd so much as glanced at the cover of *Vogue* on a grocery store rack would touch it with a three-inch acrylic nail. The store marked it for clearance, but sometimes even that wasn't enough to prod a customer into taking it off our hands. So Holt's donated it to charity.

Luckily I knew where that merchandise was kept. I made my way to the huge shelving units nearest the loading dock and saw two cardboard boxes with "hold for pickup" written on the side in red marker.

I was momentarily paralyzed at the sight. A hideous pink and orange print dress lay on the top. Using only my fingertips, I dug down and found nine more of them. Oh my God, someone had actually purchased one of those things. I didn't know if I could pick up the box or not.

Then I heard my name called. I recognized the voice immediately: Cal, the store's new assistant manager.

I hate him.

And I knew what he wanted. He'd spotted me and he wanted me to come to work today. No matter why any employee came into the store—to shop, pick up their schedule, or whatever—Cal pressured them into putting in a few hours.

No way was I working at Holt's today.

I grabbed the two cardboard boxes and took off. I rounded the next aisle, dodging the truck and replenishment team members, and headed for the loading dock stairs. Before me, through the open door, was freedom. I hit the button on the Mercedes remote and popped the trunk.

"Hey, Haley," Troy called, stepping out in front of me.

Troy worked in the men's wear department. He was just out of high school and seemed to be dog paddling his way through life.

"Where you been, Haley?" he asked, his mouth gaping open slightly. "On a shoot?"

For some reason, Troy thought I moonlighted as the porn star Rhonda Rushmore. Honestly, I haven't done much to discourage this because she was, after all, a top rated porn star. But I didn't have time for him today.

"Catch you later," I called as I hurried down the loading dock stairs and wound my way through the parked cars.

I tried to lift the trunk of the Mercedes but it wouldn't budge.

"Damn it," I muttered.

Frantically, I fumbled through the keys and hit the trunk release button on the remote. The trunk popped up.

I yanked it open and froze.

There was a woman inside. Dead.

CHAPTER 2

I slammed the trunk lid shut and dropped the boxes of clothing.

Oh my God. *Oh my God.* This was *not* happening. There was *not* a dead body in the trunk of Ty's grandmother's Mercedes.

Maybe I'd just imagined it. Maybe I'd suffered temporary vision impairment after my exposure to those awful pink and orange print dresses in the cardboard box. Yeah, maybe that was it.

I hit the remote. The trunk latch *thunked* and the lid released. Slowly, I lifted it again.

Damn.

A body was in there, all right. A woman, late twenties maybe, with bobbed bleached-out hair, dressed in shorts, T-shirt, and sandals.

And she was definitely dead. I knew that because a huge red stain had spread over the front of her white T-shirt, and her eyes were open and staring at nothing.

I slammed the trunk lid. Jeez, I'd been driving around since last night at the airport with a dead body in the trunk. How long had it been in there? Ada and I had been in Europe for a couple of weeks. Was it there all that time?

How was I going to explain this to Ty?

And the police.

Maybe I could just leave and let somebody else find the body.

I looked around. The garbage truck that had just emptied the Dumpster lumbered out of sight. The guys who had been on a smoke break were gone. Nobody milled around in the parking lot.

For a half-second I considered rushing back to the airport, taking the next flight to Paris, living in some artists' colony somewhere. Only I didn't really know anything about art, plus I didn't have any actual artistic talent. But I'm really fun at a party so maybe they'd just let me hang out with them until all of this blew over.

"Crap . . . ," I muttered.

I knew what I had to do.

I punched in 9-1-1 on my cell phone and gave them the info. I left the boxes of clothing at the car—maybe, if the women at the shelter were lucky, someone would steal the clothing and they wouldn't have to wear that awful stuff—and headed back to the store.

Troy still stood where I'd left him by the loading dock stairs, his tongue sort of hanging out, and the truck and replenishment teams were still working. No sign of the janitor. We called him Bob because no one can pronounce his name. He was from Belgrave, Botswana, Berkastan—I don't know, one of the "B" places—and spoke no known language.

"Hey, Haley," Troy said, "you want to—"

"No," I said, and kept walking.

Luckily for Cal, he was nowhere in sight. If he flagged me down to ask if I wanted to put in a few hours, I might have punched him—which I don't think I could have gotten away with, even after sleeping with the store's owner.

I had to find Jeanette, the store manager. Jeanette was in her fifties, a little on the chunky side, and easy to spot because she always dressed in Holt's stomach-turning fash-

SHOULDER BAGS AND SHOOTINGS   11

ions. Don't ask me why. She pulls down a huge salary, plus bonuses, and can afford really nice things.

The stock room door—one of them—opened into the rear of the store next to the customer service booth, the offices and training room, the restrooms, and the employee breakroom. My friend Grace, who's way cool, works in the customer service booth but she wasn't there; it was too early for the sales clerks to report for work.

I passed by the door to the employee breakroom and stopped. Technically, I was performing a service for Holt's, wasn't I? Didn't that mean I should be on the clock? I mean, jeez, finding a dead body in the company parking lot ought to entitle me to something, shouldn't it?

I slipped into the breakroom, grabbed my time card, and clocked in.

I headed down the hallway to the offices. Jeanette's door was open so I walked in, then reeled back in horror. She had on that awful pink and orange print dress.

How much should I have to endure from a crappy part-time job?

"Haley," she said, "this is a surprise. I didn't—oh goodness, what's wrong?"

"I found a dead body," I said.

She huffed irritably. "Again?"

After what happened here last fall, then again a few weeks ago, I guess Jeanette had grown a little callous. Can't say that I blamed her.

Maybe Holt's should start stocking orange cones and yellow crime scene tape.

"In the back parking lot," I said. "I already called it in."

Jeanette shot me a scathing look, then hoisted herself out of her chair and started punching buttons on her cell phone as we walked.

We waited near Ada's Mercedes, Jeanette a discreet distance away as she spoke with someone, presumably, at the

Holt's corporate office. A half a dozen emergency vehicles roared into the lot a few minutes later, lights flashing, sirens blaring, and screeched to a halt near us. Jeanette was still on the phone so I gave them a brief rundown of what had happened, and pointed to the trunk.

Apparently, Jeanette picked this particular moment to call everyone in her address book, because she stayed on the phone, away from the crime scene, well away from me. Occasionally, she gave me a nasty look—like this was my fault or something.

I'm glad I clocked in.

Finally, she walked over. "I'm going to need a statement from you," she told me.

From her tone I figured she'd been talking to the lawyers at Pike Warner, Holt's law firm.

"I don't know anything about this," I insisted, waving my hand toward Ada's Mercedes. "I'm completely uninvolved with anything to do with murder."

"Hi, Haley," a paramedic called.

Two other guys in uniform turned and waved.

"Hey, girl," one called.

"How was your trip?" another asked.

Okay, this was sort of embarrassing.

Jeanette's eyes narrowed again and she stomped away, punching at her cell phone.

I'd had enough. I was going inside. I turned to leave, only to spot a plain vanilla Crown Vic roll up. Police detectives Madison and Shuman got out.

We had history.

Detective Madison was way overdue for retirement—probably hanging around until he could finally pin a murder on me—and looked every one of his sixty-plus years. He had a jelly belly, and wore a plaid sport coat and oxfords with the heels run down. There was a gravy stain on his tie.

Shuman was the younger of the two, nice looking, somehow making his poorly matched shirt, tie, and sport coat seem endearing. Our friendship had soured because of what had happened here in January, and I hadn't talked to him since.

He still didn't look like he was ready to make up and play nice.

"So, it's déjà vu all over again, huh, Miss Randolph?" Detective Madison said, hiking up his trousers. He gave me a snarky smile and jerked his chin toward the Mercedes. "You kill this one, too?"

"You really should think about retiring," I told him.

Shuman walked over, pulling a little notebook from the pocket of his sport coat.

"What can you tell me about this?" he asked.

No hi-how-are-you, no sorry-for-the-way-things-turned-out, no thanks-for-getting-me-laid-with-the-awesome-gift-you-recommended-for-my-girlfriend. Nothing. Just business.

Jack Webb would have been proud.

I gave him the rundown: It was Ada's car; I'd borrowed it; I'd driven here to pick up the clothing; I'd found the body.

Shuman made notes, never once looking at me.

"Do you know the victim?" he asked.

"No clue," I said.

"Seen her before?"

I shook my head. "Nope."

Shuman snapped his notebook closed. "We'll talk to you more later. Don't leave."

Since the only car I had access to at the moment had a dead body in it and was crawling with investigators, I had no choice but to do as Shuman said. But I didn't want to hang around out here. I went inside.

The store had opened but only a few shoppers were on the sales floor. Mornings were usually slow. Since all the police activity was at the rear of the building and all the sales employees parked out front, nobody in the store seemed to realize what was happening out back. That suited me fine because I didn't want to talk about it.

I went into the employee breakroom. It was crowded with tables and chairs, a microwave and refrigerator. The place always smelled like those diet meals that girl, whose name I can never remember but who I hate because she's lost like sixty pounds or something, ate for lunch. The walls were plastered with posters about our rights as employees, the store's sales and credit goals, marketing plans, and other stuff Corporate seemed to think we absolutely had to know.

Nobody was in the room, which was a relief. I didn't want to run into Rita, the sales clerks' supervisor.

I hate Rita.

Rita hated me, too. I'm okay with that because I actually double-hated her since she and her friend jacked my purse party business idea. Now I triple-hated her because they were doing better than Marcie and me, having huge parties and selling a zillion more bags than we were.

Rita wasn't there. I checked the schedule that hung beside the time clock and saw that she was supposed to work this morning. Luckily, I'd missed her.

The breakroom door opened and in walked Cal. Cal was a complete moron, but like so many others, didn't know it. He was about forty, slightly balding, and he always dressed in one of three pairs of pants, a white shirt, and ties that didn't go with anything.

"Good to have you back with us, Haley," Cal said. "We're shorthanded in Juniors, so I need you to—"

"I'm not working today," I said, and stepped sideways so he couldn't see my time card tucked into its slot.

"Oh?" He leaned right, trying to see the wall of time cards behind me.

I leaned right with him. He dodged left. So did I.

"I'm just picking up clothing for a women's shelter," I said. "Jeanette knows all about it."

It was a partial lie, but so what? Those are the kind I did best.

"Well, we could still use you in Juniors," Cal said. "We're having our biggest sale of the season today, you know, and—"

Cal's words turned into blah, blah, blah and I drifted off. Finally, he left.

My day really needed a boost. I dug through my Coach satchel—luckily, I'd had it with me this whole time, otherwise it might have been hauled away with the car as evidence—and came up with a ten. I fed it into the vending machine, punched the buttons for everything with chocolate in it—just to stay mentally sharp for when the detectives got to me, of course—and sat down at one of the tables. I'd only gotten through a Snickers bar and one package of M&M's when Jeanette opened the door.

"The detectives want to see you now," she said, and disappeared again.

I followed her to her office.

Detective Madison had taken the power position in the chair behind Jeanette's desk and Shuman stood off to the side. Jeanette retreated to the corner. In that dress, she looked like a tropical sunset during a nuclear winter.

"So," Madison said, rearing back in the chair, "you want to tell us what happened?"

That was a trick question. I knew because I'd been questioned by the police before. I'd already explained myself to Shuman and he'd, of course, passed it all on to Madison. He just wanted me to tell my story again.

Under other circumstances, I might have hesitated. But not this time. There was absolutely no way Madison could stick me with this murder. I'd simply had the misfortune of driving a car that had a dead body stuffed into the trunk at the airport. I wasn't worried.

"Haley, you don't have to say anything," Jeanette said.

Madison looked excited, as if invoking my rights meant I was guilty of something.

"I'm happy to cooperate," I said.

"You're entitled to have an attorney present," Jeanette said.

Jeanette knew I was involved with Ty, the owner of the department store chain of which she hoped to remain employed, though she'd never come right out and said anything. I'm sure she figured it out, though, the night I was leaving for Europe with Ty and he called her at home and explained I wouldn't be at work for a couple of weeks.

Now she was just covering her bases. Jeanette wanted to make sure that during my next pillow-talk session with Ty, I told him that she'd been concerned about me during the police interview. Little did she realize that the only thing I was likely to mention was the hideous dress she had on.

Not that Ty would listen anyway.

"I don't need a lawyer," I said, smiling pleasantly, as any innocent person would. "The car belongs to Ada Cameron. We picked it up at the airport last night after we landed. It had been there for a couple of weeks."

Detective Madison just stared. "Go on."

I didn't really see what else there was to explain, except maybe to give them the reason Ada and I hadn't found the body in the trunk last night at the airport. If we'd had luggage instead of just a small carry-on, we'd have made the discovery there.

I guess I didn't speak fast enough for Madison because he said, "And how did you end up here at the store with the car this morning?"

"I dropped Ada off at home last night after we left the airport, so she wouldn't have to be out so late. I used the car to pick up some clothing Holt's is donating to charity."

"First thing this morning? What was the hurry?" Madison asked.

"Because I was going shopping."

Okay, that sounded kind of lame. So what could I do but give more details?

"I saw the new Sinful handbag in *Elle* last night," I said.

"Elle?" Madison asked.

"The fashion magazine," I told him.

"What does that have to do with anything?"

Jeez, what's wrong with him? Wasn't it obvious?

"I wanted to get to the mall and find the handbag before they were all sold out," I told him.

"Let me be sure I have this straight," Madison said, shifting in his chair. "You got up early after a grueling flight from London. First thing you wanted to do was go to the mall. You could have waited for Mrs. Cameron to show up, but you didn't. You could have taken your own car to pick up the charity donation, but you didn't. And all of this was because of some handbag?"

When he said it like that, it did sound kind of weird, but it was the truth.

"Yes, that's right," I told him.

Everybody was staring at me now. Shuman, Madison, even Jeanette. I started to get a yucky feeling in the pit of my stomach.

"Did you get a look at the victim in the trunk?" Madison asked.

I was kind of relieved he'd changed direction in his questioning. Guess he understood, after all.

"I saw her," I said.

"Recognize her?"

I shook my head. "No."

"You've never seen her before," Madison said, making it a statement, rather than a question.

I got the yucky feeling again.

"I have no idea who she is," I said.

"None at all?"

Maybe I should stop talking now.

"Look," I said, "I don't know anything more—"

"Well, as it turns out, we know lots more to talk about," Detective Madison said, and suddenly I knew exactly what the canary must have felt like the second the cat opened its mouth.

Madison leaned closer. "We talked to Ada Cameron. She's telling a different story. She says that she never gave her permission for you to take her car anywhere, except to your apartment. She didn't ask you to pick up the clothing for the shelter. In fact, she told you to stay home, she'd get the car from you at eleven this morning."

"Well, yeah, but I told you I wanted to go to the mall and get that—"

"Handbag. Yeah, right," Madison said and grunted. "And when you got to the store, you didn't park out front where you usually park, did you? You circled around to the back. You parked as far from the building as you could, without making it look obvious. And when you got out of the car, you looked around to see if anyone had seen you, didn't you?"

"But that was—"

"We have witnesses," Madison said. "Don't lie."

"I'm not lying!"

"The assistant store manager said he saw you in the stock room, but you ran off, like you didn't want him to see you and know that you were in the store," Madison said.

"I didn't want him to—"

"And that kid back in men's wear. What's his name?" Madison asked, glancing over his shoulder.

"Troy," Shuman said, checking his notes.

"Yeah, Troy. He told us you practically ran over him trying to get out of the store."

I was *not* getting into the whole porn star thing with Madison. Not with Jeanette standing there.

"And about the victim?" Detective Madison gestured to Shuman.

"Tiffany Markham," he replied.

"Are you still claiming you don't know her?" Madison asked.

"I don't know anybody named Tif—"

Oh God.

The little yucky feeling in the pit of my stomach doubled in size.

"Tiffany Markham," Madison said. "She's the co-owner of a purse party business, along with that woman Rita who works right here in the store. Your archrival in the purse party business. The person who's booking bigger parties than you. The person who's selling more bags than you. The person who's trying to ruin you. *That's* who Tiffany Markham is. Isn't she? *Isn't she?*"

Oh, crap.

CHAPTER 3

There was nothing left to do but go shopping. And nothing less than finding that Sinful handbag could possibly improve my mood.

After Detective Madison had finished accusing me of murder—again—at Holt's this morning, I'd left. Nobody tried to stop me, which was good, since that meant I wasn't under arrest or anything.

But no one had tried to comfort me either. Jeanette definitely kept her distance, and Detective Shuman hadn't spoken a word. After what happened a few weeks ago—the murder and all that other stuff—I figured Shuman and I would be friendly even if we weren't friends anymore. Guess he had other ideas.

A woman on the morning replenishment team gave me a ride to my apartment complex. I jumped into my Honda and headed out.

As I cruised down the 405 freeway, Ty flashed into my mind. He knew about the murder by now. Someone from Holt's—probably that bitch Sarah Covington—had called him.

I hate Sarah Covington.

She was Holt's vice president of marketing, made a ton of money, and dressed in great clothes with fabulous handbags. She got a Louis Vuitton organizer before I did, which alone was reason to hate her.

With some of the lame-ass marketing ideas she came up with, I didn't know how she kept her job, except that Ty thought she could do no wrong. He acted like the universe rotated around her. I didn't get it.

I passed an SUV, then cut off a Beemer and sped up, more anxious than ever to complete my Sinful quest.

How would Ty react to this whole thing? He loved his grandmother. What would he say when he found out I'd embroiled her in a murder investigation?

Wait a minute, I realized as I cut across two lanes of traffic. He was my boyfriend now. Officially, since we'd finally slept together. He couldn't be upset with me. He was obligated to be supportive, wasn't he? I mean, that's what boyfriends did, right?

Any minute now my cell phone would ring and it would be Ty, worried about me.

The scene played out in my mind. Him frantic, ready to abandon the crucial negotiations for Holt's International, and jet home immediately to be at my side and comfort me during this tragedy. Then me telling him no, that I couldn't let him walk out on the multi-billion-dollar deal just for me—that's the kind of supportive, understanding girlfriend I am. Then Ty, overwhelmed with glee, thrilled beyond belief that he was lucky enough to have a fabulous girlfriend like me.

I exited the freeway and drove to the Beverly Center, one of L.A.'s best shopping centers. As I took the escalator up from the parking garage, my cell phone rang.

I yanked it from my pocket, sure it was Ty. But it was my mom, according to the readout on the caller I.D. screen. It was the sixth time she'd called today.

Believe me, it was not because she missed me and wanted me to come over so we could chat and do each other's nails.

Obviously, the ex-beauty queen cult she belonged to had gone global, bounced satellite signals off of their tiaras, and learned that I was back from Europe. I hadn't taken any of Mom's calls so far, and I didn't intend to now. I let it go to voicemail and tucked my phone away again.

One thing I knew for sure was that I didn't have to worry about Ada being upset with me over this whole mess. We'd hit it off right from the start and, after our intense bonding experience shopping together in Europe, I knew she'd be totally cool with what happened. Even if she ended up having to buy a new Mercedes.

I headed for Nordstrom and immediately picked up the scent of the handbag department. My heart rate increased and I got a really great rush of adrenaline. Oh my God. The Sinful purse was here—I just knew it.

I dashed through the aisles, my gaze bouncing from display case to display case. Gorgeous handbags on my left, my right, behind and in front of me. But where was the Sinful bag?

I spotted a sales clerk at the register just finishing up with a customer. She was short and wide, and had on one of those boxy suits women over fifty thought they were supposed to wear. I rushed over.

"Where are the Sinful bags?" I asked, my breath coming in short little pants.

The clerk lowered her head and peered up at me over the top of her half-glasses.

"I just sold our last one," she said, and nodded toward the woman she'd just waited on.

I gasped and whirled toward the customer walking merrily along, swinging a shopping bag on her arm.

"No . . . ," I moaned. I couldn't have missed the last bag—not by a couple of minutes.

I was in no mood.

Maybe I could buy it from her. Or just take it. She was little, one of those petite people who were always taking up valuable floor space in stores with their tiny clothes, who ought to be rounded up and marooned on a deserted island in the Pacific somewhere. And she was old, too. She'd probably snap like a day-old bread stick if I—

"I could order you one," the clerk offered.

I whipped back around, ready to snap her in half—which I think she realized because she backed up a few steps—and tried to control myself.

Where was Marcie when I needed her? She could always talk me down in situations like this.

I drew in a calming breath and said, "Yes, that would be nice. Order me one. I'd like to pick it up tomorrow."

The clerk backed up another few steps and frowned. "I'm afraid I can't get it here that quickly. More like eight to ten weeks."

"Weeks?"

She backed up a little farther. "It's a very popular bag. The *it* bag of the season. Everybody wants one."

"Ten weeks?"

"Or less," she offered, and reached for the telephone.

I was pretty sure she was calling security and I couldn't face yet another run-in with the law today—plus my mother would never forgive me if I was banned for life from Nordstrom—so I just said, "Never mind. I'll keep looking."

I was halfway to the door, my mind zipping through a list of stores to check out, when somebody called my name. I turned and saw a young woman in a great outfit, waving. She was about my age, with dark hair.

"Haley, hi, it's me," she said, walking over. "Remember? Last fall at Holt's? I had a job interview with a recording company and you picked out the only fabulous outfit ever to grace their racks?"

"Oh my God! Jen!"

I remembered her immediately. She'd been saddled with a gift card from Holt's, of all places, to buy funky, hip clothes to wear to her interview. I'd put together a killer outfit for her. I hadn't seen her since that night.

We hugged, and I said, "Wow, you look great! I guess you got the job?"

"It's a blast," she said, and her smile—plus the terrific clothes she had on—told me that she'd hit the job lotto. "Only it's not 'Jen' anymore. Everybody at the label calls me Jay Jax. You know, 'Jay' because it's my first initial and 'Jax' because it's part of my last name. Cool, huh?"

"Yeah, really cool," I said.

"So what are you doing these days?" she asked.

I didn't know where to start, exactly. Should I tell her that I was nearly penniless now because I'd spent my savings—translation, rent money—shopping in Europe? That I still had the crappy job at Holt's? That I was a college student, barely able to stay awake in two boring classes? Or that I was, once again, a murder suspect?

I've really got to get a grip on my life.

"Just got back from Europe," I said, and waved my hand like it was no big thing. Then, because I was anxious to change the subject, I nodded toward the handbag department. "I'm here for a Sinful bag."

Jen's—Jay Jax's—face lit up. "Don't you love that bag? I got mine yesterday."

She had a Sinful bag and a cool new name, and I didn't?

I hate my life.

"There's a big party coming up. You have to come," Jay Jax said.

A party? My mood improved immediately.

"The record label is launching a new artist. It's going to be fantastic. *Everybody* will be there. I'll text you the details."

We exchanged phone numbers and she said, "Got to run. I'm here to buy a gift for the boss's wife—and both of his girlfriends. See you, Haley!"

I watched her disappear and the image of the Sinful bag grew larger in my mind until it shut out everyone and everything else. I needed that bag, and I needed to take it to that record label's party. I absolutely had to have it. And I'd get it. Somehow.

"Tell me everything. I have to hear everything," Marcie declared as she rushed into my apartment.

I'd called her during a mocha frappuccino break from my Sinful search today and she'd promised to come over right after work.

Marcie had been my best friend since forever. She was a petite, blue-eyed blonde, with a lot more brains than most blondes get credit for.

I hadn't seen her in weeks but we'd e-mailed a few times. She'd kept me up to date on things, as a best friend would, including a choice bit of info about one of Mom's friends, Cynthia Gray.

Cynthia, it seems, blamed me—wrongly—for her daughter's death in January and had left a threatening note on my door. Marcie knew this because, according to the store surveillance tapes posted on YouTube, Cynthia had screamed her confession over and over in the lingerie department of Macy's during the spring preview event for the bra and panty club, while she'd chased a model wearing a thong and a red lace demi-cup bra—thus the interest of YouTube viewers—off of the runway, through the aisles to the men's department, where they both landed in unflattering positions atop a display of Jockey briefs.

Nobody, it seemed, knew exactly what had set Cynthia off, but speculation was that the model had looked a little like her daughter. Rumor had it that Cynthia was now in "seclusion" recovering from "exhaustion," which really meant that her beleaguered husband had shipped her off to rehab somewhere.

I was relieved to know that it was Cynthia who'd left the

threatening note. I'd been afraid it had been Kirk Keegan, yet another person who—wrongly—blamed me for their troubles.

I get that a lot.

Kirk was an attorney I'd known back in my other life last fall when I'd worked for the Pike Warner law firm. He'd threatened to kill me because I hadn't fallen for one of his schemes, then disappeared. Nobody had seen or heard from him in months. Still, he was out there, somewhere.

I got a couple of Coronas from the fridge along with a box of Ritz crackers and the Cheez Whiz—nothing says *special occasion* like canned, processed cheese—and brought them into my living room. I'd laid in a lot of supplies in anticipation of Marcie's visit. We had two weeks and two continents to catch up on. This could be an all-nighter.

"So, how was it?" Marcie asked, her eyes wide as we settled onto opposite ends of the sofa.

"London was beautiful," I said, "and so was—"

"I'm not talking about sightseeing," Marcie said. "How was it with Ty? You did sleep with him, didn't you?"

She looked completely mystified that I hadn't opened the conversation with details about Ty. Not that I blamed her. After all, he and I had waited months to finally sleep together.

Honestly, I'd hoped to put off this topic for a while, but I could see by the look on Marcie's face that she was having none of it.

"Well, yeah," I said.

Marcie leaned closer and her eyes got wider. "So what was it like?"

"Uh . . . good. It was . . . good."

Marcie gasped. "Oh my God. It was awful, wasn't it?"

"No, it wasn't awful . . . exactly. It was . . . great. Really—"

"Ty's terrible in bed!" she exclaimed, looking stricken.

"He's not terrible," I insisted.

"Something went wrong. What was it?"

I couldn't hold back. Not with Marcie.

"He's a talker," I admitted.

Marcie frowned. "During?"

"After."

"Oh, no . . ." Marcie slumped back on the couch, shaking her head.

I didn't like a lot of talking—which was why I usually liked to leave before they woke up—but I could tolerate a little chatting. Ty took it to a whole different level.

"Not the how-was-it quiz, I hope?" Marcie asked, still frowning.

I have no patience for a guy who asks the did-you-like-it, was-it-the-best, and everything short of would-you-recommend-me-to-a-friend questions. I expect men to know what they're doing, to bring their A-game. I'm not giving lessons.

"Politics," I said. "The economy. Global commerce. Stuff like that."

Marcie brightened a little. "Did you pick up any good stock tips?"

"I drifted off," I told her. "The first couple of times he yammered on about that boring stuff, I figured it was no big deal. But he kept doing it."

We both just sat there for a minute, Marcie looking disappointed.

"When is Ty coming home?" she asked.

"In a few days."

"You have to tell him," Marcie said.

She was right—Marcie was almost always right—but telling Ty he was boring me out of my mind in bed wouldn't be easy. Our relationship had progressed at glacial speed. I didn't want to set us back.

"You *have* to tell him," Marcie said again.

"Yeah, I know. And I will."

She seemed satisfied with that. "So what did you buy?"

"Tons of the coolest stuff," I said, feeling excited now.

"Let's see it," Marcie said, bouncing on the sofa.

"I had it FedEx'd to Evelyn's house," I told her. "I'll pick it up tomorrow."

I'd met Evelyn Croft last fall when I started working at Holt's. She was fortyish and, I'm sure, perpetually mistaken for a librarian or middle school teacher. Evelyn had been injured in what she now referred to as "the incident" caused by "that certain someone" at Holt's last fall and, as a result, didn't work now or come out of her house.

I'd e-mailed her from Europe asking if I could have my purchases delivered to her house. She was the only person I knew who was totally reliable, at home all day, and unlikely to open my packages and try on my clothes.

After some cajoling, Evelyn agreed to accept delivery as long as she could clearly see the FedEx truck parked in front of her house; could identify the FedEx uniform through her peephole; and the driver would wait while she turned off the alarms and opened the locks and chains on her front door, a process that could be quite lengthy.

Marcie finished off her Corona. "I've got two people interested in having a purse party."

We'd started our purse party business last fall and we both loved it since we were, after all, self-professed handbag whores. It was a great way to make extra cash, plus the parties were always tons of fun.

"Business might be picking up," I told her, then explained how I'd discovered the body of Tiffany Markham in the trunk of Ada's Mercedes.

"That's awful," Marcie said.

Yes, it was awful. Detective Madison had been right about one thing: Tiffany and Rita had been our chief rivals in the purse party business. I'd wanted to leave them in our dust with superior sales, but not like this.

Marcie gasped. "Does Rita know you're involved?"

I'd thought about that. Rita already hated me, and if she

found out I was connected—even innocently—to her friend's death, she'd make things harder on me at work.

Jeez, I really hoped she didn't know I was involved.

"I just happened to find Tiffany's body," I said.

"So what's Tiffany's connection with Ada?" Marcie asked. "Why would her body have been stuffed into Ada's car at the airport?"

"Beats me," I said, and tipped up my Corona. "All I know is that Detective Madison has twisted the facts around and is convinced I murdered Tiffany."

"Wow," Marcie mumbled and sat back on the sofa. "I guess you'd better find out what really happened."

I'd solved a number of crimes in the past few months—I have mad Scooby Doo skills—and it looked as if I might have to do it again.

I nodded. "I guess I should."

CHAPTER 4

Cal had wasted no time in putting me back on the schedule at Holt's. He'd gone so far as to call my cell phone and leave a message—which was *way* annoying because I still hadn't gotten a call from Ty—stating that I was expected back at work for my usual evening shift. This didn't suit me, really, but I needed the money.

When I walked into the breakroom, a line of employees waited at the time clock. Shopping in Europe and sex with Ty seemed like a really long time ago.

"Hey, girl!" Bella called when she spotted me.

Bella—ebony to my ivory—was tall and thin, and about my age. She worked at Holt's to save money for beauty school and, in the meantime, practiced on her own hair. Tonight she seemed to be in what I could only guess was a saucer phase. She'd fashioned her hair into what looked like a satellite dish atop her head.

We hugged and I stored my bag—a really great Kate Spade tote—in my locker and got in line behind Bella to wait, along with everyone else, for a few more minutes of our lives to tick by.

"Where you been, girl?" Bella asked.

"Out of town," I said, not wanting to get into the whole Ty thing with her. "Family situation."

"Lucky you," Bella said, nodding toward the work schedule posted by the time clock. "Rita's not here for your first night back."

I glanced at the schedule and saw that Rita was supposed to work tonight, but a red line had been drawn through her name. I wondered if she was in mourning over the death of Tiffany, her friend and business partner. Or if maybe she was busy attempting to destroy the purse party books and drain the bank account before Tiffany's relatives found out about it.

I doubted Rita was that smart.

The line moved forward as we all fed our cards into the time clock and then, instead of heading out to the sales floor, everyone just stood around the breakroom. Shannon, who was the lead in the housewares department, came through the door.

I was surprised to see Shannon because, last I heard, she was off work on a totally bogus disability claim—I knew that for a fact. Shannon and Rita were good friends. They even dressed alike and, believe me, if they wore Holt's clothing, it would be an upgrade.

Shannon disliked me for no good reason, except that Rita didn't like me—unless, of course, she still held a grudge because of that vacuum cleaner incident last fall.

"Spread out, people, spread out," Shannon called, waving at us.

I had no idea what was happening so I moved along with everyone else, taking up my customary position at the rear of any gathering.

"What's going on?" I asked Bella.

"No talking," Shannon said.

Bella rolled her eyes and lowered her voice. "Some new b.s. Corporate came up with. We do stretches before every shift. Supposed to make us more attentive, improve our thinking. Avoid accidents."

Jeez, you're out of the loop for a few weeks and look what happens.

"You're kidding," I said.

"No talking!" Shannon called, glaring at me.

"We do this before every shift?" I asked Bella.

She shrugged. "What the hell? It keeps us off the sales floor for five extra minutes."

Immediately I saw the benefit of Holt's new program, and eagerly joined in as Shannon led the group through a series of neck and shoulder rolls, arm and calf stretches. I felt myself relax, which was kind of nice.

Shannon pointed to a chart hanging on the wall near the refrigerator. It was one of those big thermometers. Red was filled in up to the 88 percent line, which, I guessed, was good.

"We're doing great in this contest so far, but we need to do better," Shannon said, then jerked her thumb toward the breakroom door. "So get out there and watch out for that secret shopper. Believe me, none of you wants to screw that up and be the reason the rest of us don't get our prizes."

Shannon glared directly at me when she said that. I felt myself tense up again.

"What's that all about?" I asked Bella as we moved along with the other employees onto the sales floor.

"More b.s. from Corporate," Bella said, sounding weary. "They got employees pretending to be shoppers coming to the stores, seeing how we're handling customer service. This secret shopper gives us points if we do good, and takes away points if we do bad."

"So if I got that bitch Shannon in a headlock they'd count off for that?" I asked.

"Not in my book," Bella said. "Anyway, it's supposed to be some sort of contest. The employees get gifts, depending on how many points we accumulate. Supposed to make us work as a team, some b.s. like that."

This sounded like one of the dumb-ass schemes Sarah Covington would come up with, and call Ty a couple dozen times to discuss.

Somebody needed to take her out.

"Haley," Shannon called from behind me.

I ignored her and kept walking. I'm pretty tall—five-foot-nine—and have long legs, so I can stride away really quickly with almost no effort, a skill that has come in very handy since I got this job at Holt's.

"Haley!" Shannon trotted up next to me, panting slightly. She thrust a pamphlet at me. "Here. Read this. It's our new customer service procedures. And you'd better do exactly what it says. I want us to win the flat screens Holt's is giving away."

I took the pamphlet, shoved it into my pocket while staring directly into her face, and walked away.

Grace was in the customer service booth at the back of the store—my assigned corner of retail purgatory tonight—and I was glad to see her. We'd worked the booth together a lot and had come up with a great system for handling customers.

I sincerely doubted our methods were contained anywhere in the Holt's pamphlet riding around in my back pocket.

Grace was a little younger than me, totally cool, and she always wore her hair spiked up. I saw that she'd colored it again, this time making it a deep shade of pink. She really pulled it off.

"You're back," she said, as I punched in the code on the keypad that allowed entrance to the customer service booth.

I pulled the pamphlet out of my pocket.

"What's this all about?" I asked.

"Some woman from the corporate office came to the store and gave a long presentation on it," Grace said.

I wondered if it was Sarah Covington and if she had noticed that I wasn't in the training session, and figured that I was in Europe with Ty. That would be way cool.

"They want all of the employees to approach customers on the sales floor and ask if we can help them with anything," Grace said, sorting through a pile of clothing on the counter.

"What?"

"Yeah," Grace said, and pointed to the pamphlet. "There's a whole list of things we're supposed to say, and even a procedure for the order we say them in."

A customer came to the counter. I ignored her and glanced over the pamphlet. Listed there was a procedure for approaching, addressing, and assisting customers which ultimately, according to the pamphlet, would result in increased sales.

"We're supposed to ask a 'lifestyle question'? What's a lifestyle question?" I asked.

Grace glanced back as she approached the customer at the counter and shrugged. "Ask them about their life. Get them talking or something."

Now I knew this was definitely a program that had sprung from the insipid mind of Sarah Covington. I dropped the pamphlet into the trash can.

"I'll be back," Grace said, when she finished with the customer. She left the customer service booth.

I headed over to the inventory computer and scrolled through the list of merchandise. Not because I had any interest in the stock that had arrived during my two week absence, but because I could look at the screen and appear to be working while my thoughts drifted off somewhere else.

"Excuse me," a woman called.

I ignored her with practiced ease since it was my own personal policy to have a customer try to get my attention a minimum of two times—just to make sure they really needed me for something, of course.

"Excuse me?" she called again. "Ma'am?"

Her *ma'am* didn't come out sounding like *bitch,* which immediately caused me to perk up. Her accent was weird, too. Obviously, she wasn't from around here.

I turned and saw her standing at the counter. Short, petite, mid-thirties probably, with brown hair artfully styled. She looked classy in a Michael Kors suit and carried a Fendi bag.

What the heck was she doing in Holt's?

Then it occurred to me: maybe she was one of those secret shoppers. Oh my God. That *had* to be who she was. I thought the whole thing was pretty lame, but I sure could use a new flat screen for my apartment.

"Could I trouble you for a bit of information, please?" she asked.

Damn. Why hadn't I read that pamphlet?

Never mind. Too late for that now. I'd just have to wing it.

I recognized her accent then. Some place in the South— I knew that because Dad's relatives lived there, though my mom refused to acknowledge them. Yet this woman didn't look like "the Clampetts," as my mother referred to her in-laws. She looked cultured and refined.

My mind scrambled to formulate a lifestyle question. Jeez, how hard could it be?

Nothing came to me.

Then I decided I could simply offer her directions to the nearest Neiman Marcus, fearing she might suffer some sort of mental impairment resulting from overexposure to Holt's clothing line. I mean, really, what better customer service than that could anybody ask for?

"My name is Virginia Foster," she said, "and I'm hoping to speak with a woman named Rita. I'm sorry, but I don't know her last name. Is she, by any chance, on duty tonight?"

Up close now, I could see that she looked worn down, more weary than tired. Rita had that effect on people. And, it seemed, this woman was not the Holt's secret shopper.

"She's not working tonight," I said.

Virginia's shoulders slumped and she sighed heavily.

In a complete departure from my personal policy formed

from months of working at Holt's, I said, "Is there something I can help you with?"

Really, I don't know what came over me. Maybe it was her Fendi bag.

Virginia pulled herself up a little. "That's so kind of you. Yes, I'd really appreciate your help. I'm just not sure what to do. You see, I've just arrived from Charleston. A good friend of mine—my dearest friend, really—passed away quite suddenly and I need to talk to someone about it."

A cold chill zapped me.

"Tiffany?" I asked.

"You know Tiffany?" Virginia asked, looking relieved.

I saw no need to get into the whole I-found-her-in-my-trunk thing with her, or that I hadn't recognized her *dead*, so I simply said, "Yes, I met her once. She gave purse parties with Rita."

"Tiffany mentioned Rita a few times," Virginia said and looked a bit bewildered. "The police called Tiffany's family and told them about her . . . murder. I rushed right out. I dropped off my bags at the Hyatt and came here as quickly as I could. I don't know anyone to talk to but Rita and now she's not here, and . . ."

"Hang on a second," I told her.

Virginia looked as if she was about to cry, or maybe scream, so I abandoned the customer service booth—Grace would be back soon and if a customer had to wait, oh well—and took her into the employee breakroom. I got her a soda from the vending machine—they really should stock beer for occasions like this—and we sat at one of the tables. Luckily, we had the place to ourselves.

"So you and Tiffany were friends?" I asked.

This seemed weird to me because the one time I'd met Tiffany, she'd had on jeweled Wal-Mart sandals and a black T-shirt with "workin' it" spelled out in rhinestones across the front. Hardly the sort of person I'd expect to be friends with someone who looked as dignified as Virginia.

"Oh, yes, we were the best of friends," Virginia said, holding the soda can with both hands. "I hadn't seen her in a while, but we stayed in touch. She moved here to California a few months ago. The family didn't understand. But that was Tiffany, you know, always determined to do things her own way."

I felt like I should say something nice about Tiffany, but couldn't think of anything. After all, she, along with Rita, had tried to put Marcie and me out of business.

Finally, I came up with, "I'm sure this is hard on her family."

Virginia closed her eyes for a moment and shook her head. "Such tragedy. Goodness, that family has suffered through so much lately."

Virginia dug through her Fendi bag and pulled out a Louis Vuitton wallet—I was instantly jealous—and showed me a studio portrait of eight adults. A mom and dad in their sixties, it appeared, surrounded by what were probably their grown children and spouses. Everyone wore black suits. It was the sort of portrait that might hang over a fireplace in an old family home somewhere. Everyone looked elegant and successful.

Virginia turned the picture around and stared down at it, slowly shaking her head. "It's hard to believe Tiffany is really gone now."

I sat up a little straighter in my chair. "Tiffany is in this picture?" I asked.

"Yes, of course." Virginia turned the photo my way once more and pointed. "That's her right there."

I leaned forward and managed not to let my mouth drop open. The woman Virginia indicated looked nothing like the Tiffany I had met. The Tiffany I knew wore her hair in a bleached-out bob and dressed in whatever she could find on the Old Navy clearance rack. This Tiffany had dark hair and looked stunning in Chanel. I hardly recognized her.

Jeez, what had happened to this woman?

"Tiffany's daddy is quite beside himself," Virginia said. "He's not sure the law firm can go on without her."

"Tiffany was a lawyer?" I asked, and felt my eyes widen to the size of a Prada tote.

"One of the oldest, most respected firms in Charleston," she said.

Virginia sat there for a moment, as if gathering her strength. I guess Tiffany's death had really hit her hard.

"Did Tiffany mention her brother-in-law to you?" she asked.

I'd told her that I'd only met Tiffany once, so it surprised me that Virginia thought we'd have had an in-depth conversation about families. But people didn't always pay attention—I knew that from personal experience, of course—and could react really weird when someone died.

"Ed Buckley, her sister's husband," Virginia said. She leaned toward me as if expecting to hear some big piece of news. "Did Tiffany say anything about him?"

The only thing I remembered clearly about my one-time meeting with Tiffany was how she'd eyed my Marc Jacobs bag. At the time I figured she didn't know what it was. Now I knew different.

"Ed was killed in a car crash last year," Virginia said, as if that explained something.

"No," I said. "She didn't mention him."

Virginia looked disappointed—I had no clue why—and slumped back in her chair.

"I don't know how I'm going to explain things to her family," Virginia said, shaking her head.

I didn't know what the answers were either, but I knew where to start looking for them.

CHAPTER 5

It surprised me that Detective Shuman agreed to meet me. After all, I was sure he knew what I wanted—info on Tiffany's murder—and I expected he was in no mood to give anything away. Plus, he was still mad at me over the last time somebody was murdered at Holt's.

But here I was, sitting at an umbrella table in front of my favorite Starbucks, sipping my favorite frappuccino, waiting for my favorite homicide detective to show up. I'd called him this morning when I'd rolled out of bed and we'd set a meet time for noon. He was late but I figured I'd give him awhile longer—this was, after all, L.A.

The double blast of caffeine and chocolate in my mocha frappuccino had me buzzing pretty good, making it tough to sit still, so I pulled out my cell phone. I hadn't heard from Ada since the night we'd landed at LAX and I'd dropped her off at her house in Bel Air, which surprised me a little, since I'd called her twice already.

I punched in her number—she was on my speed dial because we were BFFs now—and her housekeeper picked up. She told me—for the third time—that Ada was unavailable. I left a message and hung up.

Huh. I wondered what was up with Ada. Was she sick? She must have been, since she hadn't called me back. I mean, what other reason could there have been?

I could ask Ty, but I hadn't heard from him, either. He was rushing to finish things up in London so he could come home tomorrow but, jeez, under the circumstances—I know that awful Sarah Covington had risked breaking a nail to call him immediately upon hearing about Tiffany's murder—you'd think he'd call me.

I dropped my phone into my purse—a great looking Dooney & Bourke barrel bag. My stomach felt a little queasy at the thought of sleeping with Ty again. Not the act itself. Afterwards, when he talked about the economy and whatever else he'd yammered on about when we were supposed to be cuddling.

Yet another unpleasant thought blasted through my brain: my mom. So far I'd managed to return all her calls during her prescheduled hair, nail, and spa appointments, so I hadn't actually had to talk to her. My luck wouldn't hold forever. Sooner or later, I'd have to explain my trip to Europe with Ty.

At least I didn't have to worry that she would show up unannounced on my doorstep; I'm not sure Mom knew where I lived.

I debated whether to wait any longer for Shuman—which would require a second frappuccino, of course—when he appeared beside my table. I hadn't even seen him drive up. Good thing I'm not hoping for a career with the CIA or something.

The sunlight sparkled in his brown hair but that was about the only thing warm about him. He wasn't glad to see me, which I expected, but it still bothered me.

"Let me get you a coffee," I said, rising from my chair.

"I can't stay," he said, not bothering to sit down. "I just came to tell you that I don't know anything about Tiffany Markham's death, and I'm never going to know anything, so don't call me again."

Shuman walked away.

I stood there for a few seconds, stunned. Okay, I figured

he would be upset with me, but this was way off the scale. I hurried after him.

"Wait! Shuman, hang on!" I called.

He stopped quickly and turned back. He was puffed up like men get when they're mad: straight shoulders, expanded chest, hard jaw line—which was way hot.

"Look, I get it," I said. "You're mad because you think I withheld information from you the last time you suspected me of murdering somebody."

"Because you *did* withhold information," he said, punching the air between us with his finger.

"Yeah, okay, I did that," I admitted. "I had reasons, though, good reasons. Reasons you'd agree with, if you weren't a cop."

"Well, I *am* a cop."

We stood staring at each other for a minute, sort of like back in January when we'd both realized things would never be the same between us.

I didn't like the feeling then or now.

"Look," I said. "I swear I don't know anything about Tiffany Markham's death. I opened the trunk and there she was. Believe me, if I'd known she was dead in the trunk when Ada and I picked up the car at the airport, I'd have said something about it then."

"Tiffany wasn't murdered at the airport," Shuman said. "She was shot in the chest at point blank range in the Holt's parking lot, and dumped into the trunk."

Oh my God. No wonder Madison suspected me of her murder.

It hit me as weird that Shuman would divulge this info, especially under the circumstances. But I decided to run with it.

"If that's true," I posed, "then how did the body get into the trunk? I had the key with me the whole time. It's impossible to get into the trunk with—oh, crap."

"What?" Shuman asked.

I ran the events of that morning through my head again—mentally stopping for a few pleasant seconds at the recollection of the gorgeous Sinful purse I'd been anxious to find—and remembered having the key clutched in my hand as I'd made a mad dash out of the stock room to avoid Cal and Troy.

"I popped the trunk while I was in the stock room," I said. "Yeah, I remember because I was in a hurry. I hit the remote, then Troy stopped me, and when I got outside to load the boxes of clothing, the trunk was latched—"

Shuman was watching me now, as if reading my thoughts.

"If Troy hadn't tried to talk to me, I'd have seen who killed Tiffany," I realized.

"Or been killed yourself," Shuman said.

I wasn't all that happy thinking I owed my life to Troy. I saw no need to mention it to him.

"It must have happened fast," Shuman said. "The killer parked next to the Mercedes, shot Markham, shoved her into the trunk those few minutes it was unlatched, and drove away."

"What about the security tapes?" I asked.

Shuman shook his head. "The cameras don't cover the entire parking lot. Only the loading dock area."

"Lots of people were in the parking lot that morning," I said.

"Nobody we talked to saw anything," Shuman told me.

I ran the whole scene through my brain. The garbage truck heading for the Dumpster. A big rig backed into the loading dock. The truck and replenishment teams arriving for work. A couple of guys grabbing a smoke. All the usual stuff. Nothing stuck out in my mind as unusual or important.

"What about motive?" I asked.

"They're taking a look at Ada Cameron," Shuman said.

Ada a murderer? It seemed like a stretch. What possible

connection could Ada have to Tiffany Markham, a purse party entrepreneur and ex-attorney from South Carolina?

Shuman and I stood in silence for another few minutes, both of us probably running different scenarios through our minds—although I doubt that fabulous Sinful purse occasionally popped into Shuman's head, like it did mine.

"Have you spoken to Virginia Foster yet?" I asked. "Tiffany used to be a lawyer back in South Carolina. They were close friends. Virginia came out after the family got word about Tiffany. She's staying at the Hyatt in Santa Clarita."

Shuman just looked at me. I couldn't tell from his expression whether he didn't already know about Virginia, or he resented my telling him something he already knew. Either way, I didn't score any points with him.

"If I hear anything at the store, I'll let you know," I promised.

"Don't bother," Shuman said. "Madison and I aren't on the case anymore."

"What?"

"We were ordered to turn everything over to our lieutenant," Shuman said.

"So whose case is it now?" I asked.

"Beats me," Shuman said, and walked away.

"It's me," I called to the closed door in front of me. "Haley."

Chains rattled, locks turned, and the security system beeped as I waited for Evelyn Croft to open her front door. I was used to the drill.

After "the incident" at Holt's last year, as Evelyn called it, she'd recovered from her physical injuries pretty quickly, but showed no sign of getting over the emotional ones. Still, all these months later, she wouldn't come out of her house.

The door opened a couple of inches and Evelyn's face appeared through the crack. I forced a big smile.

"It's me," I said again.

Evelyn looked past me and, seeing no one else, yanked open the door. On cue, I rushed inside and she slammed it closed again, then secured it at a frantic pace

"Well, Haley," Evelyn said, wringing her fingers. "It's so good to see you."

Today, she wore a khaki skirt, white sneakers, and a blue print blouse. Her hair and makeup were done. If Evelyn ever went out in public, she could easily be mistaken for a minister's wife.

"Let me get us some refreshments," Evelyn said, heading for the kitchen.

I took my usual spot on the sofa in the living room and noted that the pink and mint florals that covered every possible inch of the room had been replaced by blue and yellow florals. A few minutes later, Evelyn came in with a tray of her much dreaded tea and cookies.

"You got new furniture?" I asked.

"Slip covers," Evelyn said. "I made them myself."

I took another look at the sofa, love seat, and chair. They really looked great.

"You sewed them?" I asked.

"I love to sew," Evelyn said, and passed me a cup. "How are your classes?"

"Great," I said.

Really, my classes were awful. I hated them. In health we were studying suicide—which, at this point in the semester, didn't seem like a bad idea. In English we took a vocabulary test where I scored in the "impoverished" range and that made me feel so . . . so . . . well, never mind that now. The point was that I couldn't tell Evelyn any of those things. She had enough problems of her own.

I bit into one of the dry, brittle cookies Evelyn always served—I'd bring my own Oreos but it might hurt her feelings—while she talked. Even though she didn't get out, she watched TV news, read all sorts of newspapers and magazines, and surfed the Net for the latest local, national, and world events.

Most of the time, I didn't know what she was talking about.

But today I paid attention, anxious to learn if she'd heard anything about Tiffany Markham's murder. She didn't mention it. Hopefully, that meant the media didn't think it was a big enough story to cover, which would make my life a little easier.

By the time I'd choked down three cookies—I'd taken an extra one just to be polite, of course—and finished my tea, Evelyn's chatter had started to run down.

"Are you ready for your packages?" she asked, smiling like it was Christmas morning.

"Heck, yeah," I said.

I followed her down the hallway and into a bedroom she used for an office. It held an oak desk and sunny yellow curtains; blue flowers were everywhere. The room was immaculate and serene, like Evelyn herself.

In the corner sat a carefully stacked pyramid of FedEx boxes, my purchases I'd had shipped to her from Europe for safekeeping.

"Wow, I don't remember buying this much," I said.

I knew I'd spent my rent money—which was bad, I know—and now I vaguely recalled whipping out a credit card once. Okay, maybe it was more than once.

But, jeez, what was I supposed to do? Look at all of those fabulous fashions all over Europe and not buy them? I mean, really, this was my first trip with Ty. I owed it to myself to buy things to remember it by. Right?

"I'll bet you have some lovely things in here," Evelyn said, looking sort of dreamy.

I snapped back to reality, seeing the look on her face. Maybe I'd been wrong to send my packages here. I'd forced

Evelyn to vicariously experience my extravagant European spending spree, while she was too afraid to go to the mini-mart down the street.

Not a great feeling.

"You know, Evelyn," I said, "if you'd like to get out for a while, maybe go shopping or something, I'd be glad to take you."

"No!" she said, backing away and shaking her head frantically.

"Okay, okay," I said quickly. "But maybe we could just drive around a little. You don't have to get out of the car or anything, just sightsee."

She didn't look anxious to take me up on my bright idea, but she didn't bolt in the other direction, either. I figured that was something.

"Just think about it," I said. "Okay?"

"Well, maybe," Evelyn said quietly. "Maybe I'll think about it."

"I brought you something from Rome," I said, gesturing to the tower of FedEx boxes. "Want to see?"

She brightened a little. "Yes. Yes, I'd like that."

Of course, I had no idea which box held the glass bowl I'd bought for her, but it seemed okay with Evelyn that I opened every box and showed her what I'd purchased—except for the lingerie I'd found in Paris that I sincerely hoped would shut Ty up after our lovemaking.

I shoved everything back into the boxes and carried them out to my Honda. I hesitated a moment before I popped the trunk—luckily, there was no dead body inside—loaded everything, and waved good-bye to Evelyn.

I couldn't see her but I knew she was peeking from behind her closed living room blinds.

An hour of my life ground past in the housewares department as I straightened the displays of place mats. But this mind-numbing chore was okay with me tonight because it required that I sit on the floor where I could hide from customers.

I couldn't stop thinking about Detective Shuman and the conversation we'd had earlier today. At first, I'd thought it was to my benefit that he and Madison were off the Tiffany Markham murder case. Shuman wasn't in my corner anymore, and Madison was almost fanatical about proving me guilty of *someone's* murder. But now I wasn't so sure.

Voices from the other side of the aisle intruded on my thoughts. Damn. Customers. I ducked my head and kept straightening place mats.

Who were the new homicide detectives investigating Tiffany's murder? Shuman didn't know, which seemed odd to me.

The voices got louder. I scrunched lower and curled myself into a tiny—well, tiny for someone my size—knot, and kept working.

It was possible—very possible—that Madison and Shuman had gotten into some kind of departmental trouble over the last two murders when they'd named me—wrongly—as a suspect. And not only had I been exonerated, but I'd actually solved the cases myself which, I figured, hadn't done them any favors with their supervisors.

I'd like to think that would cause the new detectives on the case to steer clear of me. But instead, it might make them anxious to prove their colleagues right and come after me with everything they had.

It could go either way.

I shoved the last stack of place mats into the display bin. I needed more info, and I knew of only one way to get it.

Cautiously, I lifted my head and used my peripheral vision—which had expanded another 90 degrees or so since I'd started working at Holt's—and checked the aisle in both directions for the customers I'd heard earlier. No sign of them. I didn't hear them, either.

I got to my feet, only to see them two aisles over. I dropped down once more and duck-walked the other way. The entrance to the stock room was only a couple of aisles over. I could make it there easily without being spotted.

I made the turn and lurched to my feet to dash the last few yards when a girl jumped in front of me.

"Halt!" she declared, holding up her palm like a traffic cop. "Halt for Holt's!"

She looked like she was about twenty years old, with long blond bouncy curls and a perky smile, and had a Holt's name tag hanging around her neck.

"You're new, aren't you? Hi, I'm Christy," she said.

I didn't recognize her—and believe me, I would have remembered her—so she must have started working here during my two weeks in Europe.

Who the heck was doing the hiring these days?

"Halt for Holt's! Oh my God, I just love saying that!" she said and giggled again. "I *love* working here! You're going to love it, too!"

"I was just on my way—"

"Oh, no, no, no!" Christy put up her palm once more. "Wow, didn't they tell you about the Halt for Holt's program in orientation? It's so cool! See, it's like a mini-intervention. If any employee sees another employee not giving top-notch customer service, we intervene."

This *had* to be another of Sarah Covington's dumb-ass ideas.

I hate her.

"I guess you didn't realize it, but there were two customers in the other aisle looking for something," Christy said, still holding her big smile in place. "You should have helped them."

I was in no mood.

"If you saw them," I asked, "why didn't you wait on them yourself?"

Apparently my logic didn't penetrate her blond hair.

"Okay," Christy declared, "let's review the steps in our customer satisfaction program."

"I don't want to review the steps."

"First, greet the customer and make eye contact," Christy said, still smiling. "Then, ask a lifestyle question."

"I don't want to review the steps!"

"Next, point out features and benefits," Christy went on, ticking off the items on her fingers. "Have the customer try on. Suggest add-ons. Thank them and invite them back. See how this makes for better customer service?"

So far all it had done was make me want to bitch-slap her—just to get her attention, of course.

"Who knows? You might find the secret shopper! You want to win that flat screen, don't you?" Christy asked, bouncing on her toes. "It'll be so cool to win a prize—no matter what it is! Even the Holt's beach towel!"

Holt's was giving away beach towels? As a prize? That was even more lame than the sewing machine I'd won a few weeks ago.

"Just remember," Christy said, and held up her palm again. "Halt for Holt's! And always give great customer service!"

I gave her my why-don't-you-drop-dead glare but I don't think that penetrated, either. I hurried around her and went into the stock room.

I loved the stock room. The huge shelving units were filled with fresh, untouched merchandise that had a calming effect on me—I'm sure it's genetic—and it was a great place to hide out.

I climbed the big concrete and steel staircase to the second floor and wound my way through the aisles to the lingerie section. I didn't usually like to come back here—long story—but tonight was an exception. I needed some info and I knew only one person I could turn to.

I wouldn't have to do this if Holt's allowed us to use our

cell phones on the sales floor so, technically, I wasn't in the wrong here.

I phoned Ben Oliver and was surprised when he picked up. Ben was a reporter for the *L.A. Daily Courier.*

"Looking to ruin someone's life—again?" Ben asked.

I'd met him a few weeks ago when I'd given him a smoking-hot tip on a great story—which he didn't appreciate in the least. Really, *I* should have been mad at *him.* But that's not the way I roll.

"I get off work in an hour," I said. "Meet me."

"I'm kind of busy," he told me.

"I know you're not on a date," I said. "You're sitting there by yourself wearing wrinkled khaki pants and the blue polo shirt you've already worn once this week. Right?"

Silence. Then Ben said, "Starbucks. City Walk," and hung up.

CHAPTER 6

City Walk is a terrific area outside Universal Studios, a wide promenade lined on both sides with great restaurants, bars, and all sorts of shops, a must-see spot on any tourist's sightseeing list, plus a favorite of L.A. locals. It was a really cool place to hang out, which was why I was surprised that Ben Oliver was there.

I spotted him at a table outside of Starbucks sitting alone—I'd guessed right about the no-date thing—slumped in a chair beneath a giant King Kong cutout, watching the crowd walk past. Ben was in his late twenties with shaggy brown hair. I'd guessed right on the clothing thing, too—rumpled khakis and a tired-looking polo shirt.

I grabbed a mocha frappuccino—just to be sociable, of course—and sat down at the table. Ben sipped his coffee, threw me a quick glance, then stared out at the people walking past once more.

"How are things going at the newspaper?" I asked.

I knew Ben's editor had it in for him so, really, I figured things weren't good. But I decided I'd tackle it up front so we could get on to more important things—important to me, that is.

Ben didn't say anything, just kept sipping his coffee and watching the crowd.

"Heard about any good murders lately?" I asked.

That got a rise out of Ben. He cut his gaze to me.

"No," he said.

"Would you like to?" I asked, leaning forward a little.

He studied me for a minute, then turned his attention to the passing crowd once more.

"Not interested," Ben said.

I hated to throw Ada out in front of the bus yet again, but I was getting desperate here. If Ben couldn't get info on Tiffany's murder for me, I didn't have anywhere else to turn.

"It involves rich people, old money, deceit—all the good stuff," I told him. "The scandal could be huge."

"Not interested," Ben said again.

How could somebody not be interested in a huge scandal? It seemed un-American to me. Anyway, this wasn't working. I had to try something different.

"Not interested, huh?" I said, leaning back. "I guess that means you're back in your editor's good graces? Handling all the big stories again?"

"As a matter of fact, I'm covering a big story now," Ben said.

"Sitting at Starbucks?" I asked.

"I'm undercover," Ben said.

"Really? Cool," I said. My gaze darted around trying to pick a big story out of the crowd. I saw nothing. "So what is it?"

"Who got murdered?" Ben asked.

He was deliberately trying to be difficult. I knew that. But I decided to play his game—plus, if I sat here any longer, I'd be forced to get another mocha frappuccino.

"Tiffany Markham. She was some hotshot, old-money lawyer from South Carolina who chucked her life to move to California, then wound up shot to death a few months later," I said.

"What's her connection to you?" he asked.

"I found her body at Holt's," I said. "In the trunk of my boyfriend's grandmother's Mercedes."

Finally, Ben turned to me, a why-doesn't-that-surprise-me look on his face.

"It's not my fault," I insisted.

"Call *Dateline*," Ben said, looking out at the crowd again.

Now it was my turn to be difficult—something I can pull off pretty easily, if I have to.

"So I guess your editor is totally cool with you now and you don't need a huge story?" I asked.

Ben squirmed a bit, giving me my answer, then said, "I got a tip about espionage and terrorism."

"From who?" I asked.

I figured that after the way the tip I'd given him had turned out—long story—Ben would have turned and run at the offer of another tip. But I guess reporters feel obligated to check things out—reporters desperate to stop covering Little Miss pageants and chili cook-offs and get back to hard news, anyway.

And I had to agree with Ben. Espionage and terrorism were way cooler than murder.

"So what's going down?" I asked, looking around.

"This aerospace engineer is involved with a terrorist group and is selling government defense secrets overseas," Ben said.

I felt like I'd been zapped with a cattle prod. My dad was an aerospace engineer.

"What kind of secrets?" I asked.

Ben kept his gaze glued to the people passing by and lowered his voice.

"Aircraft engines," he said. "An engine designed with 'super cruise' capability allows an aircraft to fly at high performance levels but not use the after-burner. Doubles fuel usage. Eliminates the need for aerial refuel from tankers. Saves hundreds of millions of dollars in fuel costs."

At this point in any conversation of this type, I usually drift off. Descriptions of aircraft systems and engineering developments melt into *blah, blah, blah*. But this time I hung in there and paid attention.

"Something new is in development, something better than super cruise," Ben went on.

"What is it?" I asked.

"It operates with a far more advanced DEC—digital engine control—which is the heart of the super cruise."

Blah, blah, blah threatened to overtake me again, but I fought it off.

"What does that mean?" I asked.

"I don't know—yet. But that guy does. He's the one hanging out with terrorists and selling our secrets."

Ben nodded toward the crowd. I followed his gaze and realized that he hadn't been watching passersby all this time but rather the restaurant across the promenade. The Bubba Gump Shrimp Company had patio seating. Several of the booths were occupied by couples.

"The dark-haired guy in the blue shirt," Ben said, "sitting with the woman in the white blouse."

The first thing I noticed about her was her handbag. Not a designer brand, not even a knockoff, but a department store house brand, the sight of which made me a little queasy.

It's a genetic disorder, but I've learned to live with it.

This told me all I needed to know about her, but I looked a little further anyway. Mid-twenties, probably, with short dark hair cut in a simple style. No makeup, no jewelry. She had on navy blue pants and sensible flats. I didn't recognize her.

The guy was in his early thirties, I guessed, with dark hair and—

Hang on a minute.

I knew him.

Oh my God. *Oh my God.* It was Doug—Doug Eisner, my ex-boyfriend.

Oh, crap.

Doug had a girlfriend. A *new* girlfriend. *Already.*

The thought had been lodged in my brain since last night when I'd spotted them together at City Walk, and had hung with me all day.

I whipped my Honda into the parking lot at Holt's and headed for a prime spot near the door. An SUV cut me off and grabbed it. I hadn't even seen it coming. *That's* how distracted I was with Doug and this whole girlfriend-espionage-terrorist thing.

I slid into another space and cut the engine.

Doug and I had dated briefly—long story—a few weeks ago before Ty was my official boyfriend. He was nice in a lot of ways, but he was an engineer. Engineers were brilliant, but not exactly a lot of fun. Marcie and I had dubbed him "Dull Doug."

Anyway, things between us ended pretty quickly. It just wasn't working out.

Yeah, okay, it was Doug's idea to break up, but I would have done it myself anyway. He just beat me to it. Still, he'd made it sound like it was all his idea and had left me looking like an idiot.

Not a great feeling.

After seeing him last night, it miffed me, for some reason, that he had a new girlfriend already. Yeah, I had a boyfriend, too, but that's not the point.

How could Dull Doug have a new girlfriend *and* be involved in something as exciting as terrorism and espionage? It didn't make sense. Still, if he wanted to ruin his career and his life by selling defense secrets, that was his business.

But that wasn't the end of it. Doug worked for my dad. If Doug went down, that meant Dad might be implicated.

No way was I letting that happen.

Of course, it was possible that the hot tip Ben had received had been totally out in left field. Maybe if I called my dad I could find out what sort of project he was working on. Then I'd know—provided I didn't drift off during his explanation—whether or not this whole thing had any merit.

I glanced at my wristwatch. Four minutes before I had to clock in. Plenty of time.

I fished my cell phone out of my purse—a way hot Chanel hobo—and called my dad at his office. His voicemail picked up, so I left a message. Still, I didn't go inside the store. No sense rushing in and standing around for three whole minutes.

My cell phone rang. I grabbed it, then gasped.

Oh, crap. Ty was calling. I dropped the phone.

Yeah, okay, I knew this wasn't good. I should have answered on the first ring, thrilled to hear from him. He was my boyfriend—officially—and he was calling to tell me he was on the way home from London.

But I didn't know if I could take another night of him ruining my afterglow yammering about the stock market in Japan.

I glanced at my watch. One minute to punch in. I grabbed my purse and hurried into the store.

Customers crowded the aisles as I headed toward the breakroom, my cell phone at my ear, waiting to hear the message Ty had left. I almost wished Rita or that idiot Cal would see me and tell me not to use my phone, just so I could yell back that I wasn't on duty yet.

Maybe that wasn't the best attitude to start my shift with.

I breezed into the crowded breakroom and got in line at the time clock just as Ty's recorded voice explained that something had come up and he'd have to stay in London longer. He wouldn't be home tonight as promised. I breathed a sigh of relief—which was really bad, I know—but there it was.

Then I realized that he hadn't sounded disappointed. He sounded rushed. As usual. He hadn't mentioned my finding Tiffany's body, either. Or his grandmother. And Ada still hadn't returned any of my calls.

"No cell phones on the sales floor!" Shannon shouted, glaring directly at me.

I kept my phone to my ear, even though there was nothing to hear, as I fed my time card into the clock, then dropped it into my purse.

"Gather around, people, gather around!" Shannon called, waving us toward her.

I'd gotten used to the exercises we did before our shift started. I secured my purse in my locker and took my usual spot at the rear of the group. About ten employees were there today, including Marlene from the sewing department, who was about ninety years old and wheezed her way through the program, and Bob, the janitor who spoke no known language. Christy, that new girl who'd drilled me on the Halt for Holt's policy, was there, too. She gave me a big smile and a two-handed wave. I ignored her.

I followed along as Shannon led us through the usual routine of stretches and was feeling pretty good—right up to the point where she ruined everything by blabbing about the secret shopper and the contest.

I'm going to have to learn to lower my expectations.

"Those flat screens are slipping away," Shannon declared, jerking her thumb at the chart on the wall.

The big thermometer chart that indicated how close we were to our goal of achieving 100 percent customer satisfaction, based on the findings of the secret shoppers, currently showed us at 26 percent.

I wasn't taking a math class this semester, but I knew that wasn't great.

Prize categories were indicated alongside the percentage range of customer satisfaction we'd attained. Beach towel, toaster, digital camera, topping out with flat screens. Right now, we were barely in beach towel range.

"We have to do better, people," Shannon told us.

She glared at me when she said it.

"We've gotten some low scores," she said, and looked at me again. "Really low scores."

A few people in the group glanced at me.

"*Some* of us aren't trying," Shannon declared.

She shot me a serious stink-eye.

"*Some* of us are going to ruin it for the *rest* of us," Shannon declared.

Everybody turned and stared at me.

"*Some* of us had better get with the program," Shannon announced, giving me double stink-eye.

Now everyone in the group glared hard at me.

"Everybody get out there," Shannon said, nodding toward the breakroom door, "and let's win those flat screens."

I followed the group out of the breakroom. I thought Shannon might want to speak with me privately—which I'd ignore, of course—but luckily Christy bounced up and started talking to her.

As I passed the customer service booth, Bella rushed up.

"What'd you do?" she asked.

Jeez, where to start?

Bella glanced around, then leaned in and whispered, "The men in black are in the store. They're looking for you."

Oh, crap.

CHAPTER 7

"You've got to get out of here," Bella declared. She grabbed my arm and yanked me toward the door to the stock room. As we passed Jeanette's office, I caught a glimpse of a man standing in front of her desk. One of the men in black, as Bella had called them. A detective, I guessed, but dressed way better than Madison or Shuman. He had a partner, surely—these guys always traveled in packs—but I didn't see him inside the office.

Oh my God. *Oh my God.* They must be the new investigators assigned to Tiffany's murder. Why were they here? To question me? Arrest me?

No way was I waiting around for that to happen. I rushed into the stock room with Bella.

"What's your locker combo?" Bella demanded. I told her the numbers. "Find a disguise," she said, and hurried out of the stock room.

I rushed to the mannequin farm nearby and grabbed a blond wig, then hurried to the accessories department area and picked out sunglasses. A second later Bella rushed back in and stopped dead in her tracks.

"What kind of lame-ass disguise is that?" she demanded, shaking her head.

This exact disguise had worked great for me once before—long story—and I was slightly miffed at her attitude.

"Here," Bella said.

She passed me my purse, which she'd retrieved from my locker, then went to work. She pulled up my hair and wrapped a yellow print scarf around it turban style, then grabbed a fuchsia poncho—if you're going on the lam, the accessories department is the place to start—and swept it around my shoulders.

"Wear these," she said, and thrust an oversize pair of yellow sunglasses at me. I slipped them on.

"Take my car," she said, passing me a set of keys. "I got your keys. Call me when you're clear. We'll meet up and swap back."

I got the feeling Bella had done this before.

Maybe I needed to get to know her a little better.

I'd only seen one detective in Jeanette's office, so I figured his partner was probably roaming the store, looking for me. I slipped out through the loading dock and circled the building.

I'd seen Bella drive up to the store a million times, so I knew she owned an old red Chevy Cavalier—I don't think they even make those anymore. I found it easily and got inside. Scarves, headbands, combs, brushes, pins, and clips were everywhere.

Girlfriend was serious about hair.

My first instinct was to peel out of the lot but, really, where would I go? If the new detectives assigned to the case had found me here, they knew where I lived. Sooner or later they would catch up with me.

I glimpsed myself in the rearview mirror. Oh my God. I didn't even recognize myself.

I've really got to find out a little more about Bella's past.

The disguise made me feel safe, so I drew in a deep breath trying to calm myself. I needed to think.

I could call Detective Shuman. He could find out whether a warrant had been issued for my arrest, but would he do that? He'd been pretty cold at our last meeting and, really, he had no reason to help.

Jack Bishop flashed in my mind. He was a totally hot private detective—I didn't have personal experience, but I just *knew* he'd never brought up declining stock prices in the global economy after making love. We'd worked together back in the day at Pike Warner. I'd helped him out with his cases a couple of times and he'd returned the favor. If I called him, he'd help. But I didn't like burning a favor with Jack unless I absolutely had to.

I sat there for another minute, thinking. I couldn't decide what to do, but I figured getting some distance between me and the homicide detectives inside the store was the best thing at the moment.

I started the engine, then reached down to adjust the seat. My fingers hit something leather. I pulled it out.

Oh my God. *Oh my God.* A holster with a gun inside. Bella was packing heat.

This was so unfair. First, Jay Jax had a cool new name, a terrific job, and a Sinful bag, and now Bella had a secret past and a gun.

All of my friends were cooler than me!

Never mind about that now. I had to get away from Holt's.

Just as I backed out of the parking spot, I saw the detective come out of the store. He wasn't racing toward me or talking into a cell phone or gesturing to a circling helicopter, so I figured he hadn't realized I'd put on a disguise and slipped out the back.

I got a better look at him than when I'd hustled past Jeanette's office. Mid-thirties with dark hair cut short. Average height. A good build that filled out his off-the-rack suit nicely.

He got into a white sedan a couple of aisles over. From my vantage point—Bella parked in the assigned employee spaces, which was really inconvenient—I saw that his partner was already in the car, waiting for him. Guess he'd given up looking for me in the store.

They chatted with each other, then pulled away.

For a few seconds, all I could think was—*whew!*—they hadn't seen me. Then it hit me: I could go after them. I could follow them, see where they went, get a heads-up on exactly who they were.

Wow, how cool was that?

I fell into the line of cars leaving the Holt's parking lot, turned right at the light, and followed the white sedan east to the entrance of the 14 freeway. I merged onto the southbound lane two cars behind them, heading toward Los Angeles.

Okay, now my life was really cool. Maybe I should get a private investigator's license like Jack Bishop.

Why don't they teach something useful like this in college?

I wished I could call Marcie right now and tell her what I was doing—she'd be so jazzed, as a best friend would—but I didn't dare take a chance on losing the detectives.

The white sedan crept along at the speed limit. It took everything I had not to whip into the far left lane and blast by them—old habit—but I held back.

After about a mile, my thoughts wandered. Ty popped into my head. It occurred to me that during my moment of crisis in the Holt's parking lot when I was mentally running through the list of people I could turn to for help, I hadn't thought of Ty at all. And he was my boyfriend now—officially.

That probably meant something but I didn't want to spare the brain power to analyze it.

I followed the white sedan as it transitioned onto the 5 freeway, then took the 405. The detective driving the sedan never speeded up or slowed down, didn't pass anyone, didn't take the carpool lane even though he could have. Slowly, methodically, we plodded toward Los Angeles.

Jeez, this guy's driving was so boring. He probably discussed crime statistics after sex.

The gorgeous Sinful handbag bloomed large in my head and my pulse picked up a little. I absolutely had to find one. Not only did I desperately need it, but I couldn't possibly go to the record label's party Jay Jax had invited me to without one.

I was running through a mental list of stores to check when the white sedan signaled for a lane change—how weird was that—and took the Wilshire Boulevard exit. I swerved right cutting off a pickup truck, which I actually enjoyed, and followed. I almost missed them at the signal but the driver judiciously stopped for the yellow light. Under other circumstances, I would have run up on his bumper and blown my horn, but since I was undercover, so to speak, I didn't.

When the light changed, I followed them a few blocks to a huge building on the right. I'd seen it a million times but never knew exactly what sort of offices were in there. Probably something boring, judging from the outside of the building. The detectives parked in the lot. I swung into a space two aisles over, grabbed my purse and got out. They didn't look my way.

Jeez, this was so cool. They'd come to find me, and I'd followed them instead. All I had to do was tail them inside the building and see where they went.

Then it hit me: I could call Shuman and tell him. He hadn't known who took Tiffany's case away from him and Madison, and I could tell he was ticked off about it. If I told him, he'd be one up on Madison and the other detectives. Maybe he'd start to like me again.

Lots of people were coming and going from the building, so I fell into step with everyone else, keeping an eye on the homicide detectives while not getting too close. I was feeling like a real pro at this now.

Maybe I should join the military or the CIA. Of course, I'd have to bring Bella with me to do my disguises.

Inside the building were X-ray machines and security guards. Okay, that was kind of weird for an office building, but I put my purse on the conveyor belt and walked through. On the other side, I grabbed my purse and looked up.

Oh my God. Where were the two detectives I was following? I didn't see them anywhere. I'd only taken my eyes off of them for a few seconds—I couldn't leave my Chanel hobo on the conveyor belt unprotected. Where could they have gone so fast?

I hurried down the hallway thinking I'd catch them at the elevators. Then both of them jumped out in front of me from an open doorway.

I gasped and slid to a stop.

"Haley Randolph, we'd like to speak with you," one of them said. Both of them held out badges.

I whirled around, ready to make a break for the door, but stopped in my tracks. Two more detectives holding out badges stood behind me. I was surrounded.

"Look, Detective," I said. "I don't—"

"Special agent," he said. "FBI."

"The FBI?"

Oh, crap.

Oh my God. Those detectives—special agents—had known I was behind them all along. They'd led me here to the Federal Building and called ahead for two other agents to capture me in the corridor.

Maybe I'm not cut out for this undercover work. Although it was kind of cool that those guys had needed backup to apprehend me.

The realization of how it went down came to me as I sat alone in a conference room. I didn't know where I was, exactly, but special agents Paulson and Jordan, as they'd introduced themselves, had asked nicely. I didn't want to look guilty so I'd agreed to go with them.

The yellow print scarf Bella had wrapped around my head had started to itch, but I didn't dare take it off. What if they arrested me? My hair would look terrible. I couldn't have a mug shot done with turban-hair.

And where was my "official" boyfriend, at a time like this? Now, when I could use his family's prestige, their world-class attorneys—not to mention their bail money— where was he?

Right now, hearing Ty's impression of the Wall Street closing bell didn't seem so bad.

I glanced around the room. It looked more like a conference room than one of those dark, stuffy interview rooms you always see on television crime shows. There was a small table, chairs that weren't bolted to the floor, and there was no two-way mirror taking up one wall.

Maybe that was a good sign.

Or maybe they were trying to trick me into confessing something.

But what?

I flashed on the purse parties Marcie and I had been giving. We'd bought hundreds of knockoff handbags at L.A.'s Fashion District and sold them at parties for months now. Yeah, okay, I knew that buying and selling counterfeit bags was kind of, sort of, maybe just *slightly* illegal. But, jeez, who'd have thought there really was such a thing as the purse police?

Kirk Keegan—the guy who'd threatened me last fall— flared in my head like a nightmare that wouldn't go away. He'd been off my radar—officially—for a while now, but he kept popping into my thoughts. As far as I knew, Kirk had never been charged with a crime. The injured parties had preferred to avoid any negative publicity and let Kirk walk away unscathed. Still, Jack Bishop mentioned him nearly every time we got together. Why would he do that? Did he know something I didn't know?

Then another thought slammed me so hard I popped out of my chair. Doug. Terrorism. Espionage. *My dad.*

Oh my God. *Oh my God.* That *had* to be what this was about.

The FBI must have been spying on Doug and spotted Ben and me at Starbucks the night he'd told me about what he suspected Doug of doing. They must have followed me back to my car, gotten my license plate number, identified me, and learned everything there was to know about where I live and work.

Jack Bishop had followed me once—it was totally hot when he did it, of course—but now the idea seemed kind of creepy.

Who else might follow me, track my movements? Who else knew where I live and work? Who else might just appear in front of me one day?

The door to the conference room opened and special agents Paulson and Jordan walked in. I'd already forgotten which was which. I mean, really, how could I not? The FBI apparently hired people in the same way as the Rockettes. Everybody was the same height and build, only these guys didn't look likely to form up in a kick line—unless it was to boot my butt into a cell somewhere.

"Would you like some coffee or a soda?" one of them asked.

Since I didn't know which was which, I decided to think of him as Special Agent Paulson.

"Water, maybe?" he asked.

I could seriously go for a couple dozen Snickers bars. Luckily, I had my mom's pageant queen metabolism and could burn off calories quickly, but I was afraid to ask for anything. These FBI guys might unwrap a few bars and torture me with the smell of chocolate, and I'd confess to *something.*

"No, thank you," I said, glad that I sounded composed.

"Have a seat, Miss Randolph," Special Agent Jordan said, gesturing to the chair.

I sat down. The two of them took seats opposite me and Paulson laid a file folder atop the table.

Mentally, I steeled myself. I was not—*not*—going to say anything that might hurt my dad. He worked hard, he put up with a lot—he was, after all, married to my mom—and he didn't deserve to have his whole life shattered by some stupid misunderstanding.

And as for Doug? Well, I didn't want anything bad to happen to him, but he had a new girlfriend now—which still kind of annoyed me—and it was up to her to worry about him. All I cared about was my dad.

"What can you tell us about the morning Tiffany Markham was murdered?" Paulson asked.

Tiffany? Why was he asking about Tiffany? What about Doug and my dad and terrorism?

"*Who?*" I exclaimed.

Paulson took an eight by ten photo from the folder and placed it on the table in front of me. It was so unflattering, I figured it must have been her DMV photo.

"Tiffany Markham," Paulson said again. "You do know her, don't you?"

"Well, yeah," I told him. "But I figured you were going to ask me about—"

Oh, crap. I almost blurted it out.

"What?" Jordan asked.

"Nothing," I said, and it came out sounding *way* guilty.

Jordan and Paulson both stared at me, as if trying to penetrate my thoughts with death rays or something.

Then it hit me: the feds had taken over Tiffany's case from Madison and Shuman, not some other LAPD homicide detectives.

I couldn't wait to tell Shuman.

Then something else hit me: if they weren't asking about

Doug, but were interested in Tiffany instead, that meant they really wanted to talk to me about the knockoff hand-bag parties. How lame was that?

"Look, I know we all have our assigned role in life," I said, "but did you two really go to all the trouble of becoming FBI agents just to be purse police? I mean, really, there are a lot of *real* crimes happening around here."

Jordan and Paulson glanced at each other, then turned to me again.

"What can you tell us about Tiffany Markham?" Jordan asked.

I was tempted to throw Rita out in front of the bus and name her as Tiffany's business partner, but I figured they already knew that. Maybe they'd already questioned Rita, arrested her, and thrown her in jail. Was that why she hadn't been at Holt's lately?

The thought cheered me up a bit.

"I only met Tiffany once," I said.

"Did she mention anything about her family in South Carolina?" Jordan asked.

"I didn't even know she was from South Carolina until Virginia told me," I said.

"Virginia?" Paulson asked.

Jeez, these guys didn't know about Virginia Foster? What sort of investigators were they?

"Her friend, Virginia Foster. She came to California when she heard about Tiffany's murder," I said.

Then I started to get a weird feeling. Maybe this wasn't about the purse business, after all.

"This is about one of Tiffany's cases back in Charleston, isn't it?" I said. "You two *do* know she was a lawyer, right?"

Paulson pulled another eight by ten photo from the file folder and placed it in front of me.

"Do you recognize this man?" he asked.

I leaned forward and studied the picture. It was a man in his late thirties. He was smiling, and his blond hair was blowing as if he were on a boat or at the beach, maybe, and didn't have a care in the world. He was handsome and well groomed. If my mom were here, she'd raise her nose a bit and proclaim him "new money."

"I've never seen him," I said.

"Never?" Jordan asked.

I shook my head.

"How about the morning Tiffany was murdered?" Jordan asked. "Did you see him then?"

Oh my God. Did the FBI think this guy in the photo had something to do with Tiffany's murder? Was I looking at her killer? An accomplice? A witness?

I sat back again and centered my thoughts on that morning in the Holt's parking lot. Lots of people were there—I'd gone over all of it with Madison and Shuman that day, then later at Starbucks with Shuman—and nobody stuck out in my mind.

"I've never seen him before," I repeated. "Who is he?"

"Edward Buckley," Paulson said.

Then I remembered that in the breakroom at Holt's, Virginia had mentioned Tiffany's brother-in-law Ed who'd been killed in a car accident last year.

Okay, now I was really confused.

"Isn't he dead?" I asked.

Jordan looked at Paulson kind of weird, like maybe they didn't realize I knew Ed was dead, and maybe they'd said something they weren't supposed to say.

"What's this got to do with Tiffany?" I asked.

Paulson picked up the photos and stuffed them back into the file folder and they rose from their chairs.

"If you should recall anything more from that morning, give us a call," Jordan said, and presented me with his business card.

"Or if you should see . . . anyone significant," Paulson added.

I heaved a sigh of relief as they walked out of the office. Then Special Agent Paulson turned back.

"And, Miss Randolph, don't leave town," he said, then disappeared out the door.

I sat glued to my chair. Did that mean the FBI considered me a suspect in Tiffany's murder?

Oh, crap.

Another FBI agent, I guessed, escorted me downstairs and out of the building. My head was spinning by the time I got to my car.

The feds were investigating Tiffany's murder? A dead guy who maybe wasn't really dead? Dull-Doug-turned-terrorist wasn't even on the FBI's radar? I was still a suspect?

How could I begin to make sense of it all?

One thing was clear—there was nothing to do but go shopping.

CHAPTER 8

I called Bella—luckily, she ignored the lame-o no-cell-phone rule at Holt's—and she promised to meet me in the parking lot. She sounded kind of disappointed when I told her the detectives—I didn't mention they were really FBI agents—were there because I'd witnessed an auto accident, and I wasn't in trouble and heading for the Mexican border or anything. It was a total lie, but I didn't want to get into the whole thing about Tiffany's murder since neither Bella nor anyone else in the store had mentioned it and didn't seem to know about it.

Or did she?

I pulled into the Holt's parking lot and nosed into a space in the area where Bella usually parked. I glanced at the store entrance. No sign of Bella.

The gun hidden beneath the driver's seat had been in the back of my head since I'd found it there earlier. Why would Bella have it? Was it just for personal protection? Or something else?

I unwound my turban and took off the fuchsia poncho; I'd take them back during my next shift and enter them as returned and damaged in the inventory computer.

A thought crept into my brain. I didn't want to consider it—sort of like wondering what it would be like to carry a

Fendi purse to a beach party—but I couldn't stop the image from blooming in my head.

Had Bella killed Tiffany?

I felt awful thinking even for a split second that my BFF at Holt's could do such a thing, but jeez, she had a gun. Why wouldn't I think it?

I remembered back to the morning of Tiffany's murder. Bella had definitely not been in the parking lot when I'd arrived. I would have recognized her or her car. Wouldn't I?

Now I wasn't so sure. I'd been totally focused on getting those boxes of clothes for Ada and tracking down a Sinful handbag. Maybe I wasn't really paying attention.

Was she at work that morning, or later in the afternoon? I didn't remember.

What about motive? I couldn't think of a reason why Bella might have killed Tiffany. Opportunity? Shuman had agreed that the shooting had happened quickly, in the few minutes it had taken me to get inside the store, grab the clothes, and head out again. I suppose Bella could have done the deed as quickly as anyone.

I glanced at the store entrance. Still no sign of Bella.

I opened the glove box and rooted around until I found her car registration. Her home address was in North Hollywood. Not the sort of place you'd see a lot of kids walking around in white polo shirts carrying band instruments, but not a bad area, either. Would Bella need a gun for protection?

I glanced up and saw Bella crossing the parking lot, so I shoved her registration back into the glove box, grabbed my things, and got out.

"You okay?" she asked.

She looked concerned, which made me feel like an idiot for suspecting her of murder.

"It was nothing," I said, waving my hand to dismiss the whole thing. "But thanks. I appreciate your help."

"You coming into work?" she asked, nodding toward the store.

I could have gone into the store and worked my shift—I had, after all, clocked in today—but I didn't think I could face an evening of dealing with customers—not to mention the other employees. If Christy hit me with another Halt for Holt's intervention, I might rush out to the parking lot for Bella's gun and put an end to that marketing plan once and for all.

"Can't do it," I said. "Clock me out, will you?"

"Sure. At the end of your shift," Bella said slyly.

See what a great BFF she is? Could somebody that nice commit murder?

Really, I knew the answer: yes.

I scrounged a twenty dollar bill from my purse and held it out. I knew Bella was saving for beauty school and money was tight with her.

"For gas," I said.

Bella waved it away. "Don't worry about it."

"Look, it's either cash or a Holt's gift card," I told her. "You pick."

She snatched the bill from my hand, we swapped keys, and I got into my car as she headed back into the store.

I glanced around but didn't see anybody—more FBI agents, maybe?—sitting in a car, keeping tabs on me. Nobody looked suspicious. Still I couldn't shake the thought that, apparently, special agents Paulson and Jordan suspected me of Tiffany's murder and maybe someone really was watching me.

Never mind that now. I had something more important to attend to.

I pulled away from the store punching in Marcie's number on my cell phone. We met an hour later at Bloomingdale's.

"I can't believe they don't have a Sinful bag here, either," Marcie said, as we walked through their handbag department.

It was a fabulous purse department. All the best designers and all the latest bags—except for the Sinful.

"There's got to be one *somewhere*," I said.

"You know, you could always—"

"Don't say it."

I knew what Marcie was going to suggest even before she said it—that's what good friends we were—and I absolutely could not allow the thought to enter my brain.

"I'm not getting a knockoff," I insisted.

"They're bound to be all over the Fashion District," she said. "We could go down there and—"

"No," I said, shaking my head.

I simply could not buy a fake bag for myself—and certainly not the coveted Sinful bag—no matter how desperate I was to have one.

"When's our next party?" I asked, anxious to change the subject.

"I've been thinking about that," Marcie said, as we left Bloomingdale's and walked into the mall. "With Tiffany dying, maybe we shouldn't have any more parties for a while."

"Are you kidding? Now's the time to go full blast," I said.

All along I'd wondered how Rita managed to do so well in the purse party business. Now, knowing that Tiffany used to be an attorney, I figured she had been the brains behind their operation. Without her in the picture, Rita would likely fall on her face. What better time to take advantage of somebody's bad luck, swoop in, and grab all the business for ourselves?

Marcie shook her head. "There'll be a lot of police attention focused on Tiffany's life. We probably shouldn't be involved with the purses right now. It is sort of a, well, a gray area, legally."

Marcie was usually right about things. But the truth was I needed the money. I had my bills covered for now, but I'd have to do something soon. My European shopping spree had pretty much wiped out my checking account.

"Okay," I agreed. "But—oh my God."

I stopped and turned away, ducking my head. Marcie read my move immediately and did the same—as a best friend would.

"It's Doug," I whispered.

Marcie gasped. "Your ex?"

I couldn't believe it. I'd just seen Doug the other day eating at the Bubba Gump Shrimp Company, and now I'd stumbled over him again—with his girlfriend. What were the chances?

"That's him in the dull blue shirt looking in the Brookstone window," I said.

Marcie's gaze homed in on him like a heat-seeking missile. Her eyes widened.

"He's got a new girlfriend?" she asked. "Dull Doug has a new girlfriend? Already?"

It was kind of embarrassing that socially awkward, boring Doug had found a new girlfriend so quickly after we'd broken up. We called him Dull Doug, for God's sake. He probably hadn't had back-to-back girlfriends before in his entire life.

"She must be an engineer, too," Marcie said. "Look at the way she's dressed."

I glanced up. Marcie was right. The new girlfriend kind of looked like Doug—with boobs. Khaki pants, a blue blouse, flats. She carried the same department store purse I'd seen her with the other night.

"That's weird. She sort of resembles *you*," Marcie mumbled. She must have heard my outraged gasp because she rushed on. "Generally speaking, I mean. Tall, like you. Dark hair, same sort of figure. She even has your pageant legs."

Once I got past the new girlfriend's hideous clothes and her no-name handbag, I could see that Marcie was right.

"Maybe Doug isn't over you after all," she said. "Maybe he just found a replacement."

"One who won't doze off when he talks," I said.

Doug and the new girlfriend moved away from the Brookstone store, heading toward us.

"Let's get out of here," Marcie said, and we walked the opposite way. "So what's up with Ty? When did he get home?"

I knew Marcie had asked about my own boyfriend to make me feel better about seeing Doug. That's what best friends do.

"He's not here yet," I reported, as we strolled through the mall. "Something came up. He's not sure when he'll be home."

"Did he ask you to come back to Europe?" she asked.

"No, he didn't mention it."

Marcie said something but I didn't hear it. A noise started roaring in my brain, shutting out all other sounds.

Oh my God. Why *hadn't* Ty asked me to come back to Europe?

Didn't he like sleeping with me? Did he think I was boring in bed because I didn't know I was supposed to make the bull sound after he made the bear sound? Was Ty dreading the thought of sleeping with me?

Yeah, okay, I knew I'd been thinking that same thing— but this is totally different.

Marcie grabbed my arm and pulled me into Bloomingdale's again, shaking me out of my am-I-bad-in-bed trauma.

"Here comes Doug and the new girlfriend," she whispered, leading me down the aisle.

I glanced back and saw them headed our way. Jeez, how did I keep stumbling over them?

"Let's go look at shoes," Marcie said. "Judging from what she's wearing, they won't come near that department."

We browsed through the displays of stilettos and pumps—
I'm a sucker for a peek toe—and I was about to try on purple
sling-backs—that I had nothing to wear with, of course—
when Doug walked up.

"Hello, Haley," he said.

I was so stunned, all I could do was stare up at him.

He glanced back and I spotted the new girlfriend across
the department, pretending to look at a totally hot pair of
spiked heel, black leather, fur-trimmed boots. They were
from Kenneth Cole which, I'm sure, went right over her
head.

Doug looked at me solemnly.

"Haley, I know you're hurt about the way things turned
out between us," he said, "but you have to stop following
me."

"*What?*"

"I've seen you spying on Emily and me," Doug said.

"I—you—but—"

"This is for your own good," he said.

"You think I'm—"

"Haley, you have to get over me," he said. "In time,
you'll thank me for this."

Doug walked away.

I just stood there, my mouth open, as he joined his girlfriend. She glanced back and shot me a pitying expression,
then linked her arm through his and walked away.

Don't look at me that way! I wanted to scream. I wanted
to break up with Doug *way* before he broke up with me!

Oh my God. She had the gall to look like she felt sorry
for me—and she didn't even know what a Sinful handbag
was!

"Are you okay?" Marcie asked.

No, I wasn't okay.

I didn't have a Sinful bag, a boyfriend who would walk
through the mall with me, a gun under my car seat, a great
job, or a cool new name.

I hate my life.

And, right now, I double-hated it because I was going to have to go see my mom tonight.

I pulled to a stop in the driveway of my folks' home in LaCañada Flintridge, a fantastic area in the foothills overlooking the Los Angeles basin. The house had been left to Mom by her grandmother, along with a trust fund; we'd lived there for as long as I could remember.

Only Mom and Dad were there now. My older brother was flying F-16s in the Middle East and my younger sister attended college—she actually liked her classes, which was totally weird—and supported herself by modeling.

I never knew my great-grandmother, of course. She was long gone before I came along. I didn't know much about her, either. Mom was always sketchy on the details about Great-Grandma, back in the day when I had enough patience to ask her a question.

Tonight I wanted to talk to Dad. He was always tight-lipped about his work in the aerospace industry—it went with the job—but if I could somehow find out if the project he was working on had anything to do with that whole super-cruise-digital-engine-control thing Ben Oliver had told me about, then I'd know if Doug really was involved with terrorism and espionage.

I just hoped it wouldn't mean that Dad was involved, too.

I'd phoned him a couple of times and he'd returned my calls, but we kept missing each other. After seeing Doug—and the new girlfriend—tonight, I had to resolve this issue once and for all. Hopefully, Ben's tip would prove bogus, Doug—and Dad—would be cleared, and I could move on.

Juanita, the housekeeper, let me into the house.

"Is my dad home?" I asked.

She shook her head. "Your mother is in the family room."

I hadn't really wanted to talk to Mom because I'd managed to miss—or blow off—all her phone calls since I got back from Europe. I figured she'd heard that I'd been there with Ty and wanted to start planning our engagement party right away.

Not something I wanted to talk about.

I found Mom on the chaise lounge in the family room surrounded by books of fabric swatches, paint samples, and home-decorating magazines.

No wonder Dad wasn't home.

For a second, I thought about backing out of the room, but Mom looked up and saw me.

"Hi, sweetie," she said.

Ten o'clock at night and my mom had on a Chanel dress, three-inch heels, earrings, a necklace, and bracelet, with full-on makeup and not a hair out of place, as if the *E!* channel might burst into the room at any moment to do a live interview.

Tall with dark hair, we sort of looked alike except that she was stunningly beautiful while I—as she'd pointed out many times—was merely pretty.

"Where's Dad?" I asked, hoping I could head off her inevitable questions about Ty and me.

"At work," she said, flipping through the fabric samples. "I can't decide which color I like best."

"This late?" I asked. "What's he working on?"

"Some new project," Mom said, turning her head to examine a sample at a different angle.

Okay, it couldn't be this easy—nothing was with Mom—but I went for it.

"Yeah? What sort of project?" I asked.

Mom studied the sample a few seconds longer, looked up as if concentrating hard, then turned back to the fabric.

"How's Ty?" she asked.

Damn. She got me. Mom can be crafty sometimes. It's her pageant training.

"He's fine," I said. I guessed he was fine. I didn't know since he hadn't called lately.

Mom was quiet for a few minutes as she turned pages and matched a paint sample to a different fabric swatch.

"Perhaps I should have a little dinner party and invite him," Mom said.

Damn. I thought I was home free.

"Last I heard he was still in London. I have no idea when he'll be back," I said, which, thankfully, was the truth.

Mom grew quiet again and I figured her thoughts had wandered off to whatever room she was intending to redecorate.

"Do you think Dad will be home soon?" I asked.

"This new project of his is very time consuming," Mom said, tilting a fabric sample to catch the light. "It's the new advanced version of the digital engine control, the heart of the super cruise. It's designed to adapt to any aircraft engine for improved thrust vectoring capability. It redirects exhaust for a huge advantage in maneuverability. The project is quite involving."

Oh my God. *Oh my God*. I didn't know what startled me more: that Dad had told Mom about his top secret government project, or that Mom had listened—actually listened—well enough to repeat it.

"Mom, isn't that info classified top secret?" I asked.

"Only the details, not the concept," Mom said, and glanced up. "Besides, why wouldn't your father tell *me?*"

"I've got to go," I said, and left.

I got in my car and pulled away from the house, my head spinning.

My whole life I'd wondered what my dad—a brilliant aerospace engineer—had possibly seen in my mom, why he tolerated her, how he could live with her. Had I just discovered the answer?

She listened. She paid attention to what he said—and remembered it.

Was that the secret to a good relationship, a long marriage? Couples actually talking—and listening—to each other?

Did that mean that in order to have a long-term relationship with Ty, I'd have to learn about economics, stocks, and hedge funds?

Oh, crap.

CHAPTER 9

"So what's the big news?" Detective Shuman asked, as he stood over my umbrella table outside my favorite Starbucks in Santa Clarita.

I'd phoned him late last night on my way home from Mom's house and persuaded him to meet me this morning with the promise of new info—a detective can't resist following a clue. He hadn't sounded all that excited about it, though, and he didn't look pleased to be here.

Ty, Doug, and now Shuman. I'd had it with men who didn't want to be around me.

"Look," I told him, "are you going to get over it, or what?"

Shuman glared down at me—his bad-ass cop stare. It was kind of hot.

I stared right back, probably because I was buzzing pretty good from my second mocha frappuccino, and finally he dropped his tough-guy expression and sat down.

"Are we going to be friends again or not?" I demanded. "I've apologized to you for what happened before, but I'm not doing it again. You're just going to have to get over it because I still want us to be friends. Okay?"

Shuman looked at me for a couple of seconds, then grinned. Shuman's got a killer grin.

"Okay," he said.

"My final peace offering," I said, and presented him with the cup of coffee I'd bought for him when I'd first arrived. It was probably kind of cool by now, but Shuman didn't seem to mind as he gulped down a couple of swallows.

"Did you talk to Virginia Foster?" I asked.

"I'm off the case," he reminded me.

"Yeah, I know," I said. "So what did she tell you?"

"Probably the same thing that she told you," Shuman said.

I knew Shuman had talked to her—especially since he'd been forced off the case.

"Tiffany was a lawyer back home," Shuman reported. "She broke wild one day and moved to California. Left her family wondering what happened."

He was right. That's pretty much what Virginia had told me.

"Did she mention Tiffany's brother-in-law Ed?" I asked.

It had hit me as weird that she'd brought up Ed that day in the breakroom at Holt's, and more so since those FBI guys had asked about him, too.

Shuman nodded. "She made a point of it."

He did cop-face pretty well, but I'd known him long enough to realize he knew more.

"The FBI's got Tiffany Markham's case," I said.

Shuman choked on his coffee.

"I went in for questioning," I told him. "Voluntarily."

It was sort of voluntarily. I drove myself down to the Federal Building.

I didn't see a need to mention any more details than that.

"What gives?" Shuman asked, wiping his chin with a paper napkin.

"They showed me a photo of that Ed Buckley guy and asked if I recognized him," I said.

I could see that the homicide detective gears in Shuman's brain were turning big time.

"Did you?" he asked.

"No," I said. "Then they asked if I'd seen him in the parking lot the morning Tiffany was murdered."

Shuman rocked back in his chair.

"Last I heard," I said, "Ed was supposed to be dead."

Shuman sat still for a few minutes and so did I.

"Tiffany must have been at Holt's that morning to talk to Rita. I mean, why else would she have been there? Maybe Rita saw something," I said. "Did you and Madison question her?"

"The case got pulled before we heard from her," Shuman said.

"She didn't return your call?" I asked.

Shuman shook his head.

Okay, that was weird. Rita was supposed to be Tiffany's friend. Why wouldn't she help out with her murder investigation?

I got a yucky feeling in my stomach.

"Rita hasn't been at work since the day Tiffany was killed," I said.

Shuman frowned and I was sure I could read his mind.

Maybe Rita was just on vacation. Maybe she was in mourning.

Or maybe Rita had been there when Tiffany had been killed. Maybe she'd seen everything.

Maybe she was in hiding.

Or maybe she was dead and stuffed in the trunk of somebody's car.

"Oh my God, don't you just love clocking in?" Christy asked, bouncing on her toes.

She stood in line ahead of me at the time clock in the Holt's breakroom along with about a dozen other employees, all of us waiting for another few hours of our lives to grind mindlessly past so we could get on to something interesting.

Christy didn't wait for my reply—which was probably wise on her part—and said, "I can't wait to get out there! Can you? I mean, gosh, just being on the sales floor is so cool!"

She kept blabbing on about how much she loved working retail, but I blocked her out easily and checked the work schedule hanging next to the time clock.

Rita's name wasn't listed.

I wondered if anyone—like those two crackerjack FBI agents, maybe—had realized Rita hadn't been to work and figured out there might be a connection to Tiffany's murder. For a moment I thought about contacting them, asking if they knew anything, but I figured they wouldn't tell me, no matter what. And it would probably be better—for me, of course—if they forgot I existed.

The line moved forward and everyone clocked in as Shannon came into the breakroom.

"Gather around, people, gather around," she called, waving her arms as if there weren't fifteen people squeezed into a room meant for eight, who had no idea where to go.

Like trained dogs, all the employees formed up in a circle ready to begin our preshift stretches. As always I drifted to the rear of the group.

"Hey, Haley," Troy said.

He sidled up next to me, his mouth sagging open a little.

Troy worked my nerves big time. Why couldn't he be missing, instead of Rita? I wouldn't feel obligated to go looking for him.

I edged away from Troy and positioned myself behind that big guy who works in men's wear.

Shannon led the group through our usual stretching routine, then tensed us all up again—well, me, anyway—by talking.

"I know you've all seen the customer satisfaction thermometer," she said, pointing to the chart on the wall.

Our satisfaction rate had plummeted to 20 percent. Wow, how had that happened?

"We've lost a lot of ground. We're losing those flat screens, people," Shannon said. "If we don't turn this around, we'll be lucky to win those beach towels."

She glared right at me, mad-dogging me big time. A few people turned, too.

"Thanks a lot, Haley," somebody grumbled.

"Yeah," someone else said. "We'd better not get stuck with those beach towels."

Jeez, why was everyone looking at me? What did I do?

"Because *some* of us don't seem to know the program," Shannon said, "*all* of us are going to have to go through the training again."

Everybody moaned. Several more people looked at me.

"Check the schedule," Shannon said, and jerked her thumb toward the breakroom door. "Now get out there and let's earn those flat screens."

I eased my way around the knot of people hovering in the doorway and headed out to the sales floor. I'd barely made it halfway through the women's section when Christy bounded up beside me.

"Haley, I have to confess something," she said.

Unless she was about to admit to shooting Tiffany and dumping her body in Ada's trunk, I wasn't much interested. I kept walking.

"It was me," she declared.

I stopped. No way could I be this lucky.

"I did it," Christy said. "I was the one who told Shannon you didn't know the Halt for Holt's customer service points."

Where was Bella's gun when I needed it?

"It was for your own good—and the good of the store," Christy declared. She smiled and her eyes got big. "But it's going to be so great when you know the program! You can wait on customers all the time and you'll know exactly what to say! You can really help them!"

Maybe I'd start carrying my own gun.

"I mean, I'd just die—*die*—if I couldn't help a customer find the right size or color, or help them with a problem!" Christy said. Her smile got bigger. "You'll see, Haley, it'll be great!"

She bounced away and I plodded on to my assigned department.

Perhaps Holt's knew, after all, that the women's clothing they stocked was hideous beyond all reason, because the store had recently installed a sewing and fabric department and hired elderly, feeble Marlene—one of the last women on the planet, evidently, who remembers America's pre-Singer days—to give classes.

I knew this because, for no apparent reason, I was frequently assigned to work in that department. That was okay with me, though, because every time a customer asked a question, I could just refer them to Marlene; I guess I gave off an I-don't-know-a-bobbin-from-bias-tape vibe.

I got busy straightening a display of ribbon while Marlene gave instructions to a class of beginners on how to make a pair of pajama pants. I'd heard her spiel so many times, I could make them myself, in my sleep. Not that I'd be caught dead in them, but still, I could make them if I had to.

Two other customers wandered up and watched as Marlene explained the intricacies of sticking straight pins into fabric. One of them, apparently enthralled, suddenly looked at me and headed my way. Sensing a question, I left the department.

I'd seen on the schedule in the breakroom that Bella was working in housewares tonight. I found her folding a couple dozen cloth napkins somebody had thrown into the aisle.

"What's up with Rita?" I asked. "Have you heard why she hasn't been at work?"

Bella shrugged. "All I can say is good riddance."

"Did she quit?" I asked, my heart suddenly beating faster. I could stand a little good news.

"Like we'd get that lucky," Bella said.

She had a point.

"Listen, Bella," I said, "when I borrowed your car, I found a gun under your seat."

I'd wondered about it for a while and, since I'm not big on suspense, I decided to just come out and ask her.

"Oh, yeah," Bella said, and waved her hand like it was no big thing. "I always keep a gun in my car. Don't you have one?"

"No," I admitted.

"Everybody in my family has one. My sisters, my brothers. My nana's got a forty-four Magnum she carries in her handbag. She's stuck back in the seventies and that old Dirty Harry movie," Bella said. "You don't have one? Really?"

Jeez, even Bella's nana was cooler than me.

And just to prove that things could always get worse, Shannon stomped up.

"Haley, what are you doing over here?" she demanded, planting herself in front of me.

"I was helping a customer," I lied.

"You're supposed to be on a register," Shannon told me. She waved her hand toward the ceiling. "I've been paging you. You're backup cashier tonight."

I was?

"Didn't you read the backup cashier schedule?" she demanded.

There was a backup cashier schedule?

"Tonight's our Ginormous Coupon Event," she told me.

That had to be Sarah Covington's big—ginormous—idea.

"Come on," Shannon said, and walked with me toward the front of the store. "Now listen. The secret shopper could be anybody, so you'd better do a good job. Be sure you ask every customer if they want to open a Holt's charge account."

I had no intention of doing that.

"And remind them to complete our online questionnaire," Shannon told me.

I wasn't going to do that, either.

"And you'd better follow the Holt's six-step customer satisfaction program—or else," Shannon said. "Now, go. Open register five."

Three checkout lanes were open and customers were stacked twelve deep in each line. Christy was running register four.

"Hey, Haley!" Christy called. She gave me a big smile and waved. "You're going to *love* running a register!"

"I've done this before. I'm not new—"

"If you have any questions, just ask!" she told me, and turned back to her customer.

Shannon escorted a bunch of customers over to my line to avoid a line-jumping stampede, while I punched my employee number into the register.

I looked down the long line of customers. One of them could be a secret shopper. Or maybe more than one. The way our customer satisfaction stats fluctuated, apparently they were swarming our store like brides to a gown sale.

I glanced at Christy on register four. She smiled and chatted with the customers, and they smiled and chatted back as they whizzed through her line.

On my other side, Colleen manned register six. Colleen—who will probably work here forever because she's too slow witted to know what a crappy job this is—talked to her customers like they were her best friends.

Oh my God. Colleen and Christy were both working the new program. No way was I going to let them do better than me.

Yeah, okay, I know I'm competitive. Sometimes in the

gym I race the person beside me on the stationary bicycle. That's how I roll.

All I had to do was follow the steps from the customer service program. What were they? Something about pointing out benefits—that would be a stretch—suggesting add-ons—no way could I bring myself to do that—and asking a lifestyle question.

That one I could do.

The first customer was a woman in her forties. She handed me a knit top that was, even by Holt's standards, an all-time fashion low.

"I can't believe I found this here," she declared, shaking her head in wonder.

The top was tie-dyed in about a dozen vibrant shades of orange, green, and purple, with ruffles running down the V-neck.

I reeled back in horror.

"I can hardly believe it, either," I said.

"I've been looking for something like this everywhere," the woman said.

"Leave it to Holt's," I said.

I pulled myself together and scanned the tag.

"Wow," the woman declared, swiping her credit card, "it's on sale. Half off. This is my lucky day. I'll have to do something special with the savings."

"Like maybe buy some gasoline and matches to set this thing on fire," I said.

That was a lifestyle question, wasn't it?

I shoved the top into a bag. She snatched it out of my hand, gave me a dirty look, and walked away.

Three more people got in my line.

Christy waved, getting my attention.

"You're doing *great*," she said, and gave me an encouraging nod. "Keep it up!"

The next customer to step up was a woman with gray

hair and hound dog jowls. She struggled to lay two picture frames on the counter.

"Goodness, those are heavy," she declared, breathing hard.

I scanned them both—they weighed about a half pound combined—and told her the total. The woman studied the display screen.

Two more customers joined my line. I glanced at Colleen. Her line was still moving. Christy's was, too. I told the woman her total again.

"I . . . I can't see the screen," she complained. "Where are my glasses?"

She hefted her huge purse—a tote she'd decorated with red rhinestones herself, apparently—and rooted around for several minutes until she came up with her reading glasses.

"There, that's better," the woman said, settling them on her nose. "Okay, now, let me see."

The customer behind her rolled her eyes.

The woman leaned down and squinted at the display screen.

"Oh, my, yes," she said. "There it is. There's the total."

In a complete departure from my own personal customer service policy and in a desperate attempt to get my line moving again, I said, "Would you like to put this on your Holt's charge?"

She looked up at me. "Oh, no. No, no. I never charge. And you shouldn't either. No, I'll write you a check."

A check? Jeez, nobody wrote checks anymore.

The woman dived into her handbag again, scrounged around, and finally came up with her checkbook and began writing.

It would probably have been faster if she'd chiseled it into stone.

Customers in my line grumbled and shuffled impatiently. I didn't blame them. At this rate, their coupons were going to expire before they got to the register.

The woman slipped off her glasses and dropped them into her handbag again, then handed me her check. I didn't bother to look at it—if she'd filled it out wrong, oh well—and fed it into the check reader, then shoved it into the register.

"Thanks for shopping at Holt's," I said, dumping her picture frames into a bag.

"Oh, wait. What is this?" the woman asked.

Because retail stores are pathetically desperate to sell their customers—whom they've already run through their aisles and checkout lanes like a herd of cattle—one more item, they jammed all kinds of merchandise around the registers. Socks, perfume, boxed cards, gift cards. Anything, really.

The woman plucked a chocolate bar from the display and squinted down at it.

Shannon walked up to my line and glared at me—like it was my fault, or something, that this lady was taking forever.

"I could use a little taste of something sweet," the customer said. She leaned back and held the chocolate at arm's length. "Does this have glutens?"

Jeez, the last thing I needed was for her to dig her glasses out of her handbag again to read the ingredients.

"Yes," I said. "It's loaded with glutens."

I had no idea what glutens were. We probably covered that in health class. I hate that class.

"Well, I suppose it wouldn't hurt, just this once," the woman said, and laid the chocolate bar on the counter. "I'll take it."

The woman in line behind her groaned. I nearly did, too.

I scanned the chocolate bar and—thank God—the customer pulled a wallet out of her handbag instead of her checkbook.

"That will be three ten," I told her.

"Good," she said, as she unzipped her change purse. "I can finally get rid of all my pennies."

I hate my life.

*   *   *

Since it was too late to go shopping when I got off work, there was no way to soothe my frazzled nerves but to hit my favorite Starbucks on the way home. I got my mocha frappuccino—venti, with whipped cream and an extra shot of chocolate syrup, which just shows what a crappy day I'd had—and took a seat outside at an umbrella table.

The evening was a perfect Southern California evening. Few stars were visible, of course, since the city lights were so bright, and the only breeze came from the passing cars, but still, it was a great place to unwind.

I had a lot to think about—Tiffany's murder, Rita's sort-of disappearance, Doug's terrorism, my college classes that I hated, the Sinful bag I desperately needed, and the record label's party I absolutely had to have a cool outfit for—not to mention Ty. He'd left me a message on my cell phone saying he missed me and was anxious to get home. That was nice to hear. At least I think it was. He'd said it so fast I could barely make out the words.

I drew in a deep breath, closed my eyes, and let myself relax. I needed to just let everything go, mentally. For a few minutes, I wanted to—

The chair beside me scraped the concrete patio. I opened my eyes and I saw a man sitting next to me. The light was dim. Shadows fell across his face. A couple of seconds passed before I recognized him.

Kirk Keegan.

My heart banged against my chest. I sat up straight in the chair.

"You ruined my life," Kirk said calmly. "Now I'm going to ruin yours. And just so you know, I'm going to start with that boyfriend of yours."

He got up and walked away.

Oh, crap.

CHAPTER 10

Oh my God. *Oh my God*. I couldn't believe it. Kirk Keegan had just sat down beside me. Threatened me. And walked away—like nothing had happened.

I sat frozen in the chair outside Starbucks, too stunned to move.

For a second I wondered if I'd imagined it. It had been over with so fast, I wasn't sure anything had really happened—sort of like some of the guys I'd had sex with.

Was it really Kirk? I hadn't seen him in months but, yeah, it was him. I'd recognize him anywhere. Early thirties, dark hair, handsome. Really handsome. Kirk never had trouble with the women, thanks to his good looks. He was a charmer, too. Women couldn't resist that either.

He'd been an attorney with Pike Warner, where I'd worked, back in the day. We'd hung out a few times but never had any sort of relationship beyond that. I'd thought he was my friend—until he screwed me over big time. I'd shoved it right back on him and he'd disappeared—after he threatened to kill me, of course. I'd figured I'd seen the last of him.

Until now.

I grabbed my frappuccino and rushed to my car, got inside, and peeled out of the lot in full-on panic mode.

He had my home address—long story—so he must have followed me. That's why I'd had that creepy feeling lately that someone had been tailing me. It wasn't the FBI. It was Kirk. He knew where I lived, where I worked, even my favorite Starbucks. What else did he know?

Everything, probably.

Oh my God, was he following me *now?*

I looked in my rearview mirror, then at the traffic on my left and right. It was dark so I couldn't see inside the cars. Why hadn't I paid attention when he left Starbucks? I would know what he was driving.

I've got to get better at this surveillance thing.

Why can't they have a useful class like *that* in college?

I cut across two lanes of traffic and hit the entrance to the 14 freeway, heading south. Traffic was light—well, light for L.A.—but there were too many cars to know if Kirk was following me. I hung in the left lane, then swerved all the way to the right and caught the transition to the northbound 5. Nobody followed, so I figured Kirk wasn't behind me.

Not that it mattered, I realized. He knew everything about me. He could show up at my apartment or at my job any time he wanted.

Not a great feeling.

I drove for a while, gradually slowing to something close to the speed limit, gradually calming down.

I wasn't sure how Kirk thought he could ruin my life—since I thought it was pretty screwed up already—but he'd threatened Ty. I had to do something.

I fished my cell phone and Bluetooth out of my purse and called Jack Bishop, the hottest—and only—private investigator I knew. He answered on the second ring.

"I had a visitor tonight," I told him. "Kirk Keegan."

Jack was quiet for a few seconds, then said, "What did he want?"

"Revenge."

"Where are you?"

"Driving."

"I'll meet you at your place. Stay in your car until I get there," Jack said, and hung up.

I exited the freeway at McBean Parkway and took the surface streets through Valencia to my apartment in Santa Clarita. When I swung into my assigned parking spot, I saw Jack's black Land Rover sitting nearby. He appeared out of nowhere and slipped into my passenger seat. I was sure he'd already checked the parking lot and the hallway outside my apartment, looking for Kirk.

Tonight Jack had on jeans, a dark crew-neck shirt, and a black leather jacket. I didn't know where he'd been or what he'd been doing when I had called, but he got here pretty quick. I wondered if he drove around looking hot, just in case.

"Kirk sat down at my table at Starbucks. I didn't even see him walk up. He said that I'd ruined his life so now he was going to ruin mine," I said. "Do you think he's serious, or just trying to scare me?"

Jack's job as a consultant to Pike Warner meant that he handled all sorts of investigations—and not just for clients. He'd never come out and said so, but I knew he had the inside track on some of the firm's employees, too—including Kirk.

"He's serious," Jack said, his eyes roaming the parking lot. "Keegan's a smart guy. Don't underestimate him."

I knew Kirk was smart. He'd been way up the food chain at Pike Warner before he'd turned to the Dark Side.

"Keegan's the kind of guy who'd toy with you," Jack said. "Not attack you outright."

That sounded like Kirk's style. He must have been following me for a while, coming up with a plan. Ty had been out of the country, then I'd been gone for two weeks in Europe with him. Kirk must have wondered why I hadn't been at home or at work. But he hadn't given up, obviously. He'd waited since last fall to get even with me.

"Ty's in Europe," I said. "No way Kirk can get to him over there."

"Don't bet on it."

"Ty's got a lot on him right now with this whole Holt's International thing he's trying to launch," I said. "I don't want to worry him."

If I told Ty what was going on—not that I expected him to call me again anytime soon—and he rushed home—not that I really thought he would—wouldn't that just put him in Kirk's path? Make things worse?

Jack thought for a moment. "I'll check into it."

"I think I should get a gun," I said.

"No."

"Will you help me—"

"No."

"Take me to the shooting range—"

"No."

"But—"

Jack opened the car door. "I'll walk you upstairs."

I got out and we climbed the stairs to my second floor apartment. The exterior walkways were dimly lit by wall sconces and muted light shining through my neighbors' windows. Jack took my key and went inside first. He checked out the rooms while I waited by the front door.

"No sign of Keegan," he reported. "Just watch yourself. Call me if anything happens."

Jack stood near me. The heat from his body sent all sort of thoughts through my head—which was really bad, I know. Ty was my boyfriend now and I had to remember that— even though he wasn't here, and seldom called, and never e-mailed, and didn't send flowers or cards or gifts. Still, he *was* my boyfriend.

"Thanks," I said to Jack. "I owe you."

"Damn right you do." He gave me one of his killer smiles. "I'll let you know what I want, when I want it."

He left. I bolted the door.

It was a Coach day. Definitely a Coach day.

Thanks to Kirk Keegan, I needed to find a new favorite Starbucks. This was a major inconvenience, but luckily there were so many of them I had a lot to choose from.

Bright and early—well, ten o'clock was kind of early—the next morning I rolled up to a Starbucks in Glendale and parked. Glendale was a bit of a drive from my house but there was a great mall nearby so that made it okay.

I sat in my car—I had a serious Starbucks flashback from last night—waiting to see if Kirk Keegan pulled in behind me. He didn't, so I grabbed my Coach tote and went inside.

I ordered a venti mocha frappuccino with whipped cream and extra chocolate—just to stimulate my brain cells, of course—and sat down at a table. I had an English paper due today so I had brought my laptop.

Using a laptop in Starbucks was the coolest thing ever. You always looked smart. For all anybody knew, you could be writing a screenplay or a major magazine article. I pulled a scarf from my tote and tied it around my neck, which made me look positively brilliant.

I hoped someone I knew would come in and see me—someone other than Kirk Keegan, that is.

I hardly slept at all last night thinking about Kirk's threats. I knew Jack would keep his word and check into whatever it was he wanted to check into, but I couldn't just leave it at that.

What could Kirk do to ruin Ty? Lots of things, I figured, like vandalize his businesses or hurt his family. But I didn't think that would be enough for Kirk. Whatever he did, he'd want to make sure it hurt me, too. I mean, otherwise, what was the point? His plan must be something he could put into action immediately upon Ty's return from Europe, but I still had no clue of what it might be.

I sipped my frappuccino and gazed out the window into the parking lot. Maybe I should encourage Ty to stay longer—not that he seemed in a rush to get back to me anyway.

And just to prove that my life could continue to get worse, it occurred to me that once Kirk had accomplished whatever it was he had planned for ruining Ty, he might move on to everyone in my family. Or maybe one of my friends, or somebody I work with.

Never mind. I couldn't worry about that now—not with everything else I had to deal with.

I pulled my laptop out of my Coach tote and powered it up. The English paper I was supposed to write would just have to wait. I dashed off a quick e-mail to my professor containing my touch-of-the-stomach-flu excuse—a personal favorite of mine—and let him know I'd have the paper in to him tomorrow. He'd lower my grade but, oh well.

I couldn't do anything about Kirk, at the moment, so I moved on. This thing with Ed Buckley had been rambling around in the back of my head for a while. Even though Detective Shuman had acted like he was ready to make up and play nice the last time I saw him, I didn't know for sure that I could count on that. I had to check things out myself.

I Googled the newspapers in Charleston and came up with the *Charleston Post and Courier*. Tiffany's death had made the front page, unlike here in L.A. where it hadn't caused a ripple. If she'd been a celebrity or call girl or a disgraced politician, the media would have been all over it.

Virginia Foster could have written the newspaper story—it had all the info she'd given me that evening, in Holt's breakroom. Tiffany had been from an old, well-established Low Country family, a partner in their prestigious law firm. She'd been active in all sorts of civic and charity organizations.

The story gave the impression that Tiffany's death had resulted from a random shooting—not unusual for Los Angeles.

No mention of the FBI investigating the case.

Ed Buckley's death was tacked onto the story—as if Tiffany dying wasn't enough misery for one family. Described as a local businessman, Ed had died last summer in a car crash outside of Charleston. He'd left behind a wife—Tiffany's sister—and three daughters. Featured was a photo of Ed, the same one that special agents Paulson and Jordan had showed me.

No mention of the FBI investigating this death, either.

I sat back in my chair. Yeah, okay, Ed's death was sad and untimely, but I still didn't see what it had to do with Tiffany. Or why the FBI would be interested. And why would they ask if I'd seen Ed that morning in the Holt's parking lot? Didn't they know Ed had died last year?

I sipped my frappuccino waiting for the sugar, chocolate, and caffeine to kick in and give me that big brain jolt I needed to figure this out.

Nothing kicked in.

Jeez, I hoped I hadn't built up a tolerance to these things. Next time, I should bring a Snickers bar to munch along with it. Or maybe I'd do that right now.

I glanced out the window again, hoping to spot a mini-mart or drugstore in the strip mall next door, but instead I saw Doug sitting in his car. I'd know that wimpy white Kia—complete with its optional look-like-a-dork package—anywhere.

I gasped and ducked down behind my laptop screen.

Oh my God. What was he doing here? At this hour of the morning? Wasn't he supposed to be at work?

Maybe he was here to meet with his terrorist contact. Maybe I would see him passing government secrets.

As much as I didn't want to believe Doug would do something like that, it seemed obvious that he was involved in something. I mean, Mom knew all about that super cruise, digital something-or-other that Doug and Dad were working on. Ben Oliver had been tipped to the same thing and told me all about it that night at City Walk, so the whole thing must be true.

I eased up from behind my laptop. Doug still sat in his car. I could see him talking on his cell phone.

If Doug wanted to ruin his life, well, okay. But I wasn't about to stand by and let my dad's life get ruined, too, simply because he was Doug's supervisor on the project. I knew Dad wasn't involved, but after the FBI, the CIA, Homeland Security, or whoever investigated terrorism got finished, who knows how they might twist the facts.

I didn't want to screw Ben Oliver out of his big news story—or his opportunity to get back in the good graces of his editor—but I had to tell Doug that somebody had ratted him out, and he needed to walk away from this thing now before it was too late.

It was the only way I could figure to save my dad.

I shoved my laptop back into my Coach tote and left Starbucks. Across the parking lot, Doug got out of his car and headed toward the strip mall. He must have seen me because he did a double take, then walked over to meet me.

I knew I had to break this to him gently. It wasn't the kind of thing I should blurt out in a parking lot.

"Look, I really need to talk to you," I told him, and nodded toward Starbucks. "Come inside. We'll sit down and—"

"Haley, please," he said, shaking his head. "You're embarrassing yourself."

"What?"

"You have to stop following me," he said.

"I wasn't—"

"You have to let me go. I'm dating Emily now," Doug said.

"*What?* I don't want to talk about you and Emily," I said.

"You have to accept that she and I are together now," he said, and patted my shoulder. "Please, for your own sake, find a way to get over me."

Doug walked away.

I stood there staring after him, my mouth gaping open as wide as a snap closure on a metal frame purse.

Oh my God. I couldn't believe that guy. He actually thought I was so desperate and pathetically lonely that I'd stalk him?

My phone rang. I ripped it out of my purse, thinking it had better be Ty calling. Here I was humiliated in public—yeah, okay, so nobody else was around to overhear what Doug had said, but there could have been—and all along I had a gorgeous, wealthy, way-hot boyfriend who was out of the country because he was brilliantly overseeing an international, multi-billion-dollar deal—only nobody knew that because he was gone.

I snapped my phone open. "Hello?" I barked.

Silence.

I gripped the phone, fuming mad and said again, "Hello?"

More silence.

I got a yucky feeling in my stomach.

Kirk Keegan flashed in my head. Was he here? In the parking lot? Watching me? Phoning to taunt me?

I turned in a quick circle and scanned the cars in the parking lot. I didn't see anyone. Was he inside one of the businesses in the strip mall?

I got a double-yucky feeling in my stomach.

Had Kirk been inside Starbucks with me?

Why hadn't I paid better attention? Why hadn't I insisted that Jack get me a gun?

"Hello? Haley?" a woman's voice asked softly in my ear.

Since I'm not big on suspense, I said, "Who is this?"

"Evelyn," she said.

I heaved a mental sigh of relief as I pictured her standing in her blinding white kitchen, winding her fingers together while she talked.

"I was wondering if I could perhaps take you up on your offer?" Evelyn asked.

My mind spun. Offer? I'd offered to do something for Evelyn?

I didn't want her to think that I'd forgotten, of course, so what could I do but say, "Sure, absolutely."

Evelyn was silent for a few seconds. "Well, all right. If you're sure. When would it be convenient?"

"When? Oh, well, when is good for you?" I asked.

"How about tomorrow?"

"Perfect," I said.

"Thank you, Haley. I'll see you then," Evelyn said and hung up.

What had I just gotten myself into?

CHAPTER 11

Since Rita wasn't at work again today, not watching over the cashiers, timing our break—like an extra minute or two would throw Holt's into receivership—I saw no need not to abuse the opportunity. Bella and Sandy—she's white, red-headed, about twenty years old and way cool—sat at the table in the breakroom with me, all of us enjoying a Rita-free environment, an array of chips and candy from the vending machine spread out before us.

"This room smells funny," I said, sniffing the air. It actually smelled good in here, for a change.

"It's that girl with the diet meals," Sandy said, munching on a handful of Cheetos.

I realized then that I hadn't seen that girl—I can never remember her name—since I'd come back from Europe. She was always cooking those diet meals in the microwave.

"Damn. Those things stunk," Bella said, wrinkling her nose.

"Yeah," Sandy said. "But she lost eighty pounds."

"Eighty pounds?" Bella echoed, popping an entire Reese's cup into her mouth. "I hate her."

"Did you see her after she got rid of her glasses and colored her hair blond?" Sandy asked.

"She must have looked like Gastric-Bypass Barbie," I said as I ripped open a package of M&M's.

"She looked great," Sandy said, nodding wisely. "I mean, really great. Not fake great. Really great."

"I hate her," Bella said again.

"She quit Holt's," Sandy said.

Okay, now I hated her, too.

Sandy leaned in a little, signaling the universal here-comes-the-best-part moment of the conversation.

"I heard," Sandy said, "that she's trying to be a model. She's got an agent and everything."

"Maybe she'll let me do her hair when I finish beauty school," Bella said, reaching for a bag of potato chips.

The saucer phase of hair design that had captured Bella's attention of late continued. Today she'd fashioned her hair into the shape of an umbrella.

"So what's up with Rita being gone?" Sandy asked.

"Whatever it is, I hope it keeps up," Bella said.

It seemed that nobody had a clue where Rita was. Her death hadn't been announced to the store employees, so either she was off work due to something unrelated to Tiffany's death, or her body hadn't been discovered yet if she was really dead, of course.

"Have you heard anything?" Sandy asked me.

Without benefit of the facts, what could I do but speculate and spread rumors?

"I heard she had an STD," I said.

Bella rolled her eyes. "Hard to believe there's a man out there who'd get that close."

"Speaking of men," I said to Sandy, "what's up with you and your boyfriend?"

To be generous, I'll say that Sandy was not lucky at love. Probably because she was a living doormat.

She'd been dating a tattoo artist for a while now. They met on the Internet.

"We're on a break," Sandy said.

"Your idea? Or his?"

"His," Sandy told me. "He said I was stifling his creativity."

"He does tattoos."

"Artists need freedom to express themselves, Haley," Sandy said, and grabbed a Hershey bar. "I was at the movies the other night and I saw that guy my mom set me up with last fall."

"The one who would only take you to restaurants that accepted discount coupons?" I asked.

Sandy nodded. "After the movie ended, I saw him pick up one of those big popcorn buckets somebody had left behind. You know, the ones with the free refills? He took it to the concession stand and got popcorn."

"Gross!"

"You know, Haley, it just shows how financially resourceful he is," Sandy said.

"Please tell me you're not going out with him again."

"I'm meeting him after work tonight."

The breakroom door opened and Christy bounded in, her blond curls bouncing, smiling for no apparent reason.

"Hi!" she called.

We all mumbled something.

"The store is so busy today!" she said. "I love it when it's busy! And, shoot, I have to go home now."

Christy fed her time card into the clock. "Sandy, I saw you waiting on a customer in accessories today. She was a tough customer, wanting you to match up her new top to those earrings. You did a great job!"

"Thanks," Sandy said.

"And Bella, you're the best cashier ever!" Christy declared. "Your line was moving faster than—well, faster than fast!"

Christy disappeared into the rear of the stock room where our lockers were located.

"I hate her," Bella said.

A moment later, Christy returned with her handbag, froze, and gasped in shock. For a minute I thought maybe she'd spotted Rita's dead body stuffed behind the refrigerator or something, but she pointed to the customer satisfaction chart on the wall.

"Oh, no," Christy wailed. "Look! We've fallen even lower!"

I looked at the chart. Our store rating was 15 percent.

Jeez, how did that keep happening?

"We're even below beach-towel range!" Christy cried.

We might not get Holt's beach towels? Wouldn't that be a damn shame.

Christy pulled herself up and straightened her shoulders. "Don't worry, girls, we can do this! We can improve our rating! If we all pull together and follow the six-step program, we can win those flat screens!"

We all mumbled something.

"Thank goodness we get to go through the training again!" Christy declared. "I know it's just what we need! I'm going to talk to Shannon about it now and see if we can hurry it up!"

"You already punched out," I said.

"That's okay. It's worth it," Christy said, and left the breakroom.

"She's kind of weird," Sandy said.

"I hate her," Bella said.

The cell phone in my back pocket vibrated. I pulled it out and saw Shuman's name on the I.D. screen.

"Something's come up," he said when I answered.

I took that for cop-speak that he'd learned something new about Tiffany's murder. I guess he was talking in code because, wherever he was, he didn't want to be overheard.

That was way cool.

I was glad Shuman had come through, like he'd promised. Maybe that meant everything was finally, once and for all, okay between us.

"I can meet you after work," I said.

The bad part about working the late shift was that when Holt's closed for the day, most everything else was closed, too—at least all the cool places, like the handbag section of department stores.

"How about that bookstore near your favorite coffee place?" Shuman asked.

More code-talk. Oh my God, this was way cool.

"See you there," I said, and hung up.

The only place that was just about as cool as a Star-bucks—except for a handbag shop, of course—was a bookstore. It was filled with music, games, magazines, photo albums, great stuff to decorate your desk and office—oh, and books, if you were into that sort of thing.

I got there ahead of Shuman and hurried through the aisles grabbing books off the shelves, then found a table in the café and piled them up around me. It was really easy to look smart in a bookstore—you didn't even need a laptop, like at Starbucks.

I could have actually brought in my homework, but I saw no need to carry this thing too far.

I got a mocha frappuccino—thank God they had my fa-vorite drink here—and ordered a huge chocolate chip cookie—just to insure good brain power after my mind-numbing day at Holt's—and got a coffee for Shuman.

Around me, people were flipping pages and talking. I opened two of the books I'd picked up and placed them on the table.

I stared at them for a couple of seconds, then closed them again. It reminded me too much of studying.

My classes flashed in my mind. I hated them. I hated having to sit there for hours on end. I hated having to learn the material. I hated homework. I hated how the instruc-tor seemed to always know when my thoughts had wan-dered off and picked that exact moment to call on me.

Three more years of this? I didn't know how I was going to make it. How did anybody last?

But I needed a degree—even though I didn't know what sort of career I wanted yet. There had to be some way to make it easier, or quicker.

Then it hit me: maybe I could buy a college degree from somewhere.

Oh my God. That would be perfect.

People did it all the time, didn't they? People like me who were working lots of hours—yeah, okay, I was only working part time, but still—and had really hectic schedules, and couldn't spend years in a classroom.

Plus, I had tons of life experience. Surely there was a way to convert that into an actual degree of some sort.

Oh my God. Wouldn't that be the coolest thing—to already have my degree?

A scene flashed in my head.

Me, working a great job—somewhere, doing something—dressing in fabulous clothes with fabulous purses, of course. A Fendi briefcase, maybe. And, oh my God, I'd never have to set foot in a Holt's store again. My mom bragging about me—not just about my sister and brother—to our family and her bitchy pageant friends. And, oh my God, Ty. He'd come to me, tell me how proud he is, what a tremendous accomplishment this is. He'd want to whisk me away to a romantic mountaintop retreat to celebrate, but I'd tell him no, I can't go. I'm much too important now, with tons of responsibilities and dozens of people standing around, waiting for me to tell them what to do. Ty would be crushed, of course. Then, to ease his pain, I'd whip out my fabulous Louie Vuitton organizer and pick a date when I can squeeze him in. He'd be so grateful, he'd—

"Hey," somebody said.

I looked up expecting to see Ty standing over me with a look of heart-wrenching desire on his face. But it wasn't Ty. I blinked and Shuman came into focus.

I guess he'd had a long day because he was still dressed for work—sport coat, shirt, and tie that didn't quite go together. He sat down across from me. I passed him the coffee I'd bought for him and he took a sip.

He didn't say anything, just sat there. I wondered for a moment if he'd changed his mind about talking to me, or if maybe he was deliberately trying to be annoying, but decided to give him the benefit of the doubt. Homicide detectives didn't usually share info with anybody besides other cops. I guess taking me into his confidence was a little hard for him.

Still, I didn't have all night.

"So, what's up?" I asked.

"I checked out Ed Buckley," Shuman said. "He was killed—supposedly—in a car accident last year."

"Supposedly?"

"I talked to one of the detectives with the Charleston P.D. who handled the case initially," Shuman said. "Ed Buckley's car was found outside the city on a secondary road that winds through the swamps."

"I read the newspaper story on the Internet," I said. "That's pretty much what it said—except for the *supposedly* part."

"The car had gone down an embankment," Shuman said, "then went up in a big fireball."

"The gas tank exploded?" I asked. I mean, jeez, what else could it have been?

"Everybody figured the body inside was Ed's," Shuman said. "The detectives figured differently when the FBI showed up and took the case away from them."

"Just like with you and Madison," I said. "What did the detective think happened?"

"He was off the case," he reminded me.

"I know," I said. "So what did he think?"

The tiniest grin tugged at Shuman's lips, and I knew the detective in Charleston had continued to investigate the case, just as Shuman was doing with Tiffany's case—with my help, of course.

"Buckley was a businessman. He lived high. Expensive homes, cars. Very high profile," he said.

That fit with the image I'd gotten from Virginia and the newspaper article. Tiffany's family was old money—old Southern money—and Ed Buckley sounded as if he belonged there.

"He wasn't exactly the successful businessman he pretended to be," Shuman said.

"What was he into?" I asked.

"Charleston is on the coast," Shuman said.

I didn't know that since I wasn't taking a geography class until next semester, plus since there was no such thing as Charleston Fashion Week, my family had never been there.

"Lots of coastline, inland waterways, rivers in and around Charleston," Shuman said.

"You're thinking drug smuggling?" I asked. "Does the FBI investigate that kind of thing? I thought the DEA handled that stuff."

Shuman got quiet again, then said, "Could have been a joint operation. My guess is that the FBI is more interested in finding out what happened to their undercover agent who was working the case, then went missing."

A few ideas flew through my head but I didn't want to say them out loud. This wasn't a good point in the conversation to look like an idiot.

"Best guess is that Buckley faked his own death," Shuman said.

"He must have figured out that the undercover FBI guy was onto him and whatever he was smuggling," I said. "So he murdered the FBI agent, put the guy's body into his car, then set it on fire so it would look like an accident?"

"That's the theory."

"How could he do that? I mean, with DNA and everything."

"The body in Buckley's car was burned beyond recognition," Shuman said. "At the time, the cops, the coroner, and the family had no reason to suspect anything was wrong. Buckley was a well-respected businessman from a prominent family. Everybody figured it was him in the car."

"Just a tragic accident," I said.

"Undercover agents don't check in every hour," Shuman said. "A couple of days probably passed before the FBI got worried."

"So I guess when they didn't hear from their undercover guy, they went looking and found out that Ed—the guy they'd been investigating—had died in a car crash."

Shuman shrugged. "By then, it was all over with. Funeral, burial, everything."

We sat there for a minute, both quiet, both of us thinking.

"All of this is just a guess, right?" I asked. "They didn't exhume the body or anything, did they?"

"No," Shuman admitted. "They wouldn't want to do something like that and then be wrong. Not with a prominent family of attorneys involved."

"So to prove their theory, the FBI would need to find Ed Buckley alive," I said.

Shuman nodded and sipped his coffee.

The whole thing creeped me, but it made sense. It explained why special agents Paulson and Jordan had showed me a photo of Ed Buckley. If he'd actually murdered one of their agents, they'd be hunting him big time.

But that didn't answer my biggest question.

"What's any of this got to do with Tiffany?" I asked.

"Damned if I know," Shuman said.

Chapter 12

It was a Louis Vuitton day. Definitely a Louis Vuitton day.

After talking with Shuman last night and hearing about everything the FBI and the Charleston homicide detectives suspected had happened with Ed Buckley, I knew I had to talk to Virginia Foster this morning, and the only way I could hold my own against her and her Fendi bag was with a Louis Vuitton.

The Sinful handbag flashed in my head. I absolutely had to find one. And I would, somehow.

I stood in front of my bedroom closet looking over my clothes. Everything was hung in order: dresses, skirts, pants, capris, blouses, tops, jackets; then, further categorized by long sleeve, short sleeve, casual, dressy, slutty, and finally by color—dark to light.

Of course, I had nothing to wear. Not even with all the things I'd bought in Europe stuffed in there. How did that keep happening?

I might have to adopt a strict say-no-to-separates policy.

Mom always said that when in doubt, wear black, so I put on a black skirt, sweater, and peek-toe pumps and appraised myself in the mirror. The dark outfit set off my Louis Vuitton perfectly.

I didn't want to put Virginia off completely with our dueling purses. I was satisfied that my outfit made me look only slightly snooty.

Even Mom knows when you have to pull back.

Virginia had mentioned that she was staying at the Hyatt in Santa Clarita, which was near the Holt's store and the mall—I could run into Macy's and check for a Sinful bag while I was close—so I drove over.

At this point, nobody I could think of but Virginia could give me any info on Tiffany and her life back in Charleston, or explain how it was connected to her brother-in-law Ed Buckley, the missing special agent, or drug smuggling—except for the obvious reasons, of course.

Was Tiffany involved in drug smuggling along with Ed? I didn't know. I'd already majorly misjudged her the first time I met her. Was I doing it again by even thinking she might be less than the prestigious attorney everybody claimed she was?

Maybe she was hiding from the FBI? Was that why she'd suddenly left Charleston a few months ago, changed her appearance, and come to California?

That made sense.

Or was she hiding from her drug smuggling partners?

That made even more sense.

All of those ideas were possible but didn't explain why an attorney from an old-money law firm had gotten involved in drugs in the first place. Or how she'd fooled her prestigious, high-profile family.

I hoped Virginia could answer some of those questions for me.

I left my Honda with the valet and went into the Hyatt. The hotel was new, really big, and built at a busy intersection that only travelers who wanted a lot of shopping close by would find desirable—which, I thought, made it the perfect location.

The lobby was open and airy, done in creamy yellow tiles and dark woodwork. The lobby was circular with huge

columns and a round light fixture overhead. I used the
house phone to call Virginia's room. She sounded surprised
to hear from me, and more surprised to learn that I was in
the lobby.

I could have called her this morning when I got up, or
from the car on the way over, but cops on TV never did it
that way. They always thought that if they called ahead,
the person they wanted to question might bolt before they
got there, and sometimes they did. It made for some really
cool chase scenes. So since I didn't have backup—and
couldn't run very fast in peek-toe pumps—I decided I'd better go with the element of surprise.

Virginia exited the elevator a few minutes later looking
sharp in Vera Wang pants and jacket, and wearing sensible
shoes. No purse. I pulled my Louis Vuitton in front of me
where she'd be sure to see it and be jealous.

"Haley, it's so good of you to stop by," Virginia said,
and gave me a quick hug.

Up close I could see that she still looked tense, worried,
like maybe the strain of being here, away from home, sitting alone in a hotel room all day, waiting to make funeral
arrangements for her best friend, just might be getting to
her.

Not that I blamed her, of course.

"Let's go have some coffee," Virginia suggested.

We got a table in the hotel's restaurant. The place was
elegantly furnished with dark wood tables. It was pretty
quiet—too late for breakfast, too early for lunch. That
was no reason not to eat, of course.

"I'll have a slice of your sugar-free apple pie," Virginia
told the waiter as he poured our coffee.

Damn. That's why I hated dining with women who were
skinnier than me. They never ate anything good, so I always felt pressured to not eat like a truck driver in front of
them. Forget pigging out on dessert, or eating three rolls

from the bread basket, and no way could I order the mega-calorie fish fry platter when all they got was a petite salad with that crappy lite dressing.

Still, I had to stay mentally sharp for our conversation. This was no time to let a late-firing brain cell cause me to miss some vital piece of info.

"I'll have a slice of chocolate cake," I said to the waiter. "A half slice."

"Yes, ma'am," he said.

"And would you put a little vanilla ice cream on it?" I asked.

"Certainly," he said. "Perhaps some hot fudge on top?"

"Oh no, I couldn't possibly—well, okay," I said. "And make it a whole slice."

See how committed I was to solving this murder? I was willing to make whatever sacrifice was necessary to stay mentally sharp and figure everything out, by eating a slice of straight-to-my-butt chocolate cake with all the extras.

"How are you holding up?" I asked Virginia.

She sighed wearily. "More than anything I want to go home. The police haven't released Tiffany's . . . body yet. I don't know what's going on. Just one delay after another."

"I'm sure her family back in Charleston is having a rough time," I said, because it seemed like a good way to introduce Tiffany's background into the conversation.

But Virginia didn't answer. She pressed her fingers to her lips and turned away.

Oh my God, I hoped she wouldn't start crying. I wasn't good in a crying situation—unless I was the one in tears, of course.

"Have you heard from Rita?" Virginia asked.

My stomach rolled a little. Rita was hardly the person I wanted to discuss—let alone be reminded of—today.

"I've phoned her several times but I haven't heard back from her," Virginia said, sounding a bit mystified.

"She hasn't been at work lately," I explained.

Virginia shook her head. "I called her home phone number, too. Tiffany had given it to me sometime back. I've left a number of messages for Rita, but she's never returned a single call."

Okay, that was weird.

Jeez, I really hoped Rita wasn't lying dead somewhere.

Maybe I should check the trunk of my car again.

As much as I didn't want to think about Rita, this did present a good lead into what I'd come to talk to Virginia about. I rolled with it.

"So how did Tiffany and Rita meet?" I asked. "Did Tiffany ever mention it to you?"

The waiter appeared with a tiny sliver of apple pie for Virginia and a gargantuan piece of chocolate cake covered with a mountain of toppings.

I resisted the urge to lay my face down in it.

"In Los Angeles," Virginia said. "The Fashion District."

Okay, that surprised me. Lots of people who came to Los Angeles thought that just about every city in Southern California was L.A. They said they were going to visit L.A. when it was really Anaheim, or Pasadena, or just about anywhere. But Virginia knew exactly.

"Tiffany and Rita just ran into each other?" I asked.

Virginia picked up her fork but didn't take a bite of her pie.

"That's what Tiffany told me," she said.

The Fashion District was a big place and it was almost always crowded. It seemed pretty weird to me that they could meet that way, but, oh well, stranger things had happened.

Like my life, for instance.

"They got to talking," Virginia went on. "Rita had the idea for the purse party business."

Which she stole from me.

I shoved a hunk of cake into my mouth.

"And since Tiffany wasn't working at the time, she had

the time to spend in the Fashion District shopping and buying handbags," Virginia said.

Which was why the two of them could have more parties than Marcie and me.

I scooped a huge spoonful of ice cream into my mouth.

"Rita knew people who would book parties with them," Virginia said, as she toyed with a flake of her pie crust. "I understand the two of them were quite successful."

"But why would Tiffany do that?" I asked, fighting off brain freeze. "She was a really successful lawyer. Why would she leave everything—her job, her friends, her family—and come all the way to Los Angeles to sell knockoff purses?"

And be Rita's friend, I almost added.

Virginia stared down at her plate for a few minutes, then placed her fork alongside her pie and pushed it away.

"It was something Tiffany felt she had to do," she said softly. "I wish . . . if only . . ."

I was pretty sure she wasn't rethinking the apple pie and I felt kind of bad asking her anything more, but what else could I do? I couldn't have shoveled in a few thousand calories for nothing.

"So what about her brother-in-law, Ed Buckley?" I asked.

Virginia touched her fingers to her lips once more, and looked away. She shook her head.

"I'm sorry, I'm so sorry," she said, finally turning to me again. "This is all so . . . it's all so upsetting. If you'll excuse me?"

Virginia left the table without another word and disappeared out the door, leaving me alone with two desserts and the fear that I'd pressed her too hard for info.

But, jeez, all I'd done was ask about Ed. Virginia was the one who'd brought him up to me in the Holt's breakroom the other night, plus she'd mentioned him to Shuman, too.

With Virginia gone and no hope for finding out any new

info, there was nothing to do but leave—after I finished my chocolate cake, of course.

The sugar had my brain buzzing pretty good, sending all sorts of random thoughts through my head. The first was to note that Virginia hadn't touched her apple pie—it was sugar free so, really, who could blame her—the other was that she didn't seem all that anxious to find out who had killed her best friend. I mean, come on, if she couldn't keep it together to answer a few questions, how concerned about finding Tiffany's killer could she be?

Since my brain cells were firing like microwavable Jiffy Pop, I let them keep sparking in whatever direction they chose. The Sinful handbag flashed in my thoughts, followed by my Louis Vuitton and Virginia's Fendi bag.

Life was in the details—or the accessories, as my mom liked to say. It always came down to the handbag.

You can tell a lot about a woman by the purse she carried. Virginia's Fendi told me she was organized, competent, successful, had money and knew how to spend it on nice things that mattered.

Was that the sort of woman who'd fall apart in a public restaurant, over a slice of apple pie—sugar free at that?

Probably not.

I corralled a chunk of cake, ice cream, and fudge with my spoon, and slid it into my mouth, waiting for the next flurry of brilliant, sugar-coated ideas to blast through my brain.

Nothing happened.

I tried again, this time with extra hot fudge.

Virginia was hiding something, I suddenly realized. That was why she didn't seem all that anxious to help with Tiffany's murder investigation, or even talk to me, for that matter.

But why?

Then it hit me—and I hadn't even had another bite of cake.

Oh my God. *Oh my God.* The night Virginia had come to Holt's asking for Rita, she claimed she'd just arrived from South Carolina. But was that the truth? Had Shuman checked out her story? Did the FBI even know Virginia was here? Had they questioned her at all? And if they did, had they bothered to verify her story?

Maybe Virginia had lied about everything.

Maybe Tiffany wasn't really her friend, and the family hadn't asked her to come here, make the arrangements, and bring Tiffany back to them.

My mind was racing now, like a bobsled careening down a high-caloric luge run.

Why was Virginia so worried about Rita? Why did she keep calling her? Was it just for cover? Did Virginia really know something about Rita's whereabouts?

Oh my God. Virginia could have been here for days, for all I knew. And that would mean—

Virginia could have killed Tiffany, and maybe Rita.

Oh, crap.

Chapter 13

"Are you sure you want to do this?" I asked.

Evelyn lifted her chin, drew in a breath, and nodded.

"Yes," she declared. "Yes, I have to."

"Okay," I said. "Let's roll."

To my knowledge, Evelyn hadn't been out of her house in months. After what Evelyn called "the incident" last fall caused by "that certain someone," she had locked up tighter—well, tighter than her own front door. So it surprised me that now, all this time later, she was willing to go out again.

Or maybe it was simply that I'd suggested it the other day.

I released the locks, dead bolts, and chains on Evelyn's front door while she turned off her security system. I opened the door and stepped outside.

Evelyn didn't follow.

"It's okay," I said. "Nobody's out here."

I didn't know if Evelyn actually thought "that certain someone" was constantly lurking in her shrubs, waiting for her to step outside so he could cause another "incident," or if something else, something rooted deep in her psyche was holding her back.

Why couldn't they cover something important like that in my health class?

Or maybe they had.

Anyway, all I knew was that Evelyn had told me she was ready to get out of the house and had asked me to take her for a drive.

"I'm being silly," Evelyn said, lingering inside her front door, twisting her fingers together.

"You haven't been out in a long time," I said. "It's okay."

"You're very patient," she said.

Patient wasn't what I did best, but for some reason, I could pull it off for Evelyn.

She paused another moment, drew in one more big breath, and stepped outside.

I wondered if I should have brought sunglasses for her, like those prisoners get when they're released from solitary confinement. Then I wondered if I should take Evelyn's arm and help her down the sidewalk.

But she didn't seem to need either. Evelyn squared her shoulders and walked with me to my car parked at the curb.

"I've been out before," Evelyn said, as we got inside. "A few times. A friend took me for a drive."

"Yeah? Who?" I asked, as we pulled away.

"Oh, look," she said, leaning forward a little, and pointing to the house on the corner. "They've painted their trim. I wonder if I should paint mine, too."

"Your house looks great," I said. "So, who's the friend who took you driving?"

Evelyn sat back and sighed. "My goodness, it's a beautiful day."

Okay, this was kind of annoying. Twice now, Evelyn had refused to answer my questions about the friend who'd taken her for a drive. For a while I'd wondered if she was involved with a banker I knew—long story—Bradley Olsen, V. P. of the prestigious Golden State Bank & Trust but, as always, Evelyn was tight-lipped on the subject.

Jeez, I was taking her out, the least she could do was give me some good gossip to spread.

"Anyplace special you'd like to go?" I asked.

"I don't know," Evelyn said. "Let me think about it."

"How about the mall?" I suggested.

"No, I don't think so."

"We could look at handbags," I said. It came out sounding like the most fun thing in the world because, really, it was.

"Maybe the beach," Evelyn said. "I love looking at the ocean. Seeing that huge expanse of water makes me think my problems aren't so big, helps me put them into perspective."

I took the 405 freeway and headed south, planning to catch the Pacific Coast Highway at Santa Monica and drive north through Malibu, up to Ventura. The road hugged the coastline there, rising and falling with the rugged hillside. It could be a little treacherous in spots, what with the rock slides, sheer cliffs, and few guardrails, but the views were spectacular.

"Thank you for suggesting this," Evelyn said, after a few minutes. "I realized that sometimes you have to do what's best, not what's easiest. I decided I couldn't stay home any longer, pretending everything was all right when it wasn't."

Evelyn kept talking but I drifted off, thinking about what she'd just said.

I guess I'd been doing that same thing. Going to school, pretending it was all right when it really wasn't. Working at Holt's, struggling to get through a few hours there each day when it wasn't at all what I wanted to do with my life.

Yeah, okay, I didn't know specifically what I wanted to do, but it sure as heck wasn't slogging through my classes and my shift at Holt's.

I had to do something. Something drastic.

Really, *drastic* was what I did best.

I turned onto PCH, the golden sand and the beautiful blue water of the Pacific stretching out to our left, the canyons and hills of Malibu rising on our right. Definitely a postcard-worthy California day. And suddenly everything made sense, it all came clear.

Evelyn was right. Seeing the ocean put things in proper perspective.

I was tired of doing things I didn't really want to do, tired of waiting for my life to start, tired of hanging on until things got good. I needed to make them good. My life was speeding by. I wanted to have the things I wanted. Important things—like more handbags sooner.

The idea of getting a college degree from some institution that would convert my considerable life experience into academic credits sprang into my mind again.

I knew some people thought it was kind of crappy, but jeez, what was the big deal? I mean, really, what could it hurt? It's not like I wanted to be a doctor or an architect or something. Nobody was going to die or have a building collapse on them because of me.

"I agree with you completely," I said to Evelyn.

"You do?" she asked, sounding surprised.

"I think people should do what's best for them, no matter what," I said.

My heart rate picked up a little. Should I really do it? Shortcut the whole college thing and get on with my life?

Just the thought made me feel lighter, freer, like anything was possible.

I wanted to celebrate.

"Do you want to go to the mall?" I asked.

"No, thanks."

Damn.

When I finally dropped Evelyn off at her house and waved good-bye, after she was locked securely inside, I pulled out my cell phone. I had to talk to Ty. I hadn't heard from him in a while—I knew he was working, but still—and I needed to hear his voice. I was totally stoked about the idea of getting my degree right away and I wanted to get his opinion on it. After all, he knew a lot about business. Maybe he could even recommend a place. He was my official boyfriend now. Wouldn't he want to hear about the stunning new direction my life may be taking?

With the time difference between L.A. and London, it was late over there and Ty would be sleeping. I knew this because when I was in Europe, a late night for him would have been 9:30. Really. But that was okay. Ty had a lot of important meetings to go to—I think he even paid attention in them—so he had to be rested.

But so what if I woke him? Official boyfriends should be anxious to hear from their official girlfriends, especially at an all-important time like this. Right?

I drove a couple of blocks and pulled into the parking lot of a convenience store. I didn't want to be driving while we talked. He would be groggy and maybe a little cranky. I wanted to devote my full attention to Ty so I could quickly tell him exactly what was on my mind, have him tell me what a fabulous idea he thought it was and give me a few recommendations, so he could get back to sleep.

See what a considerate girlfriend I am?

I punched in Ty's number and he answered on the first ring. At least, I thought it was him. Loud music and louder voices blared in the background.

"Ty?" I asked.

"Hello? Hello? Who's this?" he shouted.

A woman's shrill laughter pierced my eardrum through the phone.

"It's me," I said.

"Who?" he asked.

"Me! Haley!"

"Haley, how—" The phone cut out, then I heard Ty's voice again. "—you?"

"What's going on?" I asked. "Are you at a party?"

Ty was at a party? He never went to a party. He didn't have a single party gene in his entire DNA. He hadn't even stayed up until ten at night when I was there with him.

"Just a little celebration for the—"

The crowd in the background roared again and I totally missed what he said.

"I want to talk to you about something," I said.

"What?" he screamed. "I can't hear you!"

"I want to talk to you about something!"

"What is it?" Ty shouted.

Okay, yelling my startling, life-changing epiphany at the top of my lungs wasn't exactly how I envisioned sharing this moment. But I didn't exactly have a lot of choices here.

"I'm thinking about—"

The line went dead.

"Damn . . . ," I muttered.

I called back but it went straight to voicemail. I hung up.

"Gather around, gather around," Shannon called. "Let's move it, people. We've got to get out there."

I moved along with the other retail zombies in the Holt's breakroom and formed up in a semicircle in front of Shannon. She led us through our usual series of stretches, then gestured to the customer satisfaction chart hanging on the wall.

"We're pushing upward, going in the right direction, *for a change*," she announced, and narrowed her eyes at me.

I glanced at the chart. We'd climbed to 38 percent.

Wow, how did that happen?

"We're out of beach towel range," Shannon said. "Now we're looking at winning a toaster. I don't know about anybody else, but I don't want a toaster any more than I want a beach towel. I want a flat screen. So let's make it happen, people."

Everyone left the breakroom and I followed along at the rear of the crowd, dragging my feet a little more than usual. I'd only gotten as far as the children's department when Christy leaped in front of me.

"Come on, Haley!" she said, smiling broadly. "Let's be partners!"

How did I keep getting scheduled to work when Christy worked? Who was doing the schedule these days?

I needed to take them out.

She took my elbow and jumped up and down.

"Come on! It will be fun!" she declared. "We'll be the best partners *ever!*"

I had no idea what she was talking about.

"I don't want to be your partner," I said, and started walking again.

"But you have to have a partner! For the training!"

A feeling of dread crept over me, sort of like when you showed up at a party with a satchel and everyone else was carrying a hobo.

"What training?" I asked.

"For the six-step program!" Christy said. "Didn't you see the schedule in the breakroom?"

There was a schedule in the breakroom?

"Come on! It'll be fun!" she said. "You're going to love this!"

I followed along behind Christy and a couple dozen more employees to the training room. The chairs were set up in rows. A screen for a PowerPoint presentation hung at the front of the room. An easel with a flip chart stood in the corner. Everything necessary to incite mass suicide.

"Let's sit here!" Christy grabbed my arm and pulled me to the front row.

No way was I sitting up there. My customary spot in

any Holt's meeting was at the rear of the room, directly behind that big guy from men's wear.

But my reaction time was off and Christy had me in the chair before I knew what was happening. Jeanette came in. Today she had on a bright yellow dress that made her look like the rear end of a school bus. She started yammering on about the exciting Holt's six-step program and its path to better something-or-other, and my eyes glazed over.

A polite round of applause brought me back to consciousness sometime later, and a young woman in a fabulous Dior suit stepped in front of the room.

My heart jumped. For a second, I thought it was Sarah Covington.

I hate her.

But then I realized it wasn't Sarah and I breathed a little easier.

"She's new," Christy whispered. "She didn't give the training last time. Last time we had the marketing V.P. herself."

"Sarah?" I asked.

"Ms. Covington." Christy nodded. "She gave the most fabulous presentation *ever*."

The new training person—whose name I missed—jumped right in with the PowerPoint slides and I drifted off again.

So if Sarah gave the last presentation, where was she now? I wondered.

Then it hit me: what if she was in London with Ty?

Oh my God. *Oh my God*. What if she was? What if she'd gone there after I left?

She probably waited until she knew I was back in L.A., then flew there on the red-eye to be at his side. Sarah was all over Ty, all the time. Everything she did, everything she thought about doing, she had to discuss with Ty first. She couldn't make a move without him. And he didn't even seem to notice how she was hanging all over him, making up things to talk to him about, just to get face time with him.

People standing up and chairs scraping the floor jarred me from my mental tirade. Thank God, the meeting had ended quickly. I headed for the door.

"No, this way," Christy said, and pulled me in the opposite direction. "Now comes the best part."

There was another part? The meeting wasn't over?

I hate my life.

Everybody broke off in pairs and scooted chairs together. Christy pushed two chairs together and pulled me down beside her.

"Remember what the object is here," the trainer said.

She cut her gaze to me like I hadn't been paying attention earlier. I hadn't, but still.

"In this exercise, you're going to learn about your partners. Learn about their lives, their backgrounds," she said. "This will make us more aware of who we're working with. This will make us aware that our customers—just like each of you—are sometimes like us, but sometimes—just like each of you—they're different than us. And this will enable each of you to better understand our Holt's customers, and provide the highest quality of customer service possible."

Now I really hate my life.

The trainer passed out pencils and pads of paper to everyone. Around us, people put their heads together and started talking.

"I'll go first," Christy said, jiggling with excitement in her seat. "Is it okay if I go first?"

"I don't care."

"Okay, first, I had the best life ever," Christy said. "My mom was the best mom ever, and my dad—you're supposed to be writing this down."

I picked up the pencil and started making a grocery list while Christy yammered on about how great her parents were, how close she was to her sister, blah, blah, blah. It sounded as if she'd had a wonderful life, so far. Nothing explained why she loved working retail so much, but maybe I'd drifted off during that part.

Christy scooted to the edge of her chair and positioned her pencil over her pad of paper.

"Okay, now tell me all about you," she said.

Thinking that if I hurried I could leave the meeting sooner, I blasted through my life pretty quickly. My beauty queen mom, my gorgeous sister, my engineer dad, my air force pilot brother, the two classes I was struggling with, the purse party business I'd put on hold, my impending financial woes, my boyfriend who'd broken up with me at a big party—no mention of Ty, of course, since he owned the store—the really great job with the law firm I'd lost last fall.

Christy jotted copious notes, for some reason, and continued writing even after everyone else in the room had finished. Just when I thought we could leave, the trainer stepped to the front of the group.

"Now I want each of you to review what you've written about your partner," she said. "Then close your eyes and envision their life. Think about it. Try to feel what it's like to lead your partner's life."

I closed my eyes—if I could only learn to sleep sitting up, meetings would be so much easier to get through—and thought about what Christy had told me about herself. That lasted about a minute, then the Sinful handbag floated into my mind.

I'd been to almost every store I could think of looking for one. I'd asked and all the clerks had reported that the bag was on back order, not expected in for weeks.

I couldn't wait weeks. The record label's to-die-for party was coming up soon and I absolutely had to walk in with the hottest bag of the season—maybe in the history of handbags—on my arm.

I'd have to expand my search. Yeah, that's what I'd do. I could fly up to San Francisco for a few days and—

Christy sniffed, interrupting my mental search grid of upscale department stores in the Bay Area. That was weird. I didn't remember that she had a cold.

Anyway, back to the Sinful bag hunt. If I couldn't find it in San Francisco, I'd try Vegas. There were tons of great shops there and—

A gut-wrenching sob tore from Christy. My eyes popped open.

Oh my God. She was crying.

Was this part of the exercise? Did I miss something?

My first instinct was to break for the door, but everyone in the room was staring—and nobody else was in tears.

Jeez, what was I supposed to do now?

Then I remembered the time I'd been so upset here at the store—long story—that I'd cried in the stock room, and Ty had comforted me. If he could figure out what to do, so could I.

Of course, Ty had a really big shoulder for me to lean on, and a strong arm to put around me, and he smelled great. But I could do this.

Gently I laid my arm around Christy's shoulder and leaned in.

"What's wrong?" I asked. It didn't come out sounding as comforting as I'd hoped, but Christy didn't seem to notice.

She looked up at me, eyes puffy, cheeks red, tears streaming down her face, and said, "I just feel so *sorry* for you, Haley! Your life is so *awful!*"

Okay, now I felt like a complete idiot. Here I'd been mapping out a North American search pattern for a Sinful handbag and Christy had actually been thinking about me and my life.

"Really!" Christy wailed. "It's just awful!"

I pulled away, a little miffed now.

"My life's not awful," I told her.

"Yes, it is!" Christy said. "Everybody in your whole family is really successful, except for you."

"I just haven't found my niche yet," I said.

"Your boyfriend dumped you at that big party in front of hundreds of people."

"I wanted to break up with him first," I told her.

"You got fired from a really great job."

"I was laid off, investigation pending," I insisted.

"And you're so bad with money you have to sell fake purses—and even that's not working anymore."

"We're on hiatus."

"People probably think you're a big loser!"

"*What?*"

"Everything about your life is just *awful!*" Christy sobbed into her hands.

All the employees had broken off their own discussions and were staring. So was Jeanette, so was the trainer.

Why didn't that trainer come over here and do something? This whole thing was her big idea. Wasn't there some action plan in her PowerPoint presentation manual on what to do if an employee went ape-shit during the exercise?

Then I knew what was going on: Sarah Covington was behind this.

That trainer was her friend. Sarah had sent her to this store on purpose. She'd probably engineered the whole exercise just to make me look stupid and pathetic in front of everybody at Holt's. This trainer was probably streaming a live feed through her laptop straight to Sarah so she could see every detail of my humiliation. Oh my God. She'd probably post it on YouTube.

Well, I'd just show her.

I stood up and faced the other employees.

"Everybody stay in your seats. Don't be alarmed. I've had medical training and I have this under control," I announced. "Pay no attention to anything Christy said. This is just a delusional episode brought on by a chemical imbalance due to an overdose of over-the-counter medications."

I yanked Christy out of her chair, put my nose in the air—channeling my mom's I'm-better-than-you attitude—and led her out of the room. She sobbed all the way to the breakroom and collapsed into a chair.

I wanted to bitch-slap her—just to get her attention, of course—but wasn't sure even that would break her mood.

Christy looked up at me with tear-filled eyes. "How do you do it? How do you even get through the day?"

"Knock it off," I told her. "I have a great life—and it's just going to get better."

"You're so brave, Haley." Christy sniffed and straightened her shoulders. "From now on, Haley, I'm going to try to be just like you."

"*What?*"

"Do you really have medical training?" she asked.

My cell phone in my back pocket vibrated. I didn't care who was calling or for what reason, as long as it got me away from Christy.

I yanked it out and answered. Stony silence rang in my ear.

Jeez, what now?

I got a yucky feeling in my stomach. I looked at the caller I.D. screen. Mom.

"Haley, something's come up," she said. "Something urgent."

That could mean anything from a death in the family to a delay in the delivery of this month's issue of *Vogue*.

"You have to come over right away," Mom said. "Something's happened at your dad's office. Something concerning Doug."

Oh, crap.

CHAPTER 14

I blasted out of Holt's after Mom called, barking my seldom-used family-emergency excuse at Shannon, and headed to my parents' place.

I figured the whole terrorism-espionage thing with Doug had finally hit the fan. Dad must have been implicated. His job would be in danger, maybe even his freedom. The family would be in crisis mode. My sister would have been called, my brother notified in the Middle East. The family lawyer would have already been consulted and would have called in a battery of attorneys who specialized in this sort of thing. We'd need a media consultant, a P.R. firm. The whole family would be put under a microscope. We'd make national headlines. Our lives would never be the same again.

Not a great feeling.

I swung into the driveway at my parents' house expecting to see the street lined with TV news vans, police cars, maybe even a few private security vehicles to handle hordes of paparazzi.

The driveway was empty, except for my mom's Mercedes.

Okay, well, maybe they were just running a little late.

I got out of my car. Juanita, the housekeeper, opened the front door.

"Is my dad home?" I asked her.

Juanita looked at me like my wanting to know if Dad was home at this hour of the day was the craziest thing I'd ever asked.

"Just your mother," she said.

"Have the reporters been here yet?" I asked.

She shook her head like that was a really crazy question, too, and said, "No."

Okay, that was good. We still had some time to prepare.

I found Mom in the family room off the kitchen stretched out on the chaise, a glass of wine in her hand. Today she had on linen pants, a silk blouse, two-inch heels, full-on jewelry and makeup, and her hair was twisted into a loose updo.

Mom's idea of casual—which seemed weird, given the throngs of media preparing to descend upon us.

"I'm glad you came right over," Mom said. She looked past me. "Where's Ty?"

"Mom, you said something urgent had come up," I said. "Remember?"

"Of course I remember." She sipped her wine. "Where's Ty?"

"Still in London, I guess," I said. "You said something had come up about Doug."

"He's in London? You're certain?"

I figured Ty was probably still sleeping it off, after the big party he'd been to, but since he'd never called me back I didn't know for sure.

I wasn't about to tell Mom that.

"Yes, I'm certain," I said.

It was kind of a lie but what difference did it make at a time like this?

Mom rose from the chaise. It was hard to tell from her stance whether she was upset or not—Mom always has perfect pageant posture—but I could see that she was.

"There's talk going around at your father's office," she said.

My heart sank, knowing for certain that he'd been implicated in this terrorism thing with Doug.

Mom's chin rose ever so slightly. "How is this going to look to Ty?"

Less than one minute into the conversation and already she'd lost me. This was a new record.

"What's Ty got to do with anything?" I asked.

"Everything, I should think," Mom told me. "He's out of the country conducting very important business and *this* happens."

"What are you talking about?" I asked.

"It's all over your father's office that you've been stalking Doug Eisner," Mom said.

"*What?*"

Oh my God. This was what she'd called me over here to talk about? This was urgent? *This?*

"You've been following him in the mall, to the dentist—everywhere," Mom said.

"No, I haven't."

"You're denying it?" she asked.

"Well . . ."

Oh, crap. I did see Doug at the mall, and he must have been going to the dentist that day I saw him outside of Starbucks.

"Doug has another girlfriend. He's moved on. You have to do the same, Haley. You told me you and Ty were involved now. How is this going to look when word gets out?" Mom said. She sipped her wine. "I don't know what I'll do about the dinner party I was planning."

This was my perfect opportunity to leave, but I didn't want to go until I made sure Dad wasn't in trouble because of Doug.

"Is there any other talk about Doug at Dad's office?" I asked. "Anything to do with the project they're working on?"

"Of course not. Why would there be?"

"I've got to go," I said and gave her my standard excuse for leaving, "I've got class."

"Let Doug go, Haley," Mom said. "Take my word for it. Holding on to a man who doesn't want you will lead to nothing but heartache."

I could have gone back to work, but no way could I force myself to walk into the Holt's store twice in the same day, so I drove home. I figured that when I got there I'd break out my emergency package of Oreos—just to give myself a boost—and figure out what to do with myself this evening.

As I approached my apartment, I spotted an arrangement of fresh flowers sitting outside my door.

I stopped and looked around, searching for whoever might have left them. I'm kind of punchy about finding things on my doorstep—long story—but I didn't see anyone, so I took them inside with me. I opened the card. They were from Ty.

Ordinarily, receiving flowers from your official boyfriend was way cool. It showed that he was thinking about you, that he cared, that he wanted to brighten your day a little.

But the last time I'd talked to Ty he'd been partying like a rock star, apparently, and had yet to call me back.

I grabbed my cell and phoned Marcie. A best friend was the only one who could help at a time like this.

"Ty sent me flowers," I reported. "He was at a party the last time we talked."

Marcie deciphered this immediately.

"I'll be right over," she said, and hung up.

By the time Marcie arrived, I'd put out a couple of Corona's, chips and salsa, and the Oreos. We settled on opposite ends of my sofa. The flowers Ty had sent sat prominently on my coffee table.

"I think Sarah Covington might be in London with Ty," I said.

"Bitch."

"I hate her."

"What happened the last time you talked to Ty, exactly?" Marcie asked.

"He was at a pub or some sort of party," I said. "I could hear all sorts of commotion—the fun kind—in the background."

"Do you think Sarah was there?" Marcie asked.

"That was probably her I heard laughing like a hyena," I said.

"Do you think she lured him there and tried to get him drunk just so she could sleep with him?"

"Maybe," I said.

"Sarah probably likes talking about the economy after making love," Marcie said and tipped up her beer.

I gasped. "Oh my God, she probably does. And she probably actually understands what the Dow Jones is and what NASDAQ stands for—it does stand for something, doesn't it?"

"Yeah."

"She's probably got it stitched on a pillow on top of her bed," I said.

"Bitch."

"And she probably already knows how to play Naughty Stock Trader," I said.

I took another swig of beer trying to wash the scene from my mind. As much as I didn't like Ty's buzz-killer after-lovemaking talk, I wasn't ready to chuck our relationship.

Marcie nodded toward the flowers. "I don't think Ty sent those because he's done something wrong. It's not his style."

Ty was the confrontational type. That's one of the things I liked best about him.

"You're right," I agreed. "But it still irks me that Sarah has more in common with Ty than I do."

"You could learn about all that stuff," Marcie said. "That way you could talk to Ty about it."

"Yeah, I guess I could," I said.

But, really, I didn't know if I could pull it off. I'd watched *60 Minutes* once. I didn't make it past minute three.

I sipped my beer and popped an Oreo.

"At work today, this girl named Christy told me she thought my life was awful," I said.

"Your life's not awful," Marcie insisted, as a best friend would.

"Yeah, it is, kind of," I admitted. "I hate going to school."

Marcie thought for a minute. "Why don't you go for a different major? Try theater. Remember that girl who went with us to that club wearing that fuchsia sun dress who'd just left her husband?"

"The one who moved out and didn't tell him?" I asked.

"Yeah, and he came home and the house was empty. He got married again, by the way, to this girl who's a complete idiot, and they went on a cruise and six weeks later she left him, too," Marcie said. "Anyway, that girl at the club is in college, too. She's majoring in theater. I saw her the other day and she said that in one of her acting classes everybody walked around in a circle and pretended to be a towel."

"Sounds like an easy A, but I don't think I could do that," I said. "Besides, I'm sick of working at Holt's, too. I need to do something totally different."

"That's cool," Marcie said. "We'll just figure out what you want to do and you can go do it."

Was it really that simple?

"I'm thinking of looking into one of those colleges that will convert your life experience into a degree," I said.

"That's cheating," Marcie said. "It wouldn't be right."

I liked the idea, but maybe Marcie was right. Marcie was almost always right about things.

"So maybe you can find a great career without a college degree," she said. "What kind of job do you want?"

"The kind where I can wear great clothes, tell everybody what to do, and make tons of money," I said.

Marcie nodded, thinking it over.

"What sort of qualifications do you have?" she asked.

"I worked as a file clerk, a receptionist, a life guard, and, you remember, those two weeks at the pet store," I reported. "I did accounts payable at Pike Warner, which didn't turn out so great, but I still have it on my résumé. And, of course, Holt's."

Marcie sipped her beer and thought for a few minutes.

"You know, finding a college that will convert your life experience into a degree might not be such a bad idea, after all," she said.

"I'll check into it," I said.

"Good idea."

We finished our beers and Marcie got up to leave. She gestured to the sewing machine sitting in the corner of my living room.

"You're not sewing yet?" she asked.

"No time," I said, and didn't bother to add that I had no interest in it, either.

Marcie shrugged. "Well, you're looking for a change in your life. Maybe you should start your own clothing line— or maybe a handbag line. We could show them to our customers at our purse parties, see what they think."

This wasn't the first time Marcie had suggested I design my own purses. In fact, a couple of other people had said the same thing.

"I'll think about it," I said.

I guess Marcie heard in my voice that I still wasn't feeling much better about things.

"Let's go shopping," she said. "I'm dying for a new Sinful purse myself. There has to be some out there somewhere."

That kind of cheered me up.

"Okay," I said. "But if we spot Doug, we're leaving. He's telling everybody at my dad's work that I'm stalking him."

"You're kidding."

"No."

"He's an idiot," Marcie said.

Maybe even a bigger idiot than Marcie thought, if what Ben Oliver had said about that whole terrorist-espionage thing was true.

I went into my bedroom and stared at the clothes in my closet—I still didn't have anything to wear—and finally came up with jeans and a black sweater. It wasn't very imaginative, but it looked good.

We were heading out the door when my cell phone rang.

My heart rate picked up a bit. It was probably Ty. The scene sprang into my mind. Him calling to see if I got the flowers that he'd selected so lovingly, just to please me. Him telling me how much he misses me, and that he's ditching the final negotiations for Holt's International to come home to me.

Then I heard sniffles coming through my phone. Christy flashed in my mind. Was she still sitting in the Holt's break-room crying?

"Haley?" a woman's quivering voice asked.

Jeez, what now?

"Who's this?" I asked.

"Virginia Foster," she replied, gulping back tears. "This . . . this is all my fault. Tiffany's murder. It's all my fault!"

Oh, crap.

CHAPTER 15

Virginia looked as if she'd been crying, but she covered it up with fresh makeup pretty well. It helped that the lobby of the Hyatt where we sat was kind of dark. We shared a small sofa away from the few other people in the area. Behind us was a floor-to-ceiling window that offered a view of the hotel's outdoor patio seating and pool, amid blooming flowers and swaying palms.

Marcie had understood when I told her I had to go talk to Virginia instead of going shopping, and she'd promised that if she found a Sinful purse, she'd buy one for me, too.

You can't ask for a better friend than that.

"Thank you for coming over," Virginia said, and drew in a ragged breath. "You've been so kind, and continue to be kind, while I've not been completely truthful with you."

I was dying to hear Virginia confess to Tiffany's murder and it took everything I had to sit still.

I don't think I could be a detective. I don't have the patience for a long-winded, extremely polite suspect.

For a minute during the drive over here, I'd considered calling Detective Shuman so he could hear Virginia's confession himself, but decided against it. We were getting along well, finally. I didn't want to blow it by dragging him here expecting to break the case, only to have Virginia change her mind and clam up.

I wanted to let Virginia tell her story in her own way—
that's how they do it on TV, anyway—but still, I didn't have
all night.

"So what happened?" I asked.

She gazed across the lobby, but I don't think she was actually seeing anything. I noted several men wearing business suits, carrying briefcases, and milling around.

"I didn't know things would turn out the way they did.
How could I have known?" Virginia shook her head. "If
I'd only known . . ."

"Maybe you should start at the beginning," I suggested,
and resisted the urge to add, "and talk faster."

Virginia drew in a breath and sat up a little straighter. "I
work for an insurance firm in Charleston. Last fall there
was a convention here in Los Angeles. I attended, along with
hundreds of other people. There were organized bus tours
to all sorts of places. Several of my friends and I took a
tour of the downtown area. All of those *districts* are there,
you know, one city block after another, all running together.
Clothes, jewelry, fabric, flowers, toys. Everything. I'm sure
you're familiar with them."

A man dressed in a golf shirt paused across the room and
put his cell phone to his ear. He turned away so I couldn't
see his face.

"We had a fabulous time," Virginia said, and smiled
faintly at the memory. "Looking at everything, shopping,
taking it all in. Very different from Charleston, of course."

"So what happened?" I asked.

A young woman in a fabulous Chanel suit sat down across
the lobby and dropped her purse on her lap. My heart
jumped. Oh my God. Was that a Sinful bag?

"I saw Ed," Virginia said.

I had to go ask her where she got it. What if she'd just
bought it a few minutes ago? What if there was only one
left in the display case?

"Right there. On the sidewalk. Only a few feet away," Virginia said. "I couldn't believe it. It didn't make sense. Ed was dead but I was looking right at him."

Something jarred me out of my Sinful stupor.

"What?" I asked. "You saw Ed? Dead Ed?"

"At least, I thought it was Ed. But it couldn't have been, of course. I'd attended his funeral. I thought perhaps I'd spotted Ed's brother, or his cousin. So I moved on with my friends, walking and shopping, and a few minutes later, of all things, I saw him again," Virginia said.

"Where?" I asked.

"A few blocks from where I'd initially spotted him," she said. "Seeing him once, well, I figured it was just a fluke, an odd occurrence. But seeing him a second time?"

"Was he with anybody?" I asked.

Virginia thought for a moment. "Not that I noticed. He walked with purpose, as if he knew where he was going and was in a hurry to get there."

If Virginia had spotted Ed twice—alone—within a couple of blocks, he wasn't strolling along taking in the sights, so he probably wasn't a tourist. He was there for another reason.

"Did you talk to him?" I asked.

"About what?" Virginia wondered. "Stop a total stranger on the street and tell him that he looked like a dead man I'd known from all the way across the country?"

Yeah, okay, I guess that made sense.

"I took his picture," Virginia said.

I gasped. "You did?"

She nodded. "I had my camera in my hand so I just snapped his picture. I thought it might be interesting, an oddity, to show friends back home."

"You took a picture of him?"

"I regretted it, though, after I took it. He saw me and I could tell he wasn't happy about it. I suppose I should have asked first." Virginia grew quiet for a moment, then said, "And given the way things turned out, I have more reason to regret it."

I didn't need the Hubble to see where this was going. Virginia hadn't killed Tiffany. She thought she was at fault for other reasons.

"So you showed the picture to Tiffany when you got back home?" I asked.

"As I said, I thought it was Ed's brother, perhaps. But Tiffany knew Ed had no brother," Virginia said.

"Tiffany thought it was Ed?" I asked.

I glanced toward the woman with the Sinful bag. She was gone. The guy in the golf shirt still had the phone to his ear. He cut his gaze at me, then turned away again.

"Looking back, I believe she was always suspicious of Ed. I don't think she believed his stories. She wasn't taken in by him like her sister and everybody else," Virginia said. "A few weeks later, Tiffany told me she was going to Los Angeles for an extended vacation."

I put myself in Tiffany's place, mentally. She was a lawyer. She had contacts everywhere. I figured she'd made some calls, found out about the missing undercover special agent, and like the FBI and Charleston detectives, figured Ed had faked his own death. Or maybe one of those guys had told her that outright.

"That wasn't like her. Not at all," Virginia said, looking troubled again. "She asked me for a copy of the picture of Ed and I knew—I knew—she suspected it really was him, that he was alive, and she was going to Los Angeles to find him."

"Why would she come out here herself? Why not hand everything over to the FBI?" I asked.

"Tiffany had to be careful. She had her reputation to consider—and that of her family's law firm," Virginia said. "And there was her sister, of course, and her three little nieces. Insurance payouts, the estate settlement. Tiffany could hardly make the accusation that Ed was really alive, of all things, unless she knew for sure."

"And the only way to know for sure was to come out here herself," I concluded.

"Tiffany made me swear not to tell anyone what she was doing," Virginia said. "I didn't like it, but I gave her my word. A promise is a promise. Now, of course, I wish I hadn't."

"You think it's your fault Tiffany is dead?" I asked. "Because you didn't stop her from coming out here, and you didn't tell anybody what she was planning to do?"

Tears filled Virginia's eyes.

"That's how it looks, doesn't it?" she asked. "Do the authorities have another theory? An explanation for her murder?"

I wished I could say something to make Virginia feel better, but I couldn't. In fact, I agreed with everything she'd said.

Why would the FBI take the case away from LAPD, question me about the morning of Tiffany's murder, and show me a picture of Ed if they didn't believe he was still alive and responsible for Tiffany's death?

I figured that Tiffany had been in the Fashion District looking for Ed when she'd hooked up with Rita. She'd probably seen it as a good cover—I mean, really, why would anybody be friends with Rita if they didn't have to? Tiffany could spend a lot of time shopping and buying purses for their business and not draw any undue attention to herself, while she looked for Ed.

And, obviously, Tiffany had been looking in the right place. She found Ed or Ed had found her. Either way, he'd followed her or lured her to the Holt's parking lot and shot her in the chest to shut her up and keep his secret safe.

"Did you tell the police what you suspected? Did you show them his picture?" I asked.

"No," Virginia said. "You see, like Tiffany, I had no proof

either. Just a photograph I'd snapped at a distance, in a crowd of people, of a man who looked a bit like Ed. How would that help anything?"

Obviously, Virginia didn't know everything that was happening with Tiffany's murder investigation.

"I know a homicide detective who can help you," I told her. "Detective Shuman."

"Oh, yes, I met him. He came by and we spoke briefly." Virginia clasped her hands together. "Oh, goodness, I don't know what's right or wrong anymore. I don't know what will help, or what might create more problems. I don't want to send the authorities off on a wild goose chase after Ed if Tiffany's death had nothing to do with him."

"You can trust Detective Shuman," I told her. "Just tell him everything you told me. He'll know how to handle things."

Virginia sighed with relief. "All right. I'll do that."

My mind spun with what to do next: call Shuman, explain everything to him, have him speak with Virginia—

"Would you like to see it?" Virginia asked.

Lost in thought, I didn't understand what she meant.

"The picture of Ed," Virginia said. "Would you like to see it?"

"You have it with you?" I asked, a little stunned.

She dug through her Fendi bag, came up with a photo, and handed it to me. It was a four by six color snapshot taken from a distance showing a group of people milling around on a crowded sidewalk. I recognized the Fashion District in the background.

"That's him," Virginia said.

She pointed. Slightly off center in the photo was Ed Buckley.

My breath caught.

I hadn't recognized him from the color photo special agents Jordan and Paulson had showed me because Ed Buckley had changed his appearance since that photo was taken.

His hair was now dark, he'd grown a mustache and goatee, his ear was pierced, and he looked like he'd dropped a few pounds. Ed looked nothing like the man I'd seen in photographs who'd lived the high life in Charleston.

No, I hadn't recognized Ed Buckley from the photo the FBI guys had showed me.

I now recognized Ed from the Holt's parking lot, the morning Tiffany was murdered.

I walked Virginia up to her room on the fifth floor and made sure she was locked in safely for the night. I didn't want to alarm her, but there was a definite possibility that she was in some danger.

Ed Buckley had already killed an undercover FBI agent and Tiffany Markham. I doubted he'd have any reservations about doing the same to Virginia if he somehow figured out she was in L.A. and would soon be cooperating with law enforcement to bring him down.

It was kind of a long shot, but it could happen. Kirk Keegan had learned all my personal info, followed me, sat down at my table at Starbucks, and threatened to ruin my life, starting with ruining Ty's, so I had some experience with this sort of thing.

The elevator doors opened and I walked down the hallway into the lobby. I dug my phone out of my bag—a fabulous Fossil tote—and punched in Shuman's number.

I probably should have called FBI special agents Paulson and Jordan with the news but, really, I didn't especially like them. They hadn't been all that nice to me, plus they'd made me look like a complete idiot the day I'd been questioned at the Federal Building.

I wanted Shuman to know first. I wanted him to have first crack at the new info. I didn't like that the FBI had taken the case away from him and Madison—well, Madison I didn't care so much about—but they'd treated our LAPD guys like they were incompetent. I didn't like that.

I wasn't sure the FBI would believe me, anyway. Even if they did, I might end up stuck in their conference room—going through major Snickers bar withdrawal—for days before they finally decided my info had merit. Or, they might twist it all around so that I looked like a suspect—then I'd never get another Snickers bar.

I couldn't take the chance.

Shuman would know what to do with the info he got from Virginia. He was the professional, after all. He had training. He had a badge. He'd know how and when to turn it over to the FBI.

Jeez, I can't be expected to handle absolutely everything, can I?

Shuman didn't answer his phone, so I left him a message detailing everything I'd just learned from Virginia and telling him he ought to get to the Hyatt right away and talk to her.

Satisfied I'd done all I could do—and knowing that the mall was just a few blocks away and there might be a Sinful handbag there at this very minute—I headed for the sliding doors on the other side of the lobby.

Halfway there, it hit me that the lobby was totally empty.

I got a yucky feeling in my stomach.

Where were all the businessmen with their briefcases who'd been hanging around when Virginia and I were down here just a few minutes ago? The guy in the golf shirt who'd been talking on his cell phone? The woman with the Sinful purse?

Had they really been who they appeared to be? Or were they really someone else?

Kirk Keegan flashed in my head.

Could one of those men have been Kirk? Had he followed me again, spied on me again?

Or worse, was he outside the hotel right now, waiting for me?

And what about Ed Buckley?

I hadn't recognized him in the old photo the FBI had

showed me because he'd changed his appearance so much. Had he changed it yet again? Was he here, checking up on Virginia?

Jeez, why hadn't I paid more attention?

All I'd really looked at was that woman carrying the Sinful purse—and even she'd gotten away before I could ask where she got it.

Crap.

CHAPTER 16

"You're never going to get a date if you keep dressing like that," I said.

Ben Oliver looked up from his laptop and saw me standing over him. He frowned.

"Get away from me," he said.

He was seated at an umbrella table at Pacific Park, the amusement park on the Santa Monica Pier. The pier was one of the oldest in California and still had a hippodrome with a really great carousel in it. Everything else was for tourists. Lots of restaurants, shops, souvenir stands, a video arcade, rides, and all kinds of carnival games. The gorgeous California spring weather made this the perfect spot to spend an afternoon—or write a news story, as Ben seemed to be doing.

After talking to Virginia at the Hyatt last night, I knew I needed more info on everything that happened back in Charleston with Tiffany and Ed. I decided Ben could help me. Since he seems really good at holding a grudge, I knew I couldn't show up empty-handed, so this morning I'd hunted him down and was ready to trade favors.

I sat down on the bench across from him. Just as I expected, Ben had on khaki pants and a polo shirt, the same sort of clothes I'd always seen him wear. At least the shirt wasn't blue this time, but it was a little rumpled. His hair still looked a little shaggy and I'm pretty sure he hadn't shaved this morning.

Ben Oliver would be my reclamation project, and maybe he'd get laid in the process. Was that a deal or what?

"I know things didn't work out so great with us before, so let me make it up to you," I offered. "I'll give you a makeover. I'll take you shopping, pick out a whole new look for you, get your hair styled. It will improve your love life. I promise."

"How did you find me here?" he asked, and started typing again.

"I called your office. The girl who answered the phone seemed more than anxious to rat you out," I told him.

"I'm working," he said. "I think better outside."

I doubted that was true today. Spring break had brought tourists and locals out in droves. Around us kids yelled, babies cried, barkers lured people to their games of chance with promises of a winner every time, the roller coaster swept by clacking on its tracks.

"So how about it?" I asked. "A whole new you in one short afternoon. What do you say?"

"I like myself the way I am," he told me and kept his gaze glued to his laptop.

Okay, so my makeover idea wasn't working out as I planned—which I didn't understand. I mean, really, who wouldn't want a makeover?

Anyway, I needed to try something different. I'd learned long ago that getting your way—some people call it nego-tiating—meant that you had to be ready to go with a dif-ferent tactic on a moment's notice. That's how I roll.

"What are you writing about?" I asked, and leaned around to get a peek at his laptop screen.

He angled it away. "Something important. Something I have to finish. Go away."

"Is it your terrorism-espionage-aircraft-thingy story?" I asked.

"Shh!" Ben growled and glanced around.

I hadn't told Ben that Doug—the subject of his story—was actually my ex-boyfriend. I didn't want to get into the whole breakup thing with him and I didn't want to tell Ben that Doug worked for my dad. I figured the less Ben knew, the better—for me, anyway.

But now I needed more info on Tiffany's murder and I was prepared to give something to get something in return. Not my favorite method of getting my way, but what choice did I have?

"Hey, I've got a great idea," I said. "I'll talk to that engineer you're spying on and find out what's really up."

Ben looked up, horrified.

"Oh my God," I said. "I'll be just like an undercover newspaper reporter. Wow, that will be so cool."

"No."

"I'll get close to him, gain his confidence."

"*No.*"

"I'll get all the details," I said. "And don't worry. I'll be really smooth. He'll never suspect a thing. Don't think for a minute that your story—your big, career changing, ticket-to-*20/20* story—will be jeopardized in any way—"

"No!"

We sat there, locked in a stare-down, and I gave him my I'm-going-to-win smile. Ben read it immediately.

He plowed his hands through his hair and sighed heavily. His bangs fell over his forehead. It made him look kind of hot.

He closed his laptop. "What do you want?"

"Just a little info and, you know, it isn't like this won't benefit you, too," I pointed out.

"I doubt that."

"Remember the woman I told you about who'd come to California and ended up shot—"

"Tiffany Markham. Trunk of the Mercedes. Holt's parking lot. Lawyer from Charleston. Old money, old family. Yes, I remember," he said. "What about it?"

"The FBI is investigating her murder. They think her brother-in-law Ed Buckley was smuggling something— drugs, maybe—and murdered an undercover FBI guy who was onto him, then faked his own death to cover it up. They think Ed's alive and well, living in L.A. somewhere."

Ben stared at me. I could almost see the wheels turning in his brain. He didn't jump on the story like I'd hoped, though.

"It's true," I told him. "Ed's here. I talked to a witness who saw him in L.A., and another witness who saw him in the parking lot the day Tiffany was murdered."

"Who?" Ben asked quickly. He'd grabbed hold of the story—I could see it in his face. He had that two-for-one-sale-price look in his eyes.

I wasn't ready to name names yet—even if one of them was mine.

"Here's what I'm thinking," I said. "Cops leak info to reporters all the time. So I figure a reporter in Charleston must have gotten wind that something was up when this whole thing with Ed Buckley went sideways."

Ben didn't say anything, just kept staring. I hadn't lost him, so that was good.

"Ed was probably into drugs, but I need to know for sure," I said.

"Whatever he was doing in Charleston, he's probably still doing here," Ben added.

And that would make it easier for him to be found.

"Can you talk to somebody reporter-to-reporter?" I asked.

Ben stewed for a moment, making faces like the idea in-trigued him but he wasn't sure he wanted to commit—sort of like when you're considering buying a red handbag but don't think you should carry it except during Christmas.

You can carry it anytime, of course.

Ben shifted his shoulders and leaned forward a little.

"If I do this, you'll give me the story—exclusively?" he asked.

"Sure," I said.

"You'll give up your witnesses?" he asked.

"Absolutely."

"They'll cooperate?"

Okay, Ben was getting a little technical here, but what could I do but agree?

"Yes, of course," I told him.

Still, he hesitated, no doubt having flashbacks of the disastrous—for him—way things had turned out a few weeks ago.

Not that I blamed him, of course.

And, really, I figured I did owe him. I'd gladly turn everything over to Ben and let him break the story.

"You'll stay away from Doug Eisner?" he asked, narrowing his eyes at me.

No way was I staying away from Doug—not after the way he'd told everybody at my dad's office that I was stalking him. I intended to confront Doug—that's what I did best—and set him straight once and for all, but only about the two of us.

"You're only pursuing this story because you want the truth to come out, right?" I said. I gestured to his laptop. "That's why you haven't broken the story yet, isn't it? Because you don't have all the facts yet?"

"I'm not going to ruin somebody's life just to get a story—and screw myself in the process when the whole thing blows up in my face," Ben said.

I nodded. "The truth is all I care about, too."

Judging from the look on Ben's face, I didn't think my sidestep of the truth scored any points with him. But with the prospect of this whole Tiffany Markham murder I was dangling in front of him, he seemed willing to let it go.

Or maybe not, I realized, when he again asked, "You'll stay away from Doug Eisner?"

What could I say but "yes."

"You swear?"

I was in too deep to back out now.

"I swear," I told him.

Ben brooded for another moment, then said, "I'll get back to you when I have something."

I stood up. "Let me know if you change your mind and still want that makeover."

"Go away," he said, and opened his laptop again.

Leaving the pier on a day as gorgeous as this one was tough, but I had things to take care of before I started my shift at Holt's that evening. I got into my car and drove out of the pier parking lot.

I was tempted to turn left into the Third Street Promenade, a favorite shopping area of mine. After all, a Sinful handbag just might be waiting in one of the display cases there for me to claim it as its rightful owner. For a moment, I thought I heard it call to me.

Still, I had a lot to do today.

I hate it when I have to do the right thing.

I'd promised Ben that I wouldn't talk to Doug about the terrorism-espionage thing, but that didn't mean I couldn't talk to him about the other stuff he was doing—which I considered even more criminal.

Anyone in my place would think the same.

According to Mom, Doug had been yapping to everyone in sight—or, at least, at his office—about how I was stalking him and Emily, the new girlfriend, making him, I'm sure, the envy of every geek in the place. No way could I let that continue, even though I had enough problems of my own dealing with Ty and the possibility that Sarah Covington was with him in London.

Ty settled in my mind as I merged onto the northbound freeway and darted across two lanes of traffic.

I needed to call and thank him for the flowers he'd sent.

I still didn't feel so great about receiving them, though. I wasn't sure if they were I-miss-you flowers or I-screwed-up flowers.

Since I wasn't big on suspense, I decided to find out.

I hooked the Bluetooth on my ear and punched in Ty's number. As the phone rang, I glanced at the clock on my dashboard trying to figure out what time it was in London. Before I finished my calculations—guess I'll have to take a math class sooner or later—Ty's voicemail picked up. Jeez, didn't he ever answer his phone? I left a message thanking him for the flowers and asking him to call me.

I considered telling him that I really missed him a lot and that I couldn't wait for him to get home, but couldn't quite pull it off. The thought that Sarah might be with him, listening to his messages, soured my mood big time.

For a moment I thought about flying back to London and surprising him—or at least, I'd tell him that's why I'd done it. I could just show up unannounced and see for myself what was going on.

But that didn't really sit right with me, either. I didn't like not being able to trust Ty.

Then I realized that showing up in London didn't mean I didn't trust Ty—it meant I didn't trust Sarah.

Then it occurred to me that I didn't have to head for the airport to find out if my suspicions were true. All I had to do was call the Holt's corporate office and ask to speak to Sarah.

Wow, this was a great idea, I decided as I scrolled through my cell phone contact list. If Sarah was there, that meant I was worried for nothing. If she wasn't there, that meant—

Oh, crap.

I closed the phone.

If I called the corporate office and was told Sarah wasn't there, would that really mean anything? Maybe she was just out of the office.

If I pressed and learned that Sarah had gone to London, did that mean something was going on between her and Ty?

I thought about it for a few minutes as I wove in and out of traffic, and finally I decided that all it meant was that I didn't trust Ty.

Not a great feeling.

We were having enough problems with our relationship—although I wasn't sure Ty was aware of them—without me making things worse by imagining things, bad things.

I sat a little straighter in the seat, feeling better about myself that I was doing the right thing by believing in Ty, in our relationship. Everything would be fine between us. No, not just fine, great.

Of course, a little reinforcement wouldn't hurt, I decided.

So just to prove to myself that I'd done the right thing, I picked up my cell phone once more and punched the speed-dial number for the Holt's corporate office.

I asked to speak with Sarah Covington.

"She's not available," the receptionist told me.

This meant nothing, I told myself. She was probably just out to lunch or something.

"When do you expect her back?" I asked.

"Ms. Covington is out of the country," she said.

Okay, still no reason to panic. The world was a really big place. She could be anywhere.

"Would you like to leave a voicemail?" the receptionist asked.

I knew she was giving me the runaround—that's what people in her position did—so what could I do but channel my mom's I'm-better-than-you-and-I-know-it attitude?

"This is Ada Cameron's personal assistant," I told her. "I must speak with Sarah right away."

"Yes, of course," she answered. "I'll put you through to the London office right away."

Oh, crap.

I closed my phone and tossed it aside.

CHAPTER 17

I did a slow burn as I drove. Sarah Covington was in London.

I hate her.

She was in London with Ty. She'd probably waited until I left, then invented some lame excuse to go over there and be with him, just as I'd suspected. The whole thing made me so angry I could hardly see to drive.

So what could I do but take it out on somebody else?

I grabbed my cell phone and called Doug.

"It's Haley," I barked when he answered.

I heard him sigh wearily.

"Haley, please, you have to stop this—"

"Stop talking!"

I was in transmit mode, not receive mode. I had to hand it to Doug, though. He picked up on it right away.

I glanced at my dashboard clock and saw that it was almost noon.

"I have to talk to you—*now!*" I told him.

"Very well," he said, and drew in a patient breath. "I suppose it would be better if we spoke in person. Let me find us a location."

I heard his keyboard clicking in the background.

No way would I let him pick the spot. By the time he

finished analyzing locations on the Internet, I wouldn't see him for two days.

Besides, I wanted to meet him on my own turf, a place where I felt strong, a place where absolutely nobody would recognize him.

"Pasadena," I told him. "Paseo Colorado."

"I'm not familiar with—"

"The mall on Colorado Boulevard," I said. "Meet me outside the Coach store."

"The what store?"

"Coach!" I screamed and hung up.

By the time I'd found a spot in the underground parking garage and taken the elevator up to the street level, I'd calmed down—but only a little—thanks to the great location. The open air shopping area had lots of great stores and restaurants, and it was, after all, in the heart of gorgeous Pasadena.

Really, it's almost impossible to be in a bad mood when you're in Pasadena.

But I hung on to my anger as I walked up to the display windows of the Coach store. I wanted to blast Doug big time, and I needed to be in the right frame of mind to do it.

Still, the bags in the window looked great.

I pressed closer to the glass.

Oh my God. The new spring line had arrived.

Yellows, pinks, blues, greens. Clutches, satchels, hobos. Wallets, mini skinnies, wristlets. I needed every one of them—with a new outfit to go with each one to properly show them off, of course. Plus I still absolutely had to have a Sinful purse.

Jeez, I had so much to do.

Where was Doug? I didn't have all day to stand around here waiting for him.

I turned and saw him walking toward me and it irritated me a bit that I still thought he was kind of good looking. Tall, dark hair, dressed in khaki pants and a pale blue, button-up shirt—the engineer's uniform—looking calm and composed.

If only he hadn't been so dull, maybe we could have worked things out.

But never mind about that now. I had to put an end to his gossiping about me at his office.

I turned away from the fabulous array of bags in the Coach display windows so as not to lose my focus.

"Good afternoon, Haley," Doug said, stopping in front of me. "I think I should tell you right up front that—"

"Stop," I told him, and resisted the urge to put my palm in front of his face. "You don't get to talk. You get to listen."

He looked like he wanted to say something, but he held back.

"First of all, I'm not stalking you," I said. "Just because I *happened* to run into you a couple of times means nothing. I'm *way* over you."

Doug said nothing.

"Second of all, I couldn't care less that you have a new girlfriend," I said. "Got it?"

Doug nodded thoughtfully. "That's indeed gracious of you, Haley, given how crushed you were at our breakup."

My temper spun up again—and not even spotting a Sinful bag right now could have unwound me.

"I wasn't crushed! Didn't you see what kind of handbag I had with me that night?" I demanded.

Doug frowned. I don't think he knew what I was getting at.

"It was a fabulous bag and absolutely everybody there was jealous of me!" I said.

Now I was sure Doug had no idea what I was talking about.

"Listen," I said. "Just stop talking about me. Okay? Very soon now you're going to have really big problems of your own to worry about."

"Are you threatening me?" Doug asked.

Jeez, what an idiot. He was probably stupid enough to sell our secrets to terrorists and not even know it.

"I'm not threatening you," I told him.

"It sounds as if you are, Haley," he said. "And I must tell you, I don't find that attractive in a woman. To be quite honest, you've spoiled any chance at all for us to get back together."

"I don't want us to get back together!" I told him. "And I'm not threatening you! I'm talking about your new terrorist buddies you're selling secrets to!"

Oh, crap. I didn't mean to say that.

Doug pondered my words for a moment, then said, "Spreading lies about me won't make things better, Haley. Oh, yes, it might assuage your pain for a while, but in the long run it will only make you look and feel small."

Now I wished I'd told him to meet me in the parking garage. At least there I could bitch-slap him and nobody would see me—plus I wouldn't run the risk of being denied entrance to the Coach store for being a security risk.

"Perhaps you should get some counseling," Doug said.

Okay, I'd had it with him.

"Somebody ratted you out," I said.

"I understand there are excellent drugs on the market to help with the emotional and mental problems you're experiencing," he said.

"That whole super-cruise-digital-engine-something-or-other project you're working on," I said. "Your secret is out, Doug. Everybody knows what you're doing."

"You shouldn't take dinner hour talk with your father and try to use it against me, Haley. It's disrespectful."

"I know this newspaper reporter—"

"Please, Haley, stop." Doug pushed his chin a little higher. "Because of our past relationship, I won't say anything to your father about this."

"Doug, are you listening—"

"Please, Haley, get some help," he said and walked away.

*   *   *

Either Doug was a complete moron, or he was telling the truth.

The idea came to me as I pulled into the Holt's parking lot. I killed the engine and sat staring at the blue Holt's sign.

Doug had fried my last nerve this afternoon when I'd tried very nicely—okay, not nicely at all—to get him to stop running his mouth about me. He just didn't get it. He just refused to accept what I was saying.

And as if that weren't irritating enough, he'd completely blown off my warning to back out of his dealings with the terrorist group. How much plainer could I have been?

So, it seemed to me, that could only mean that Doug really had no idea what I was talking about. He really wasn't involved with terrorists or espionage or selling our government secrets.

Then why had Ben Oliver been tipped off that he was?

I sat there, watching customers coming and going from Holt's. I couldn't make myself get out of my car.

Ben had told me he'd received an anonymous tip detailing Doug's involvement, everything right down to the type of project it was. It made sense that whoever had called Ben would want to stay anonymous. Whistle-blowers didn't want to get themselves involved and endanger their own reputations or careers.

The whole *anonymous* thing was kind of sketchy. I mean, anybody could call up the newspaper and tell them anything. It didn't mean it was true, which was why Ben was being careful to check out the facts before going ahead with the story.

But if it wasn't true, why would anybody make up something like that about Doug? Even if Doug was accused and eventually cleared, it was a career killer. It would always follow him. He'd have a tough time getting a job in aerospace again—or anywhere else that required a security clearance or even a background check.

A jealous colleague, I figured. Who else would want to ruin Doug's life?

The thought stuck in my head as I left my car and hurried into the store. As I approached the breakroom, I saw that all the employees were heading out, starting their shift. That meant I was late.

Crap.

I went inside and saw that everyone was gone. Shannon had written my name on the white board with a red marker—yeah, just like fourth grade. If you got your name on the board five times in one month, you got fired.

I punched in and walked leisurely to my locker—no reason to hurry now. I slipped my cell phone into my pocket and stowed my purse. The list on the clipboard hanging beside the time clock indicated I was assigned to the customer service booth tonight. I noted that Grace was working there, too, so if I was going to squander several hours of my life for a lousy seven bucks an hour, at least she was a cool person to do it with.

Doug flashed in my mind again. I couldn't stop wondering why someone would try to ruin his career—if he was really innocent, of course.

What could Doug have done to cause a coworker to want to do this to him? How awful could it have been?

I'd known engineers all of my life, thanks to my dad's job, and while they could show a little professional jealousy from time to time, they didn't usually turn on each other. They worked together on projects. They did team-building stuff. Really, one engineer couldn't do much without the work of lots of other engineers.

Plus, engineers were so weird—which was okay because they knew they were weird—they socialized with each other almost exclusively. They partied—which really meant that they each drank a lite beer and talked about the project they were working on—and, since they weren't particularly athletic, they played ball on teams they'd organized themselves.

So it didn't make sense to me that suddenly, after working together for a long time on a project, one of them would make such an outlandish claim against Doug.

But if it wasn't a coworker, who could it have been?

I headed for the customer service booth. I was late—really late—but I knew Grace would be cool about it, that's the great thing about working with her.

When I got there, she was busy at the inventory computer, probably doing a return for the customer waiting at the counter standing off to the side. About eight people were waiting in line, so I was forced to help the next person.

A woman with short gray hair, wearing stretch pants, top, jewelry, and Crocs—all in aqua blue, for no apparent reason—stepped up to the counter holding the Holt's sale ad in her hand. She pointed to a pair of angels swinging gardening tools.

"Can you tell me where to find these figurines?" she asked.

Customers think that the employees working in the customer service booth should know where everything in the entire store is located. It's crazy. I mean, really, if something wasn't sitting next to the time clock, why would I notice?

I had no clue where to find the figurines.

"Housewares," I said.

"I tried there," she said. "I didn't see them."

Damn.

"Try the last row, on the bottom shelf," I said.

"Thanks," she said, and left.

The next customer stepped up to the counter. A couple of seconds passed before I realized it was Detective Shuman. He had on his usual mismatched sport coat, shirt, and tie, so I figured he was still working.

"I need to talk to you," he said. "When can you take a break?"

I glanced at the six people in line behind him, then at Grace still working at the inventory computer.

"Now's fine," I said, and left the booth.

"Someplace quiet," Shuman said.

I pushed through the double doors leading to the stock room. No one else was there, as usual, during the evening.

"Did you find anything on Ed Buckley?" I asked.

"Nothing here in L.A. He must be using an alias," Shuman said. "I went to see Virginia Foster."

My stomach tingled—in a good way, not an I-could-kill-somebody-for-a-Snickers-bar way—and I figured he'd gotten some new info on Tiffany's murder. But he didn't say anything right away, just looked kind of troubled.

Not a good sign.

"So what happened?" I asked.

"She wasn't there," Shuman said.

He came all the way over here to tell me that?

The tingle in my stomach turned into a lump.

"Nobody's seen her. I checked with housekeeping. She didn't use her room last night," Shuman said.

I started to feel a little sick now.

"Maybe she went to Disneyland," I said.

"She's missing," Shuman said.

His expression hardened and morphed into his cop look.

"Do you know where she is, Haley?" he asked.

"How would I know?" I asked.

"Because according to witnesses at the hotel," he said, "you were the last person to see her."

Oh, crap.

CHAPTER 18

I had to hurry. I knew I could be living—shopping, actually—on borrowed time.

I dashed away from my car and headed straight for the handbag department in Nordstrom.

After Shuman had come to Holt's last night and told me how Virginia Foster had vanished from her room at the Hyatt, I figured it was just a matter of time before the FBI showed up and accused me of being involved somehow. And I had no reason to think they would stop there. They'd probably twist everything around until they charged me with Tiffany's murder and thrown in their undercover agent's death, Ed's smuggling, and Rita's disappearance to boot.

That's why I'd headed to The Grove first thing this morning. I absolutely had to find a Sinful purse on the off chance that I could make bail in time to go to the record label's party that Jay Jax had invited me to.

Everyone has their priorities.

Not a lot of shoppers were out at this time of the day. Mostly moms pushing baby strollers, a few older couples, wives who shopped while their husbands worked.

This was good news for me because if I spotted a Sinful purse, I intended to take out anybody who stood in my way. I could not—absolutely could not—walk into that party without a Sinful bag.

Or a date?

Ty flew into my mind.

I intended to invite him to the record label's party—if he ever returned one of my calls, that is. No way was I going through what happened a few weeks ago—long story—with him. But that wasn't why I was thinking about him at this particular moment.

Whether Ty did or didn't get back from London in time to go to the party with me didn't change the problems we had—or at least our one big problem: I thought I would lose my mind if he kept talking about the stock market and all that other crap after sex, and Ty didn't seem to be able to talk about anything else.

Somehow, we had to work this out.

I realized then that I was standing outside a Barnes & Noble. Inside this bookstore were probably all sorts of books, magazines, and newspapers that could teach me how to live in Ty's world—a little, anyway. Hopefully just enough that he didn't constantly kill my afterglow—or be tempted to sleep with Sarah Covington because she knew what he was talking about.

All I had to do was go inside and buy them. I could spend a few hours reading, learning just enough to get by—sort of like with my college classes—and things would get better for us.

Our relationship deserved that much, didn't it?

I glanced down the walkway at Nordstrom. Right now, at this moment, the very last Sinful handbag could be sitting in the display case, waiting for me. Somebody else who definitely didn't deserve it as much as I did could walk in and scoop it up.

I stood there for a really, really long couple of seconds looking back and forth between the two stores.

What should I do? Put my shallow, materialistic, crazed obsession with the hottest handbag of the moment ahead of my official boyfriend and the future of our relationship?

What kind of girlfriend would I be if I did that?

How would I look going to that party without a Sinful bag?

I dashed to Nordstrom.

Anyone in my place would have done the same thing.

I was tempted to pause at the doorway and stretch my hamstrings—just in case I had to go over the counter after an uncooperative sales clerk—but didn't waste the time. I charged inside and ran into a young woman leaving the store. She dodged left, just as I did, then we both went right at the same time, then both stopped and shared the apologetic smile the awkward situation called for.

But she got a weird look on her face, kind of like she'd seen a ghost—or maybe a Gucci handbag teamed with Coach shoes.

"Haley . . ." she gasped.

Oh my God. *Oh my God.*

Emily.

It took me a few seconds to recognize her because she looked so different than when I'd seen her out with Doug. Today her short bobbed hair was spiked up in a chic do, she had on really great makeup, and she wore a fabulous yellow sundress I'd seen in Banana Republic.

Emily looked terrific. Fantastic. She looked better than— well, *me.*

Jeez, what had happened to her? Where had this ultra stylish look come from? Had she just had a makeover this morning?

Then I glanced at the handbag slung over her shoulder. Marc Jacobs. I peered into her shopping bag. Oh my God. She'd just bought Dooney & Bourke's new purple satchel— I wanted one of those—plus a Betsy Johnson tote.

Hang on a second. Something was majorly wrong here.

Emily's cheeks had gone white—even under that great makeup she wore.

"This . . . this isn't what you think," she said.

"You're a fraud," I said—actually, I think I shouted it. "You're not who you're pretending to be at all, are you."

She glanced around embarrassed at the scene I'd caused.

"I . . . I can explain," she said.

"This whole thing with Doug is just an act, isn't it?" I said.

She didn't answer, but I didn't expect her to—or need her to. I already knew.

When I'd seen her with Doug she'd looked plain and simple—dull, just like him. But that wasn't the real Emily. *This* was the real Emily. I could tell it in the clothes she wore, her hair and makeup, and especially by her handbags.

You didn't carry a Marc Jacobs without knowing what you were doing. And you certainly didn't buy a Dooney & Bourke plus a Betsy Johnson at the same time without being a fully committed, crazed handbag aficionado—or handbag whore as Marcie and I call ourselves.

And then I got angry—and not because she'd bought that terrific Dooney & Bourke purple bag I wanted—but because of what she was doing to Doug.

He probably thought he'd found the woman of his dreams. Someone dull, just like him. Someone he might have a future with. Maybe marry, buy a house, have kids with. And all along, Emily had been someone completely different. Not at all who Doug thought she was.

"I know what you're doing," I told her. "I know what you're up to."

Emily's white cheeks got a little paler.

"Knock it off," I said. "Stay away from Doug. If you ever come near him again, I swear I'll rat you out quicker than you can say 'Donatello Versace spring runway show.' Got it?"

She gave me a single nod, then raced around me and out the door.

I stood there fuming for a few minutes, then dashed to the handbag department. After a quick sweep of the display cases, I left doubly annoyed because there wasn't a single Sinful handbag in the place.

I hoofed it back to my car and headed for the freeway, forming yet another mental list of stores I could search in pursuit of the purse of my dreams. But instead I turned south and caught the 10 freeway to Santa Monica—which just proves how super annoyed I was.

Driving with Evelyn the other day had reminded me of how much I like looking at the ocean. She was right, seeing that huge body of water made your problems seem smaller, somehow. And, it was a great place to think.

I needed to think—but not about a handbag, for a change.

Leaving the freeway, I took the surface streets to Pacific Coast Highway and headed north.

I couldn't get Emily out of my head. I couldn't stop thinking of what she'd done, how she'd deceived Doug and how it would probably hurt him when he found out the truth.

Why would she do that? Why would she pretend to be someone she wasn't? Someone *way* different from the person she really was.

Was it simply because she wanted Doug to like her?

I got a yucky feeling in my stomach.

Was I so different?

A few minutes ago I'd been standing outside the bookstore planning to buy anything and everything that might help me fit into Ty's world, just so he'd like me better than I feared he liked Sarah Covington—and to improve our sex life, of course. But still, I'd been driven by the need to have Ty like me.

And how many times had I told Sandy to dump her crappy boyfriends? But she never did. She'd proved time and time again that she was willing to put up with anything just to have a boyfriend.

The yucky feeling in my stomach got yuckier.

Maybe I should have kept my mouth shut and stayed

out of Doug and Emily's relationship—if you could call it that. Maybe it would have worked out, after all.

Weirder things had happened.

PCH rolled up and down hills, hugging the edge of cliffs as I drove northward. Not a lot of traffic, which was always a plus—especially since I wasn't paying all that much attention to my driving.

With this scenery, almost nobody did.

Emily and Doug wandered into my thoughts again. Yeah, sure, women changed to get a man, to keep a man, to please a man. But Emily had changed a lot. Judging from the way she'd been dressed when I saw her in Nordstrom, she'd changed completely, as if there was nothing of her true self there at all.

And she'd done that for *Doug? Dull Doug?*

Something wasn't right. Something else was going on.

I fished my Bluetooth out of my purse and punched in Jack Bishop's number. He answered on the third ring.

"There's this guy," I said. "His name is Doug Eisner."

"Your ex?" Jack asked.

How did everybody know about Doug? Were we picked up on security cameras somewhere? Had Ben Oliver followed Doug around, shot footage with me in it, and posted it on the Internet? Had Doug splashed me all over his Facebook page?

"Can you check out his new girlfriend?" I asked.

Jack didn't answer for a minute.

"This isn't some jealousy issue between the two of you, is it?" he asked.

Jeez, did *everybody* think I still had the hots for Doug?

"You wish," I said. "Her name is Emily. I need to find out everything about her."

"A first name? That's all you've got for me?"

"You'll figure out the rest."

"Damn right I could," Jack said. "But why should I?"

"Because I saw her earlier today carrying a Marc Jacobs handbag," I said.

Jack was quiet for a moment. "So?"

"A Marc Jacobs," I said again.

Jeez, why didn't he get it?

"And she'd just bought a Dooney & Bourke *and* a Betsy Johnson," I added, since he seemed to need further explanation.

Jack didn't say anything.

"Look," I said. "She's not who she's pretending to be."

"And you know this because of the purses she bought?" Jack asked.

"Yes," I said. Thank goodness, he finally understood.

"I'll check her out," Jack said. "You owe me."

I already knew that.

I hung up.

I was late for work again.

I knew that because when I got to the employee breakroom, nobody else was there and my name was written on the white board again. But luckily I'd missed Shannon's supposed pep talk about the secret shopper and the customer satisfaction thermometer chart that was falling again, even after a repeat of the training program.

Somehow we'd fallen below beach towel range and were now in the you'll-be-lucky-to-keep-your-jobs category.

Jeez, I wonder how that kept happening?

I clocked in, stowed my purse—keeping my cell phone with me in direct violation of Holt's policy—and headed out to the sales floor.

Tonight I was assigned to the ILA department—that's retail speak for Intimates, Lingerie, and Accessories—which meant I was no doubt destined to spend the next few hours straightening displays of socks.

I hate my life.

"Haley?" a woman called.

Just in case it was a customer, I kept walking.

"Haley, I need to talk to you," she said, a little louder.

Just in case it was Shannon, I walked faster.

"Haley? Stop, please," she all but shouted.

I recognized Jeanette's voice. She sounded like she was in store-manager mode.

I stopped and turned, then gasped in horror. Jeanette had on a dress with wide horizontal bands of white, red, and black. She looked like a cargo ship backing into the harbor.

"I need to discuss something with you," Jeanette said.

Yeah, okay, I knew I'd been late two nights in a row but, jeez, it wasn't the end of the world. And it certainly didn't rate a conversation with the store manager. Surely she had something more important to do—something that would benefit Holt's—than to talk to me.

I'd have to find a way to work this into my next conversation with Ty—if he ever called me again.

At this point, the natural instinct was to rush ahead with an explanation of why I was late, followed by a promise that it wouldn't happen again. I'd learned long ago to fight that instinct. Just in case.

"There's a special project coming up, Haley, and I'd like you to take charge of it," Jeanette said.

See what I mean?

"I'm kind of busy working intimates," I said, in keeping with my strict never-volunteer-for-anything policy.

"Our annual Blue Jeans Blowout sale is coming up and all of our denim merchandise has to be tagged," Jeanette said. "I need someone to take charge of it who works well with little or no supervision, and I think that person is you."

Did she have me mixed up with someone else, or what?

I shook my head. "I don't know, Jeanette."

"You'll work your entire shift in the stock room," she said.

My entire shift? In the stock room? No customers? With management approval?

Cool.

"If it will help out our Holt's team, I'll be happy to take it on," I told her.

"Shannon will explain everything to you," Jeanette said, then walked away.

Though she hadn't said so, I was pretty sure Jeanette intended for me to go find Shannon and get the particulars about my new assignment, rather than report to the accessories department right now.

At least that's the way I'm choosing to interpret it.

Knowing that Shannon spent most of her shift in the front of the store watching the cashiers, like a vulture hovering over a dying carcass, I headed to the rear of the store. Sandy waved to me from the shelves of handbags she was straightening.

Since I'm genetically predisposed to turning away at the sight of nondesigner handbags, it took a great deal of effort for me to walk over and talk to her. But hey, that's what friends do. Right?

"You're here," she said. "I didn't see you in the break-room just now."

"I'm handling a special project," I said. "Jeanette asked me personally to take it on."

"Oh." Sandy grinned. "I thought maybe you were out with your boyfriend."

I froze. How would she know about Ty? I'd never told a soul about him—not here at Holt's, anyway.

"How did you know about him?" I asked.

Sandy shrugged. "I saw you two in the parking lot after work a few weeks ago. Can't say that I'm crazy about the little white Kia he drives, but he seemed like a nice guy."

Oh my God. She had to be talking about Doug. He was the only guy I knew who drove a Kia. She thought Doug was my boyfriend—still—not Ty.

"Doug and I broke up," I said.

"Too bad," Sandy said. "He was kind of good looking."

I walked away feeling a little rattled by what Sandy had said.

No way did I want anyone at Holt's to know I was dating Ty. Guess I'd gotten lucky that Sandy had been behind the times and was really talking about Doug. Since I'd been away in Europe for a while, it made sense. Doug was the last guy anybody here would have seen me with. In fact, Doug was the last guy anybody in North America would have seen me with.

My cell phone in my back pocket vibrated. Immediately I thought of Jack Bishop and hoped he'd already wrapped up his investigation of Emily.

I yanked the phone out of my pocket as I hurried into the stock room and checked the caller I.D. screen. It was Evelyn.

Okay, that was weird.

"Haley, something's happened," she said, sounding more rattled than usual.

Knowing Evelyn, this probably meant someone had rung her doorbell.

"Are you okay?" I asked. "Do you want me to come over?"

"No, no, I couldn't ask you to leave work."

"Really, it's no problem. Really."

Evelyn drew in a breath. "Could you come by in the morning?"

"Sure," I said. "What's up?"

"Something's happened," Evelyn said. "And you're the only one who can help me."

Oh, crap.

CHAPTER 19

"So, how are your classes?" Evelyn asked.

"Great," I said, as I pulled away from the curb in front of her house.

I'd driven to Evelyn's house first thing this morning, as she'd requested last night, and was surprised to see that she wanted to go out again. She'd been ready to leave, dressed as if she'd just walked off the set of *Little House on the Prairie,* in a long pale green skirt, a print blouse, and flats. It had taken only about ten minutes to actually get her out of her house, down the sidewalk, and into my car. Progress, Evelyn style.

She still hadn't explained her emergency.

"So what's up?" I asked, as we cruised out of her neighborhood.

"I'm thinking of making new curtains for my kitchen windows," she said.

This was her emergency?

"You want me to take you to the fabric store or something?" I asked.

"Oh, no, that's not why I asked you to come pick me up," Evelyn said. "Something's come up and, well, I need your advice."

Oddly enough, people don't usually come to me for advice. Now I was completely lost.

"I've been invited to a party," Evelyn said.

I nearly ran my car up onto the curb.

Evelyn was considering going to a party? A real party? She hadn't been the party type even back before "the incident" last fall. She'd hardly been out of her house in months—and now she thought she was ready to party?

I decided this wasn't the best time to point that out.

"Do you think I should . . . attempt it?" Evelyn asked.

"What kind of party are we talking about?" I asked.

"I don't have all the details yet," she said. "It will be a large event. Lots of people, I understand."

"A big crowd won't . . . bother you?" I asked, and was pleased that I hadn't said *freak you out* instead.

Evelyn didn't answer. I glanced over and saw that she was staring out the windshield, but didn't seem to be seeing the freeway entrance ahead of us.

"I think . . . I think I'd like to go," she finally said.

"You're sure you're up to it?" I asked.

"Yes, I believe that I am," she replied, then drew in a breath. "I believe that it's . . . time."

If Evelyn thought the time had come to hit the party scene, who was I to discourage her?

"Then you should do it," I told her. "And, you know, if you get there and don't like it, you can call me. I'll come pick you up."

I glanced over and saw that she was looking at me. Evelyn gave me a gentle smile.

"Thank you, Haley," she said softly.

"So, where would you like to go today?" I asked.

"Actually, I'm thinking about going to the mall," Evelyn said.

I nearly ran the car up onto the curb again.

Evelyn wanted to go to the mall? To go shopping? After she'd just told me she wanted to go to a party?

Jeez, if Evelyn got any wilder, I didn't know how I'd handle it.

I shifted immediately into shopping mode as I merged onto the freeway.

"What kind of dress do you need?" I asked.

"Cocktail length," she replied. "But I think I'd like something that looks young, and fun."

Immediately, a dozen stores flashed in my mind, prioritized by location, driving distance, and cost.

"What kind of budget are you thinking of?" I asked—translation, how much are you willing to spend?

Evelyn thought for a moment. "Since it's a special occasion, I think I'd like to buy something extra special."

Translation, unlimited budget.

My favorite kind.

"Great," I said. "We'll get you the perfect dress. Don't worry. I'm all over it. And we'll get you the perfect shoes to go with it—and, of course, the perfect handbag. And the day of the party we'll schedule you for a mani and a pedi and get your hair done."

"Oh . . ."

I glanced over to see that Evelyn had gone considerably paler.

Committing to going to the party was a big deal for her. I guess facing a battery of spa pampering on the same day might be too much for her.

"I know a place that will send someone to your home for those things," I said. "My mom uses them all the time."

"Really?" Evelyn said, sounding slightly less traumatized.

"It's a specialized service," I said—translation, it will cost a fortune—"but it's really worth it."

Evelyn was quiet for another moment. I glanced over to see if she was considering it.

"Yes," she finally said. "That will be fine. Thank you, Haley. I knew you were the right person to ask for help."

"So, who are you going to the party with?" I asked, and made it sound really casual.

I was still wondering if Evelyn was seeing the vice president of the GSB&T. I figured this was the perfect time for her to admit to it.

"A friend," she replied.

"Yeah? Who?"

"Do you think a red dress would be too much?" Evelyn asked.

My cell phone rang. I checked the I.D. screen and saw that it was Jack Bishop. I gave Evelyn an apologetic look and answered.

"I need to talk to you," he said. "Now."

"I'm kind of busy," I said. "Where can I meet you later today?"

"You're not that busy," he said. "Pull over."

I glanced in my rearview mirror and saw Jack's black Land Rover hugging my back bumper.

Jeez, where had he come from? How long had he been following me? I'd never even noticed.

I've really got to get better about looking around.

I took the next exit and pulled into a Chevron station. Jack swung in behind me.

"This will just take a minute," I said to Evelyn as I got out of my Honda.

"Well, all right," she said, twisting her fingers together.

As I walked away, I heard the car doors lock.

Jack stood at the hood of his Land Rover. Today he wore really nice-looking black trousers, a green silk shirt, and sunglasses. He looked way hot.

"How did you find me?" I wanted to know.

"It's all part of the service," he told me with a grin that was also way hot. "Talk to me about Emily."

I figured Jack had learned something but was cautious about spilling it all at once.

I didn't get a good feeling.

"Like I said, she's dating Doug, a guy I went out with a few weeks ago," I said. "He's an aerospace engineer and

Emily looked just as dull as him—until I saw her at Nordstrom looking totally different."

"She's an actress," Jack said. "She's worked a little.
Mostly she's a cocktail waitress."

This hardly seemed like info I needed to drop everything
to hear about. I knew there was more.

"I saw her with your old friend Kirk Keegan," Jack said.

For a second, I thought Jack had slapped me, that's how
hard his words hit me. I went from stunned to shocked to
angry in less than a minute.

"Damn it, I knew something wasn't right about her," I
said. Then my anger gave way to confusion. "If she's hanging out with Kirk, why is she dating Doug?"

"You tell me," Jack said.

Then it hit me.

Oh my God. *Oh my God.*

"Kirk said he was going to ruin my life, starting with
my boyfriend," I said. "Kirk thinks Doug is my boyfriend."

It made sense. Almost nobody knew I was dating Ty. Doug
was the last man anyone had seen me with. Sandy had
thought the same thing. Why wouldn't anybody else?

"Kirk used Emily to try and set up Doug, thinking Doug
was still my boyfriend," I said. "Kirk used Emily to steal
my boyfriend, which was easy since we'd broken up. Then
Kirk intended to ruin Doug's career so we could never get
back together again."

Jack nodded. "That's Keegan's style."

"Kirk had this whole terrorism-espionage accusation thing
going against Doug. He must have used Emily to make it
happen," I said.

The whole nasty business came clear to me.

"Emily pretended to be Doug's girlfriend to learn a little
about the project he was working on, then tipped off the
newspaper reporter that he was selling our government secrets to a terrorist group. Even after the accusation turned

out to be nothing, Doug's career would still have been trashed."

Jack was quiet for a moment.

"Any chance this Eisner guy was doing that?" he asked.

"No, I don't see it happening. Not his style," I said. "But you know it's Kirk's style to get a girl to help him with his dirty work."

Jack didn't comment, but we both knew it was true—long story. Kirk had a way about him that women—most women—couldn't refuse. Emily, an aspiring actress and struggling cocktail waitress, would be easy prey for him.

"When I saw Emily at Nordstrom, I figured she was pretending to be someone really different just so Doug would want to date her," I said. "I told her to stay away from him or I'd rat her out big time. I didn't know Kirk was behind everything."

"But Emily thought you did," Jack said.

I got a yucky feeling in my stomach.

"She went straight to Keegan," he said. "Told them they were busted."

The yucky feeling got a little better. In fact, I felt really relieved.

"That means the end of Kirk Keegan's threats against me," I said. "So, good news, huh? It's over."

"Not so fast," Jack said. "If you think Kirk was out to get you before, just wait until he finds out you've screwed him over—again."

Oh, crap.

I wish I could say Jack's prediction about Kirk coming after me again didn't bother me. It did.

Kirk would probably think I'd deliberately provoked him, after Emily reported to him what I'd said to her when we'd run into each other at Nordstrom.

Just my luck. I'd thought she was simply deceiving Doug

into thinking she'd be his perfect girlfriend. But, instead, she'd thought I'd figured out what Kirk was up to.

No wonder she'd looked so scared when she saw me.

Well, nothing I could do about that now.

Of course, Kirk might figure out that Ty was my official boyfriend now. He'd worked for Pike Warner and he knew that Ty's family had lots of money and lots of connections. Hopefully, he wouldn't go after Ty.

Hopefully.

Anyway, there was nothing I could do about that now, either.

Right now I had something important to do. Right now, I had to ruin someone's life—again.

Evelyn had wanted to go back home—I think seeing Jack kind of scared her—so I'd dropped her off with the promise that we'd go shopping for her party dress another time, and called Ben Oliver at the newspaper. He wasn't in, but the same woman I'd talked to before—I got the feeling they'd dated, which explained a lot—was more than happy to once again tell me in great detail that Ben wasn't at his desk or in a meeting and probably wasn't out covering a story, either, even though that's what he was being paid to do at that particular moment. She also told me where I could more than likely find him.

I needed to tell Ben that the big terrorism-espionage-digital-engine-thingy story he was working on—the one that would surely put him back in the good graces of his editor, change his life, and possibly propel him to journalistic stardom—was going nowhere.

I wasn't great at delivering bad news, but I didn't have a choice.

I hate it when I have to do the right thing.

Ben sat in the back corner of the Starbucks on Wilshire— where did people meet before Starbucks opened?—typing furiously on his laptop. I got a mocha frappuccino—a grande, which I needed for moral support—and approached his table.

He spared me a quick glance and kept typing.

"Go away," he said.

"I need to talk to you," I said, and sat down.

"Not now."

Ben looked really intense, and I got a really bad feeling. I leaned around a little trying to get a glimpse at the screen.

"That's not your Doug-might-be-a-terrorist story, is it?" I asked.

Ben's fingers froze on the keyboard. I guess something in my tone must have tipped him off.

"Yeah. What about it?" he asked, in that way that dared me to answer.

"Well, I, uh . . ."

"You stuck your nose in it, didn't you," Ben said.

"Well, sort of, but not exactly."

Ben glared at me. He looked as if he could seriously kill me.

I get that occasionally.

And when I do, there's no option left but to lie. It works best. Believe me.

"I talked to my dad," I said. "He's an aerospace engineer. He said that all the info you were tipped to is common knowledge."

Yeah, okay, so my dad hadn't said any of that. But, jeez, if my mom knew it, everybody on the planet probably knew it. Plus I wasn't getting into the Emily-Jack-Kirk story. It would only cloud the issue.

"The whole thing with the anonymous tip was probably just somebody's idea of a prank or something," I said.

Ben kept glaring at me.

"So, essentially, the story is, well, it's not a story at all," I said.

"You did something," he said. His jaw was set and I swear I could see steam coming out of his nose—which was kind of hot. "You screwed this up for me."

"Look, don't blame me if your anonymous tip turned out to be crap," I told him. "And besides, I gave you a real story. Tiffany Markham's murder—"

"Which is crap, too," Ben said. He slammed his laptop closed. "I talked to a reporter in Charleston like you asked. He says nothing's going on. Oh, yeah, he'd heard of that Ed Buckley guy and some wild story about him smuggling diamonds, but it was all cocktail party gossip because his wife couldn't stay out of the jewelry stores."

"But—"

Ben shoved back from the table and grabbed his laptop.

"So thanks *again* for making me look like an ass!" he shouted, and stomped away.

"I could still give you that makeover," I called.

I don't think he heard me. He was already out the door.

Customers in Starbucks were staring and, since I didn't want the manager to come over and ask me to leave for causing such a ruckus, I grabbed my frappuccino and left.

No sign of Ben in the parking lot. I considered calling his boss at the newspaper and suggesting he be put on suicide watch but decided I should stay out of it.

I felt really bad about Ben's big story turning out to be nothing. It wasn't my fault, technically, but I still felt bad. And I *had* presented him with another fantastic story.

I doubted he'd take me up on my makeover offer.

I climbed into my car and pulled out of the parking lot. Really, Ben had a point. What more could he do about Tiffany's murder? For that matter, what could the cops or the FBI do?

Sure, everybody was investigating, checking on things, doing whatever it was law enforcement people did. But they didn't have much to go on. According to Detective Shuman,

Ed Buckley was using an alias here in L.A., and since Virginia Foster had disappeared—jeez, I really hoped she wasn't dead—nobody even knew what Ed looked like now.

Except for me.

Oh my God.

The signal light up ahead changed to red and I stopped in the line of traffic. A dozen thoughts flew through my head.

Not only had I seen the one and only photo of Ed that Virginia had snapped on her trip to L.A. last fall, but I'd also seen Ed in person the morning he'd shot and killed Tiffany in the Holt's parking lot.

The guy behind me blew his horn, jarring me from my thoughts. I glanced in the rearview mirror thinking maybe it was Jack, but I didn't recognize the car. I drove forward. By the time I reached the next corner I knew what I had to do.

I had to find Ed Buckley myself.

CHAPTER 20

I followed along with Shannon and the other employees in the Holt's breakroom through the stretches that were supposed to make us better workers, trying not to think too hard about the next few hours of my life that would pass in a blur, never to be recovered.

"All right, people, listen up," Shannon called. She gestured toward the customer satisfaction thermometer on the wall and its barely discernible red line. "I know things look bad."

She looked straight at me, for some reason. A few employees did, too.

"But we've still got time to turn things around and get those flat screens," Shannon said. "I've got a feeling things are going to get better."

She looked at me again. Several more employees glanced my way, too.

Jeez, what was going on?

"I've got a *really good feeling* things will get better," Shannon added.

Now everybody looked at me.

"So let's get out there and provide some flat-screen-quality customer service," Shannon said, and jerked her thumb toward the breakroom door.

I lumbered along with the crowd and took a glance at

the work schedule hanging near the time clock. I wasn't assigned to a department tonight.

"Hi, Haley!" Christy appeared next to me, a ridiculously big smile on her face, her blond curls bouncing. "Wow, isn't this great! We're going to be the only Holt's store to sky-rocket all the way to the top of the customer satisfaction chart this close to the end of the contest! Isn't it fantastic!"

"Yeah. Great," I mumbled.

Why wasn't I assigned to a department tonight?

"Gosh, I'm so glad I work here! This is a super place to work!" Christy said. "I love retail! Don't you?"

"Yeah," I muttered, checking the chart once more.

Christy left the breakroom and I followed along behind everyone else, not sure where I should report. Then it occurred to me that perhaps Holt's had come up with a new position—they could have covered it in a meeting where I'd drifted off. Perhaps the store now had roving employees who just walked around, checking on things, then jumped in where needed.

Obviously, I was the perfect person for that position.

I headed toward the shoe department—I really should check out the stock room there—when Shannon planted herself in front of me.

"Not so fast," she said. "Jeanette has you on a project."

Oh, yeah. Our Blue Jeans Blowout sale. I'd forgotten all about it.

I followed Shannon down the aisle and into the big stock room at the back of the store. It was silent in there, as always at this time of the evening. Employees rarely came back here, unless some customer threw a big enough fit to have them check on something, which didn't happen all that often.

Shannon stopped near the loading dock where the big steel and concrete stairs went up to the second floor and the conveyor belts and hanging conveyors ran alongside it. Several big work tables stood nearby amid the jumble of mannequins, unsalable merchandise, and returns.

"Okay, here's your project," Shannon told me.

She pointed to what looked like hundreds of big brown boxes stacked in the corner.

"What's in them?" I asked.

"Blue jeans," she barked, as if I were as stupid as, well, as stupid as I thought she was.

Obviously, Shannon didn't know I'd slept with the store's owner and we were now officially boyfriend-girlfriend. Maybe if I talked about futures in the Asian market, Ty would fire her for me.

She stomped over to one of the shelving units and tossed a box of plastic merchandise tags onto the work table. I'd seen them before—they'd probably told us the official name at orientation, but I'd drifted off. They were the kind with a long pin that went through the fabric and connected to a big bulky plastic thing on the other side that caused the security alarm to beep if somebody tried to walk out the front door with them. The tags could only be removed with a special gizmo at the checkout registers.

"Put one of these on every pair of jeans," Shannon told me.

My eyes widened. "How many pairs are there?"

"Two thousand."

"Two thousand?"

"Misses', juniors', womens', girls', boys', infants', toddlers', men's, plus size women's, extended size men's," Shannon said. "We're talking blowout here, Haley. Remember?"

"Well, yeah, but—"

"I'm coming back to check on you—often," Shannon threatened. "I'd better find you working. These jeans have to be tagged in time for the sale. Don't go out on the sales floor. Understand? *Don't* leave this stock room—no matter *what.*"

She stomped away.

I hate my life.

*   *   *

It was a Prada day. Definitely a Prada day.

First thing this morning, Evelyn and I had hit the mall in search of the perfect dress for her to wear to the party she'd decided to attend. Shopping is a highly fluid situation. You have to be ready to dig in, try on, or cut and run when a store just doesn't have the right vibe. I'm very gifted in that arena.

It's an art, really.

Evelyn didn't seem to see it that way but, I had to hand it to her, she hung in there with me through four stores and dozens of dresses. When we finally found the perfect dress, I felt like Columbus must have felt when he'd discovered the beautiful, lush continent of America. I don't think Evelyn shared my thrill of victory. She was mostly tired at that point.

We pushed on to the shoe department, where Evelyn perked up considerably, the handbag department—no Sinful bag, I checked—and finally the jewelry counter where we pronounced her look complete.

I drove Evelyn home. I was pretty sure she took a nap after I left.

But I was pumped. My day had gotten off to a terrific start, an omen of things to come. So with my gorgeous Prada bag looped over my shoulder in what I hoped conveyed a casual yet sophisticated look, I headed downtown where I hoped my good luck would continue.

I was shopping for a killer.

I turned off of Olympic Boulevard onto Maple and cruised up the ramp to the rooftop parking garage Marcie and I usually used when we came to the Fashion District to buy knockoff designer handbags for our purse party business.

Downtown Los Angeles had undergone major changes in the past few years. Historic buildings had been converted to individual housing units, upscale shops and restaurants had gone in, a grocery store had opened. The Fashion District had changed, too, but not nearly as much.

I parked and took the steps that led to a men's clothing store in Santee Alley. The District covered some ninety blocks, but The Alley was its heart. The stores that opened onto Santee Street and Maple Avenue used the alley between them to create a shopping experience reminiscent of bazaars around the world. The place was always jam packed with shoppers, loud music blared, and venders hawked their merchandise in English and Spanish.

Nearly everything could be bought and sold in The Alley—wholesale and retail—and most was counterfeit. Sunglasses, electronics, perfumes, iPod and cell phone cases, cigarette lighters, shoes, clothes, and, of course, handbags.

My heart rate picked up as I headed through The Alley. I was surrounded by purses, and even though they were knockoffs, I still got a rush.

Gucci, Prada, Burberry, Chloe, Dolce & Gabbana, Louis Vuitton, Marc Jacobs, Kenneth Cole, Treesje, Ferragamo. Clutches, satchels, hobos, buckets. Leather, fabric, patterns, colors. They hung from peg boards, over doorways; they were piled on tables and lined up on shelves.

Marcie and I always shopped together for our purse parties. I'd never been here alone. Where was she when I needed her? I fished my cell phone from my purse and punched in her work number.

Oh my God, what was I doing?

I hung up before she answered. Jeez, what had I been thinking? My sole purpose for being here today was to find Ed Buckley. I couldn't afford to get so caught up in the handbags on display that I forgot that. I had to be vigilant, stay focused.

Yeah, okay, that wasn't one of the things I did best, but today I absolutely had to force myself.

My plan was to search the area until I spotted Ed, just as Tiffany had done.

Maybe it wasn't the greatest plan in the world, but it was all I had. Didn't Tiffany deserve that much effort? And what about Virginia Foster, who was missing and maybe dead. Honestly, I didn't care that much that Rita might have been a casualty of this, but she probably had a family somewhere who deserved to know the truth. I owed Ben Oliver a story, too. And I wanted Shuman to show those FBI guys up.

Really, what are friends for?

And if I didn't find Ed, who would?

I was sick of always thinking that maybe I was being followed, and that those guys from the FBI might jump out at me and arrest me. I wanted to put an end to this so my life could get back to normal or, hopefully, better than normal.

Just as I slipped my cell phone back into my purse, it rang. I looked at the caller I.D. screen and saw that it was Ty.

Okay, that was weird.

I stepped off to the side, out of the way of the crowds roaming through The Alley, hoping I could get a good signal amid the tall buildings that surrounded me.

I'd given up trying to calculate the time difference between here and London, so I answered, hoping he wasn't calling in a drunken stupor from a pub or party somewhere.

I wasn't in the mood.

"Haley," he said when I answered. "How are you doing?"

I looked down at the phone, then put it to my ear again. "Ty?" I asked.

He sounded kind of down or something. I hadn't heard that tone in his voice before.

"Are you okay?" I asked.

"Everything here is taking longer than I thought," Ty said, "and, well, I need to get home."

My stomach got kind of mushy hearing him say that. Ty had a great voice. Everything about him was way hot.

"When can you get here?" I asked.

"A few more days."

"By Saturday?" I asked.

He paused for a moment. "Probably not. Why?"

"There's a smoking hot party I'm invited to," I said. "I want you to come with me."

"I can't make it. There's no way I can get things wrapped up here by then."

"I'll ask Marcie to go with me," I said.

Ty didn't say anything and for a minute I wondered if we'd lost our connection. I pressed the phone closer to my ear.

"There's something I need to talk to you about," he said, sounding really serious all of a sudden.

The warm gooey feeling in my stomach morphed into a knot.

Since I'm not big on suspense, I said, "Yeah, okay, what is it?"

He paused again.

I hate pauses.

"I can't get into it now," Ty said.

Oh my God. What did he want to tell me? That he'd realized we weren't right for each other? That he wanted to break up with me because I didn't talk dirty-stock-market to him? What could it be?

I decided to play it cool. No way would I dissolve into a desperate, clingy, whiny girlfriend right here on a public street.

"Sure, that's great," I said, "because there's something I want to talk to you about, too."

Ty didn't say anything. I figured he wanted to ask me what it was about, but didn't dare.

"I'll call as soon as I know when I'll be home," he said. "Have fun at the party."

Ty hung up. I tucked my phone away and started walking again, feeling not so great about our conversation.

Just as I'd started to replay the whole thing in my mind again, I got jostled from behind.

Oh my God. Had somebody just tried to pick my pocket? Steal my purse?

I looked back and saw a young Hispanic woman pushing a baby stroller. She mumbled an apology and kept going.

Nothing bad had happened, but it could have. I tightened my hold on my handbag and walked a little faster, renewing my resolve to remain attentive.

I reached the end of Santee Alley and turned east toward Maple. The sidewalk was narrow and crowded with colorful umbrellas used to shield both merchants and merchandise from the California sun. Vendors eyed me as I walked past; a white girl here alone was an uncommon sight.

Had Tiffany felt this way? I wondered. She'd walked these same streets, looking for Ed Buckley. It must have seemed really different from the quiet, staid atmosphere she was probably used to in Charleston.

I scanned the crowd ahead of me, then looked across Olympic Boulevard at the shoppers streaming back and forth. No sign of Ed. Yet. But I'd spot him, sooner or later. And when I did—

What would I do?

Jeez, I've got to get better about thinking things through.

Since my apprehension of Ed was imminent, I decided it would be good to have some backup in place. I called Detective Shuman.

"Can you meet me?" I asked when he answered. "I'm in the Fashion District looking for Ed Buckley."

"*What?*"

How could I have a clear connection with Ty all the way in London but Shuman couldn't hear me a few blocks away?

"I said I'm in the Fashion District—"

"*Alone?*"

"Yes," I said.

"Have you lost your mind?" he demanded.

Okay, so maybe he could hear me just fine.

"Where are you—exactly?" Shuman asked.

"Olympic and Maple."

"Don't move," he said and hung up.

A few minutes later I spotted Shuman hoofing it up Maple toward me. He looked like exactly what he is—a cop.

As if the police don't have anything more important to do, they occasionally raided the Fashion District, rounding up counterfeit merchandise and arresting merchants. I know all about copyright infringement and, yes, it's wrong to rip off somebody else's products, but jeez, people are killing each other all over the Southland. Maybe the cops could prioritize a little better?

Vendors, merchants, and shoppers eyed Shuman and his angry-cop face as he strode up to me.

"What the hell do you think you're doing?" he demanded.

"You're ruining my rep," I said. "Come on."

We crossed Olympic and went into an enclosed shopping area on the corner. The place was lined with vendors and merchandise, just like outside. But this place was newer, cleaner, a little more upscale and a lot cooler thanks to the air conditioning.

We found the closest thing to a quiet corner available and Shuman lit into me.

"What are you doing looking for Buckley? The man is a murderer. Have you forgotten that? What are you thinking coming down here all by yourself?" he demanded.

"I'm not by myself," I pointed out. "You're here with me."

I'm pretty sure Shuman didn't appreciate my attempt at humor.

He drew in one of those big breaths that makes men's chests expand and their shoulders raise—which is always way hot—and let it out slowly.

"Tiffany Markham knew Ed was here somewhere," I said. "She found him. So can I."

"And it got her killed," Shuman said.

"It will be different for me. Ed knew Tiffany. They'd been in the same family for years. They'd sat across the Thanksgiving dinner table from each other, she'd gone to his kids' birthday parties," I said. "Even though she went to great lengths to change her appearance, he'd seen through her disguise because he knew who she was."

"And it got her killed," Shuman said again.

"Ed doesn't know me. If he happens to see me in a crowd, my face will mean nothing to him."

I guess Shuman figured he wasn't getting anywhere pointing out the obvious.

"Why are you doing this?" he asked.

"Because *it* won't leave me alone," I told him. "And besides, I saw him. I saw Ed. I can identify him."

Shuman stilled, giving me cop-face.

"Virginia Foster showed me the picture she'd taken of him," I said. "I recognized him. I saw him in the parking lot the morning Tiffany was murdered."

Shuman drew in an even bigger breath.

"Why didn't you tell me this?" he asked.

"You're off the case, remember?"

"Did you tell the FBI?" he asked.

"No way," I said. "Look, I'm not in any real danger here."

"Unless Ed remembers you from that morning at Holt's," Shuman said.

Oh, crap. I hadn't thought of that.

"Ed was probably too busy to notice me, remember me, or think that I got a good enough look at him to point him out as Tiffany's murderer," I said.

"Probably?"

"Probably," I said. "I'm not going to try and catch him, or anything. Just locate him. And then I'll call you."

I could tell Shuman didn't like it, but really, what could he do?

"Be careful," he said. "And don't do anything crazy."

"I promise," I said, and resisted the urge to cross my heart.

"Call me right away if you spot him."

"I've got you on speed dial," I told him, and touched my Prada bag where my cell phone lay at the ready.

Shuman stewed for another couple of minutes, then left.

I spent the next few hours patrolling the Fashion District, looking for Ed Buckley. I found myself wondering how Tiffany had managed it. Had she just stumbled across him? Or had she, somehow, known where to look?

Maybe I needed a better plan.

Too bad I couldn't ask Virginia for more info.

I was walking north on Santee Street when something across the street caught my attention. I froze, did a double take, then gasped.

Oh my God. *Oh my God.*

With no regard for my personal safety, I dashed across the street, dodging cars and ignoring rude gestures—which I deserved—and raced to the display window of a tiny clothing store. I pressed my palms against the glass, too stunned to move.

There, in the center of the window display, sat a Sinful handbag.

Chapter 21

Please, don't be a knockoff. Oh, please, please, please, don't be a knockoff.

I silently repeated this chant, as if the handbag gods could hear me and somehow make my wish come true.

Cupping my hands against the store window, I leaned closer to block the glare and get a better look at the Sinful purse on display. My trained eye swept the detailing quickly and my heart started to pound.

The bag looked perfect. It looked genuine.

So as not to rush into the store looking scattered and frantic—which might cause the clerk to alert security—I closed my eyes for a moment, attempting to find my center and relax.

That lasted about four seconds.

My eyes popped open and I rushed inside.

All sorts of accessories filled the shelves—bracelets, necklaces, earrings, scarves, wallets, wristlets, socks, hats, and—yes—handbags. A few other customers milled around, checking out the jewelry.

What was the matter with them? How could they look at jewelry when a Sinful purse lay merely steps away?

The clerk behind the glass counter eyed me as I lifted the handbag from the display window.

Thanks to the advanced training Marcie and I had acquired picking out handbags for our purse parties, I knew exactly what to look for.

My gaze raced over the detailing: hardware—securely fastened; designer name—positioned properly, spelled correctly; tag—printed accurately.

My heart pounded in my chest. Oh my God, I'd found a genuine—

Hang on a minute.

I flipped the bag over and examined the stitching on the bottom. My heart sank.

The stitches were crooked, irregularly spaced. No way would a genuine bag in this condition have gotten past an inspector. This purse was a fake.

Crap.

I put the bag back and left the store, but couldn't bring myself to walk away just yet. I lingered for a moment at the window.

The quality of the bag was excellent. It had nearly fooled me—*me*. And if I, with my trained eye, could barely tell the difference, chances were good that almost nobody else could either.

Maybe I should buy it—just in case I couldn't find a genuine one in time to take it to the big party on Saturday.

"Nice knockoff, huh?" somebody said.

I turned and saw a man standing next to me. Late twenties, I guessed, maybe thirty already. Tall, dark brown hair, rugged build, dressed in jeans and a polo shirt. Handsome. Really handsome.

My heart started beating faster again—but for an entirely different reason.

"It had me fooled for a minute," I said. "I'm dying for one of those."

"Why don't you get it?" he asked.

The thought raced through my head for a fleeting second, but I couldn't do it.

"I'm addicted to the real thing," I told him.

He nodded, though I'm not sure he knew what I meant.

"Luke Warner," he said, as he stepped forward and offered his hand.

I took it. A wave of heat ran up my arm as I introduced myself.

"Shopping?" he asked.

This didn't seem like the best time to tell him that I was there searching for a murderer, so I just nodded.

Luke gestured down the block. "I'm here for a business meeting."

We couldn't seem to think of anything else to say, just stared at each other—sort of like in tenth grade—then both realized we were staring and not talking—*really* like tenth grade—and we looked away.

"Well, I'd better go," I said, backing up.

Luke took a step toward me and nodded toward the Sinful purse in the display window.

"Searching the shops for a real one of those?" he asked.

"It's a Sinful," I said.

Luke grinned. He had a killer grin. It reached his eyes which, I realized, were an incredible shade of green.

"Sinful, huh? Sounds intriguing." He said it in that deep, seductive, Barry White voice men use when they want to cause a woman's toes to curl.

My toes curled a little.

"Maybe I'll see you around," he said.

"Yeah, maybe," I said, which sounded really lame, but hearing the Barry White voice caused my brain to switch to half-function, sometimes.

I gave him a little wave and hurried away. At the corner I glanced back.

Luke was watching me.

"Okay, people, gather around," Shannon called as she waved the employees toward her in the breakroom.

While everyone else formed up in a semicircle ready to

start their stretches, I punched in, locked up my purse, and breezed past them.

Shannon gave me major stink-eye.

"I'm on a special project, remember?" I called.

I gave her my I'm-better-than-you eyebrow bob and I left the breakroom.

So far, those few seconds were the only thing I liked about the special project Jeanette had put me on and I'd agreed to.

Note to self: stick with my say-no-to-volunteering-policy *regardless*.

In the stock room I saw that the mountain of blue jeans on the work table and the wall of boxes that still held hundreds of dozens of pairs remained just as I'd left them last night. No one had come in on the morning or afternoon shifts and put a single tag on a single pair of jeans.

Jeanette really had given this project to me, only me.

I hate my life.

Now, I hate denim, too.

I got to work tagging jeans, wanting to get the project finished and these next few hours of my life over and done with. I pushed hard, staying focused, minimizing my movements, concentrating on not wasting a single second. Time flew by. I glanced at my watch. Fifteen minutes had passed.

Crap.

I pulled out my phone and called Marcie.

"Come by the store," I said when she answered her cell. "I've got something really cool to tell you."

"You're getting a lunch hour tonight?" she asked.

"I'm on a special project."

Nobody had specifically said what my hours would be for this project. But since I'd single-handedly taken on the monumental responsibility of ensuring that the Holt's Blue Jeans Blowout actually had jeans on the shelves, surely I was entitled to something more than my usual fifteen-minute break.

"Cool. Catch you later," Marcie said, and we hung up.

Another half hour dragged by—I knew because I checked my watch every ninety seconds—and I figured Marcie had to have arrived at the store by now. I went to the break-room.

She'd been to the store a few times and this was where we always met. She wasn't there yet and I should have gone back into the stock room, but oh well. She'd be along soon.

I got some cash from my wallet and fed it into the vending machines, then sat down at one of the tables, M&M's, Snickers bar, and soda in hand, and started flipping through a month-old copy of *People* magazine. Marcie came through the door a few minutes later.

She sat down across the table from me and glanced around the room, taking in the signs and posters that are plastered all over the walls.

"What's that?" she asked, pointing to the customer satisfaction thermometer chart.

"Some contest," I said, pushing the M&M's closer to her.

"Looks like you're doing pretty bad."

I glanced over and saw that the band of red had actually crept upward, back into beach towel range. Wow, how had that happened so fast?

"So what's the big news?" Marcie asked.

"I went to the Fashion District today," I said.

She looked hurt. "Without me?"

Shopping for knockoffs in Santee Alley was one of our all-time favorite things to do. We had a fabulous time selecting which bags we thought our customers would like. Most of the vendors knew us now, so haggling had been cut to a minimum—which was sort of disappointing—and we always left with huge shopping bags filled with dozens of purses.

Who wouldn't want to spend an afternoon that way?

I could see that Marcie was disappointed that I'd gone without her—not that I blamed her, of course—but I couldn't tell her the real reason I was there. No way could I get into the whole Tiffany–Ed thing with her.

But I could definitely get into the whole Luke thing.

"I was just scouting things out," I said, "for when we start having our purse parties again."

Marcie helped herself to a handful of my M&M's, which seemed to make everything all right for her.

"I found a Sinful bag," I reported.

Her eyes got bigger. "Was it—"

"A knockoff," I said.

She looked as crestfallen as I'd felt in the shop today.

"You didn't get it, did you," Marcie said. She hadn't even asked it as a question. She already knew the answer, as a best friend would.

"I was tempted," I admitted. "I met a really hot guy there."

Marcie's eyes widened. "You're just now telling me this? I've been here for five whole minutes and only now you're sharing this?"

"His name is Luke," I said, and felt my stomach start to tingle a bit. "He's tall and has a great build, and the most gorgeous green eyes you've ever seen in your entire life."

Marcie frowned. "What about Ty?"

"Who?"

"Haley . . . ," she said in that singsong way that always brings me back to reality.

I hate reality.

"Look, I'm not saying that anything is going on between Luke and me," I said. "I'm just saying that I met him and he's really good looking. That's all."

"When's Ty coming home?" she asked.

"Not until next week," I said. "Want to go to a really great party on Saturday?"

"Of course," she said.

"Remember that girl last year who had that great job

interview at that cool place and I got her that totally hot outfit to wear?" I asked.

"Sure," Marcie said, decoding my words as only a best friend can.

"She invited me to an awesome party on the Queen Mary. The record label is launching a new artist," I said. "They've rented the whole ship for the event."

"What are you going to wear?" Marcie asked.

Marcie has priorities, just like me.

"Something I got in London, I think," I told her. "You should wear that print dress we bought in that shop on Melrose."

Marcie needed only a couple of seconds to recall exactly which dress I was talking about.

"Perfect," she declared. "Wouldn't it be cool if you could find that Sinful bag to take?"

Marcie had read my mind again, as only a best friend can.

We talked for a while longer, making plans for the party, then Marcie left. I couldn't face a stock room full of denim jeans yet so I got another Snickers bar from the vending machine—just to keep up my energy, of course—and started flipping through *People* again.

My mind wandered.

I thought about the hours I'd spent in the Fashion District today, the streets, stores, and vendors I'd checked out in my search for Ed Buckley.

Luke floated into my thoughts.

I pushed him out.

Maybe Ed wasn't in the Fashion District at all. Maybe Tiffany had scoured the place and realized he simply wasn't there. Where else would she have looked? Where else should I look?

I needed to review all the info I'd gathered.

Luke floated into my thoughts once more. I'd met him

in the Fashion District surrounded by great fashions. I wondered if he talked about clothes after making love.

Yeah, okay, I knew that was bad. Ty was my official boyfriend now—though maybe I wouldn't be thinking about Luke if Ty was actually here rather than half a world away. But still, I shouldn't be thinking about Luke. I should be thinking about Ty.

No, really, I should be thinking about Ed Buckley.

I searched through the discarded magazines on the counter by the microwave and found an old flyer announcing a Holt's blood drive—when had that come in?—got a pen from my purse and sat down again.

I wrote down everything I knew and everything I'd been told about Ed, and what it might mean.

Maybe it meant nothing, I thought. Maybe I should be thinking outside the box.

The picture I'd seen of him that was taken during his old life in Charleston showed him on a boat. Should I be checking for him at a marina instead?

He'd been suspected of drug smuggling. Would he find connections for that in the Fashion District? Somewhere else?

Tiffany might have known some tiny scrap of info about him that led her in a totally different direction. Could I figure it out, too?

I sat back and looked at the list.

There was nothing to do but go back to the Fashion District again tomorrow.

Maybe I'd find Luke—I mean, Ed—there, after all.

Chapter 22

Shops in the Fashion District opened by 10 A.M. and I was there the next morning when the doors opened. I had no clue how long it would take to actually find Ed Buckley, but I was in it for the long haul—or until I couldn't stand it any longer. Shoppers filled the sidewalks on Main Street as I strolled along, taking in the warm sunshine.

There were things in the District that you might not expect to find, like lots of guys on bicycles. Bikes in heavy traffic on narrow streets didn't usually mix well, but that didn't seem to stop them.

Some of the guys sported yellow shirts and helmets. They were the clean and safe team and the safe team officers who patrolled the area to help out with questions or directions. Other guys just rode bikes around, swerving in and out of traffic and disappearing into alleys.

Almost all of the buildings showed their considerable age. Though some had been refurbished, others hadn't; they displayed only crumbling remnants of their past glory when craftsmanship and workmanship counted more than profits.

Last night I'd checked the Internet and zeroed in on the section of the District that specialized in accessories. I turned west on Eleventh Street, hoping I'd pick up the vibe of a Sinful bag somewhere.

I have a sixth sense about purses.

Since it seemed that, so far, I'd had no sixth sense about locating Ed Buckley, I figured why not pursue the handbag of my dreams. Maybe one would lead me to the other.

When I turned the corner onto Main Street, I saw Luke Warner walking toward me. He looked way hot today—hotter than yesterday, if that were possible.

I got a whole different sort of vibe—and it had nothing to do with handbags. Yeah, okay, I knew I shouldn't feel that way, but there it is.

"Are you following me?" Luke asked, giving me a playful grin as he stopped in front of me on the sidewalk.

"Only if you are sporting a Sinful handbag," I told him. "And then I might kill you for it."

He chuckled and glanced around. "Wouldn't be the first time that had happened—especially here."

I followed his gaze to the tall old buildings that lined the street, some with open windows on the top floors.

"I wonder what, exactly, goes on up there," I said. "I figure it probably isn't legal."

"It's a twilight economy here," Luke said. "The largest collection of counterfeit fashion merchandise in the country and cash-only transactions."

When Marcie and I came to the Fashion District to buy bags for our purse parties, we usually found everything we needed in Santee Alley, we dealt with vendors we knew, and were out of there in a few hours. After spending most of yesterday and this morning here, I could feel the undercurrent of a completely different social and economic system.

"With around a thousand shops and merchants from Pakistan, Vietnam, the Middle East, Mexico, Egypt, and lots of other places, things happen fast," Luke said. "The Koreans have a big stake here now, but who knows how long that will last."

"Are you here for another business meeting?" I asked.

Luke shrugged. "I own a couple of places down here."

"Stores?" I asked.

"Buildings," Luke said. "It pays to subdivide the space. Rents can run high. Five thousand a month for three hundred square feet in the good blocks. Up to fifteen thousand a month in the expensive areas. I'm down here every day to keep an eye on things."

I got that gooey feeling in my stomach. I know my official boyfriend owns a whole chain of department stores, but hearing that Luke owned several buildings in the Fashion District and was down here ready to mix it up to protect his turf, if need be, seemed a lot more appealing than Ty sitting at the Holt's corporate office reading spreadsheets and listening to Sarah Covington's lame-ass marketing schemes.

"So what are you doing down here again today?" Luke asked.

"Still shopping," I said.

"You know, I can get you one of those purses you're looking for," he said.

I froze. I thought for a moment that I hadn't heard him correctly, or maybe I'd been struck dead and gone to Heaven.

"The Sinful bag. Right?" Luke asked.

Oh my God. Luke had actually paid attention to what I told him yesterday, he remembered it, understood how important it was, and now was offering to get it for me. I must have gone to Heaven because this sort of thing doesn't happen on Earth.

"You can do that?" I asked, the words barely coming out of my mouth. "You can get me a Sinful? A *real* Sinful?"

"Sure."

I just stared at him. Jeez, it seemed too good to be true.

"Can you really pull this off?" I asked.

"I always deliver," Luke said, giving me a grin that curled my toes. He pulled out his cell phone. "Give me your phone number."

We traded numbers, then just stood there staring at each other, a duplicate of yesterday's tenth grade moment. The silence screamed louder than words.

"You know, this isn't such a safe place," Luke said, his grin suddenly morphing into something between concern and fear. "You shouldn't be here."

"I come here a lot," I said. "I'm okay with it."

Luke stepped closer. Heat from his body wafted over me. I smelled his aftershave. My stomach got really gooey.

"No, you should go home," he said quietly.

"Really, I'm fine here," I told him.

Luke eased closer. "You're in over your head here, Haley. Please. Leave everything to me."

Okay, that was weird.

But it was nice to think he cared about my safety—really nice. My gooey stomach warmed up considerably.

"Where are you parked?" Luke asked. "I'll walk you back to your car."

Suddenly, patrolling the Fashion District looking for Ed Buckley didn't seem like much of a priority. Besides, I could watch for him in the crowd on the way to my car.

We left Main Street and walked east on Twelfth Street. I eyed every face and glanced into the shops we passed.

"Almost all of the merchandise down here comes in through the Port of Los Angeles in Long Beach, about a half hour from here, in container ships. Very little of it is inspected. The fashions here get knocked off and are put out for sale in Santee Alley in about three weeks, while Macy's has to wait about six months to get theirs," Luke said. "The manufacturers have unregistered factories operating outside of California law."

"Aren't they worried about the police?" I asked.

"Have you noticed the teenage boys on bikes who ride through the District? They're spotters. They watch for the cops," Luke said. "Lookouts are posted outside the LAPD's Central Station, just a few blocks away. They know which cars belong to the inspectors. When they pull away, cell phones ring all over the area and the place clears out."

I stole a quick look up at the top floors of the buildings we passed and wondered if people worked there, and what sort of conditions they faced each day. Maybe they'd sewn the two thousand pairs of jeans I had been putting tags on for the Holt's sale.

I saw no faces at the windows. I figured the seamstresses, if they were up there, weren't allowed to get up from their sewing machines. Occasionally I saw fluorescent lights burning in the ceilings, so I knew somebody used the rooms for something.

It creeped me out a little, made me think I was being watched.

Luke walked with me all the way to Santee Alley, then up the stairs to the rooftop parking garage off Maple where I'd left my Honda. He got that concerned look on his face for a minute and I thought maybe he was going to caution me about not coming back to the Fashion District, but he didn't.

"Is it all right if I call you?" he asked.

"Sure," I said.

The valet brought my car. Luke waved as I drove away. As I turned to go down the ramp, I glanced back. Luke was watching me, his cell phone up to his ear.

I pulled out onto Maple and crept along with the traffic. I couldn't help wondering why Luke had given me the lowdown about what went on in the Fashion District. Was he trying to impress me? Or was it something else?

And what was the deal about finding me a Sinful handbag? If he could pull that off, yeah, okay, that would impress me.

I'd have to talk to Marcie about it. This was definitely a best friend conversation.

Hearing about the spotters and inspectors, the illegal sweatshops, and the international merchants from Luke didn't do much to endear me to the place, but it wasn't enough to keep me from buying purses there for the parties Marcie and I threw, and it sure as heck wouldn't keep me from looking for Ed.

I decided that I'd continue my search in my car. I could cover more ground, quicker. And who knows? Maybe Tiffany had decided to do the same thing and that's how she spotted Ed.

I covered the Fashion District. The blocks were short, the traffic slow, so I had time to check out the pedestrians on the sidewalks. Big trucks created major slowdowns as they double-parked to unload boxes. Men with handcarts moved merchandise from store to store. Lots of action on the streets. No Ed.

The Textile District adjoined the Fashion District so I cruised the area from Maple to San Julian and Eighth to Olympic. The signs on stores advertised fabrics for all sort of occasions: prom, bridal, bridesmaids. Hundreds of bolts of fabric sat on display in front of the dozens of stores. Shops carried everything from novelty fabrics to silks to upholstery. Lots of colors and textures. No Ed.

A block away I hit the Flower District. Merchants displayed their wares outdoors here, too. The sidewalks outside the shops were lined with cut flowers, potted plants, dried and silk arrangements. Some places featured funeral wreaths and crosses like you see at the cemetery, which kind of creeped me out. Still, no Ed.

I made another pass through the Fashion District—I'd leave the toy and jewelry districts for tomorrow—and caught the 10 freeway west. My cell phone rang.

I jumped in my seat and my heart did a little flip-flop.

Was it Luke calling? Already? He said he'd call. And if he called now, this quickly after I'd seen him, that meant—

Crap.

What it really meant was that I was thinking too much about Luke and not enough about Ty.

Not good.

I glanced at the caller I.D. screen and saw Evelyn's name. I let it go to voicemail. Yeah, okay, I know that sounds bad, but I couldn't deal with her just then. Besides, if she really had an emergency, she'd call back.

Traffic moved along at a steady pace as I approached the transition to the northbound 405 freeway that would take me home. But instead, I stayed on the 10 and headed for the ocean.

Luke popped into my mind. I pushed him out. He came back again.

I was supposed to be thinking about Ty, my official boyfriend, not some guy I'd just met yesterday. Yeah, okay, so he was a really hot-looking guy who seemed interested in me. Ty was a really hot guy who was definitely interested in me.

Luke wanted me to stay out of the Fashion District because he thought I wasn't safe there alone.

Ty still hadn't asked me about finding Tiffany's body in the trunk of Ada's Mercedes.

Luke had walked me back to my car.

Ty was still in London.

Luke promised to get me a Sinful handbag.

Ty didn't know I wanted one.

I exited the freeway and took the surface streets to Pacific Coast Highway and headed north through Malibu. Luke and Ty kept flashing in my brain, first one, then the other.

I glanced out the window at the sun sparkling on the blue waters of the Pacific, waiting for it to soothe my thoughts. It didn't, because I noticed a black SUV in my rearview mirror that was hanging on my back bumper.

I hated tailgaters—I tailgated myself, occasionally, but this was different. I couldn't even see the guy's headlights in my rearview mirror, he was that close. The windshield had been tinted so I couldn't see inside clearly.

Jack Bishop popped into my head. He drove a black Land Rover and he'd followed Evelyn and me the other day—I still didn't know how he managed that. Maybe this was his new way of getting my attention.

Well, I'd just show him.

I hooked my Bluetooth on my ear and punched in Jack's number. He answered right away.

"Funny. Very funny," I said. "Now get off my ass."

"Can't think of another place I'd rather be," Jack said. "But what are you talking about?"

I got a weird feeling.

"Where are you?" I asked.

"Riverside," he said.

Riverside was inland about sixty miles.

I got a weird feeling.

"What's up?" Jack asked.

"Some guy is—"

The SUV bumped me from behind. My car lurched forward. I yanked the Bluetooth off my ear and grabbed the steering wheel with both hands.

He hit me again. My car veered right but I held it on the road.

The SUV cut around me on the left and hung beside me, door handle to door handle. I glanced over. The guy's passenger side window rolled down.

Kirk Keegan was behind the wheel.

"Hi, Haley," he called.

"Get away from me, you crazy—"

Kirk speeded up and cut in front of me, then hit the brakes. I slammed on my brakes. He hit the gas again and cut left, then fell back beside me again. Other cars on the road scattered. Kirk tucked in behind me. I stomped the accelerator to get away but he did the same. He swerved to my right side, then banged his big SUV against my Honda.

My car darted left into oncoming traffic. Kirk followed. He held his SUV against the side of my car, pushing me farther left toward the shoulder, trying to run me off the road. And here, along this stretch of the PCH, that meant taking a header over the cliff and into the ocean.

An RV lumbered toward me. I was in the wrong lane, facing the wrong way. Kirk nudged me left again.

I hit the brakes, then cut right. My front fender tagged Kirk's back bumper. He spun. The back end of the SUV went around. Tires squealed and smoked. The SUV flipped over the guardrail and disappeared over the side of the road, out of sight. I screamed, hit the brakes, and slid to a stop on the shoulder. I ran across the highway.

At the bottom of the cliff, the waves of the Pacific crashed over the jagged brown rocks. I spotted Kirk's SUV upside down in the water, the current dragging it out to sea.

"Isn't this just the best thing *ever?*" Christy declared as I walked into the breakroom.

I had no clue what she was talking about.

Nor did I care.

"Look! See? We're doing *sooo* great!"

Christy channeled Vanna White and rushed to the customer satisfaction chart on the wall. She pointed to the big thermometer as if I'd just asked to buy a vowel.

"Isn't it fantastic! We're out of beach towel range! We've shot completely through the toaster category! We're hovering at the very top of the digital camera prize range!" Christy bounced on her toes and clapped her hands. "We're almost to flat screens!"

"Great," I muttered.

Under other circumstances, I might have worked up some enthusiasm for the store's sudden burst of excellent customer service, but tonight I couldn't. Not after what I'd been through.

I punched in, stowed my purse in my locker at the rear of the breakroom, then saw my name written on the white board.

I was late again. You'd think having a detective from the Los Angeles Police Department call in for you and explain that you'd be late for work because you'd been in a car accident would be an acceptable excuse for being late.

Apparently, it wasn't good enough for Holt's.

I erased my name and went to the stock room.

Of course, surviving a car accident would have also been a good excuse to stay home. But I didn't want to be alone. I wasn't ready to talk to anyone about it either—not even Marcie—and I sure as heck didn't intend to call my parents. That left coming to work.

The Mount Everest of blue jeans awaited me, just as I'd left them at the end of my shift yesterday. It was okay, though. I wanted to stay busy.

At least I had a choice, unlike those women in the sweatshops.

I started tagging jeans, determined to ignore what I'd been through on PCH this afternoon, determined I wouldn't let my boiling emotions get the best of me.

I wasn't about to give Kirk Keegan the satisfaction—even posthumously.

All kinds of emergency vehicles had shown up. Police, fire department, ambulance, tow trucks, search and rescue, divers. A helicopter. News vans. Dozens of drivers who'd witnessed the whole thing. Campers from down the beach. The old couple in the RV told the story to anyone who would listen—and lots of people did.

I'd called Detective Shuman and told him what had happened. He offered to come to the scene. I let him.

Jack Bishop called a dozen times before I got back to my car and my cell phone. He told me not to mention that I knew the driver. I took his advice.

The investigating officers' preliminary work determined it was a case of road rage gone bad. I let them believe it.

When they gave me the go-ahead to leave the scene, a couple dozen men were still trying to figure out how to drag Kirk's SUV out of the water and up the cliff to the road. I didn't want to be there when that happened.

I walked away from the whole thing unscathed—except for my damaged car and my rattled nerves.

"Haley?" someone called.

I looked up from the pair of men's blue jeans I was tagging at the work table and saw Grace standing in the stock room doorway.

"There's this really hot-looking guy out here who wants to talk to you," she said.

It's not like I know so many hot-looking guys that I'd wonder who was here to see me. Jack, for sure.

Grace disappeared out the door and Jack walked in, only—oh my God, it wasn't Jack.

Luke strode into the stock room looking concerned and worried, and hotter than Jack had ever looked. He pulled me into his arms and held me close.

"Are you okay?" Luke asked.

I leaned back a little and gazed into those gorgeous green eyes. My emotions raced, along with my heartbeat.

"Yeah, I—I think so," I said, but the words came out in a raspy whisper. I wasn't okay at all. I gulped down my emotions. "How did you know?"

"It's all over the news," Luke said. "I recognized your car and license plate number from this morning at the Fashion District. I was scared to death for you."

"How did you know to find me here?" I asked.

"You told me where you worked."

"I did?"

Luke touched his finger to my chin. "Are you sure you're okay?"

"Yeah, I'm—I'm . . ."

I burst out crying. Luke pulled me against his chest and held me.

CHAPTER 23

My banged up but thankfully drivable Honda got me to the Fashion District a little later than usual the next day. I wish I could say it was because of a wild night of lovemaking with a totally hot guy, but all Luke did was take me home, walk me to my door, and leave.

It was bad to think about sleeping with Luke when I already had an official boyfriend—I knew that—but I was really upset last night and Luke showed up in the right place at the right time.

That was more than I could say for Ty.

To be fair, Ty might have at least said the right thing if he knew Kirk Keegan had tried to kill me yesterday. I still hadn't called him. Since I didn't know what he intended to talk to me about when he got home, I wasn't about to tell him anything.

I walked along Los Angeles Street, peering in shops, stores, and alleys, and at pedestrians on the sidewalk, hoping I'd spot Ed Buckley somewhere. I glanced up at the tall buildings, the open windows. I couldn't shake the idea that I was being watched, followed, especially since that's exactly what Kirk Keegan must have been doing.

Not that I wanted him dead, of course, but knowing that Kirk couldn't hurt me, or threaten me or anyone I knew ever again was a relief. He was out of my life for good, finally.

I figured Detective Shuman would call to let me know that Kirk's SUV and his body had been recovered, but I hadn't heard from him yet. Maybe he thought I'd rather not know all of the gory details. Maybe he was right.

I stopped on the corner of Los Angeles and Pico, and realized I'd been so caught up in my thoughts, I hadn't been looking for Ed.

Jeez, I've got to get better at this.

I turned around and headed up Los Angeles Street once again. I forced my thoughts onto the mental image of Ed Buckley and studied every face that passed me by.

That lasted for about half a block.

Luke's face jumped into my thoughts.

It was kind of weird that he'd spotted my car on the news broadcast, recognized the make, model, and license plate number. But I was glad he had. I needed somebody last night.

A man with a goatee walked past me. My heart jumped. Ed had a goatee.

Oh my God, he'd walked right past me and I'd barely noticed him.

I swung around and followed him until he disappeared into a shop. He turned my way as he stepped through the doorway and I realized it wasn't Ed.

I kept walking.

"Okay, people, gather around," Shannon called, as I tucked my time card in its slot. "As you can all see, we're kicking butt in this contest."

A cheer went up from the dozen or so employees gathered around me in the breakroom, ready to start our shift.

"We've reached flat screen range!" Christy yelled. "I knew we could do it!"

Another big cheer went up.

"Okay, people," Shannon said. "We've only got a couple of days left on this contest. That means we have to keep up the good customer service. I don't want any screw-ups this late in the—"

Shannon stopped and turned to me. "What are you doing in here?"

Everybody else turned, too.

"You're supposed to be in the stock room tagging blue jeans," Shannon barked.

All the other employees glanced at each other, then glared at me again.

Jeez, what did I do?

"Fine," I said. I channeled my mom, put my nose in the air, and left the breakroom.

I wasn't *fine,* of course, and by the time I got to the work table covered with a zillion pairs of blue jeans in the deserted stock room, I was starting to boil.

My morning had been crappy—beyond crappy, really. I hadn't found Ed Buckley in the Fashion District. I'd walked and walked and walked but hadn't seen him.

I hadn't seen Luke, either. For the past two days I'd run into him down there nearly every time I turned a corner, then the one time I really wanted to see him, where was he?

He hadn't called, either. He'd come all the way to the store last night to see if I was okay, he'd listened to me cry, he'd made me feel better—but he couldn't call the next day? Jeez, it wasn't like we'd slept together or anything.

And where was my supposed official boyfriend in all of this? He'd called me the other day with some cryptic line about wanting to talk. So why didn't he call me so we could talk?

My cell phone in my back pocket vibrated. I whipped it out, mentally daring it to be either Ty or Luke calling, ready to blast them with what I thought of them.

It was Evelyn.

Crap. I'd forgotten to call her back.

"Haley, I've had a change of heart," Evelyn said when I answered. "I've decided not to go to that party after all."

Okay, that really ticked me off. I'd gone to a lot of time and effort to put together the right look for her—dress, shoes, bag, jewelry—and everything was fabulous. And now she wasn't going?

"Why not?" I asked.

"I'm just not up to it," she said softly.

Had it been anybody else, I would have blasted them.

"Just put everything back in the bags with the receipts," I said. "I'll return it to the stores for you."

"Thank you," Evelyn said.

"No problem," I said, and we hung up.

But it was a problem. A major problem. Another one to throw on the heap of other problems I was dealing with.

Shannon burst through the stock room door.

"You're not supposed to be on your cell phone," she shouted. "You're supposed to be tagging jeans. The sale is almost here, and you'd better get them finished. And don't come out of this stock room until you're done."

She stomped away.

Fuming, I stared down at my phone. Maybe I would call Marcie right now. Maybe I'd call Ty, too, and Luke, and every other person I knew on the planet.

I was in no mood.

The Sinful bag popped into my head. Usually thoughts of handbags soothed me, but the record label's party was only days away and I still didn't have a Sinful. Luke had promised he'd get one for me. But would he? Could he? Since he hadn't called me all day, I didn't know.

The stock room door swung open again. I looked up, expecting to see Shannon, ready to blast her, and saw that it was Sandy.

"There's this really hot guy outside who wants to talk to

you," she said, giving me the universal you're-so-lucky smile, and disappeared again.

Oh my God. *Oh my God*. Luke. Luke was here. He hadn't been in the Fashion District this morning, and he hadn't called because he intended to come see me in person.

My heart raced. How was my hair? Did I have time to put on lipstick? Where was a Tic Tac when I needed one?

The stock room door swung open. Doug walked in.

Doug? *Doug?* What was Doug doing here?

He walked over to the work table and stopped in front of me, looking calm and composed, as always.

"Haley," he said, as he drew himself up a little and straightened his shoulders. "I forgive you."

I just stared at him.

"Emily broke up with me," Doug said. "I now know the pain I inflicted upon you when I broke off our relationship. I understand your desire to cling to me, to go to extreme measures to have me in your life again. I'm going through that myself right now, so I understand how you feel."

I opened my mouth, but no words came out.

"I'm taking a page from my own playbook. I'm letting Emily go," Doug said. "I hope you, too, can find the strength to finally let me go."

Doug left the stock room.

Oh my God. I couldn't believe it. I couldn't believe what Doug had just said—or that I'd stood there too stunned to say anything.

Okay, that was it. I wasn't taking any more crap from anybody today—and I was starting with Doug. I threw jeans and tags across the stock room and marched out the doors onto the sales floor.

I looked up and down the aisles. Where was he? He couldn't have gotten far. I was going to tell him, once and for all, that he meant nothing to me, that I was glad we broke up—I had wanted to break up with him first—and that he was a complete idiot.

I stomped down the aisles to the front of the store. All eight of the checkout registers were open, customers were stacked ten deep in line, loaded down with merchandise. People were talking loud. Kids were running around. Babies were crying. I spotted Doug outside, crossing the parking lot. I started after him.

"What kind of service is this!" somebody yelled.

I froze. A man standing at the checkout was waving a package of men's black socks and screaming at the clerk.

Oh my God, it was Christy.

"I stood in this line for twenty minutes! Twenty minutes! Just to return these socks!" he screamed. "And now you tell me you won't take them back!"

"I'm sorry, sir, but as I explained, all returns are handled at the customer service booth at the rear of the store," Christy said sweetly. "That's our policy."

"I don't give a damn about your policy!" the man shouted. He slammed his fist down on the counter. "I want you to give me a refund! Now!"

Christy's eyes got big and she shrank back from him. "I'm—I'm sorry, sir, but it's just not possible."

"Don't tell me it's not possible, you idiot! You've got money in that cash register! Open it and give me my refund!"

Christy gulped. Tears pooled in her eyes. "I would if I could, but—"

"I'm sick of your excuses!" the man screamed. "I want—"

"*Hey!*" I shouted and ran over. "You don't get to talk to her that way! You don't get to treat anybody in our store that way! You don't come in here shouting, disturbing our other customers, and expecting us to make an exception for you that we don't make for anybody else! We don't do business that way! And if that doesn't suit you, you can go shop somewhere else!"

"I'll do that!" the man said, and stomped away.

I watched him go out the front door, my heart pounding, my palms sweating.

Damn, that felt good.

Then I realized the store had fallen silent. Nobody talked. No babies cried. No kids ran through the aisles.

I turned and saw everybody staring at me. Every customer, every checkout clerk, every sales person on the floor. Shannon glared at me. So did Jeanette.

Oh, crap.

I'd searched every store in Los Angeles and the surrounding areas numerous times for a Sinful handbag and had repeatedly come up empty. I figured I'd have to face the fact that I simply would not find one in time for tonight's big party.

I hate it when I have to face facts.

Especially facts I don't like.

I walked along Pico Boulevard in the Fashion District amid the crowds of early morning shoppers, peering into shops, stores, and alleyways, as usual, not spotting Ed Buckley, as usual. I hoped not finding Ed wasn't a fact I'd have to face also, but it wasn't looking so good.

Of course, that wasn't the end of things not looking so good in my life right now. After the way I'd blasted that customer at Holt's yesterday—even though he deserved it—I probably wouldn't have my job much longer. After Ty came home next week and we had our "talk," I probably wouldn't have an official boyfriend, either.

I still hadn't heard from Luke. And just why he'd come to Holt's that night to comfort me, only to ignore me afterwards I couldn't figure out.

The morning seemed warmer than usual—or maybe I was more out of sorts than usual. I stopped on the corner of Pico and Wall Street and looked around.

I couldn't keep living like this. I had to focus on something positive. Something I could control.

Maybe I'd never find Ed down here. Maybe I'd never see Luke again. Maybe Ty would break up with me.

But there was no reason for me to ever want for a special handbag again.

Over the past few weeks, a number of people had suggested I start my own handbag line. The thought had stuck to the lining of my brain like cellulite on thighs. I decided to check it out.

I hoofed it up the street, crossed Olympic and plunged into the Textile District. I'd driven through here in my search for Ed, but seeing it up close was way better.

I ducked in and out of stores along the street, marveling at the fabrics. These were different from the limited amount of material Holt's stocked. The bolts of fabric were presented differently, too. In Holt's, a few yards of material was wrapped around a long, rectangle piece of cardboard. Here, the fabric was wound around long round rolls.

Every color, every texture imaginable was here. Every kind of trim, beading, and thread a designer could want. Marlene, who ran the sewing department at Holt's, would probably lose what was left of her mind if she saw all of this.

The Textile District was just as busy as the Fashion District. Crowded sidewalks, trucks double-parked, hand-carts loaded with merchandise pushed from store to store.

My imagination went crazy. Seeing all the fabric possibilities, gorgeous handbags started to bloom in my head. Maybe I could really do this. Maybe I could really design my own line of purses.

The scene flashed in my head. Me at the helm of a handbag empire—in a fabulous office, wearing a fabulous outfit—surrounded by dozens of assistants, all waiting for me to come up with the design for the next handbag to take the fashion world by storm. Me at Fashion Week, being hailed as the latest fashion genius. My picture on the cover of *Elle, In Style, Vogue* magazines. Everyone—absolutely everyone—clamoring for the next Haley bag.

I turned onto Ninth Street and checked out the fabrics displayed on the sidewalk as I headed west. The Textile District was big and I didn't want to miss anything.

That's how we fashion icons do things.

Ahead of me on the sidewalk, a guy pushed a handcart loaded with three rolls of fabric wrapped in black plastic and tied on the ends. I knew it was fabric because I'd seen store clerks ripping them open in shops all over the Textile District. I decided to follow him, check out the new fabric when it was unloaded in the shop. Maybe I'd be the first to see it, the first to buy it, the first to turn it into a gorgeous handbag.

At the corner of Ninth Street, the guy kept going. He crossed Santee Street.

Okay, that was weird. All the fabric shops are in the opposite direction.

He kept going. I kept following. At the corner of Ninth and Los Angeles Street, he glanced around.

I saw the side of his face.

Oh my God. It was Ed Buckley.

CHAPTER 24

Ed kept walking, pushing the cart loaded with the three fabric bolts in front of him. I followed at what I considered a discreet distance of about a half block. He turned north on Spring Street, then left on Seventh.

He seemed pretty calm for a guy wanted by the FBI, a guy suspected in two murders and the disappearances of two people. No shades, no hat pulled low, no attempt at any sort of a disguise.

I couldn't imagine where he'd be headed with three bolts of fabric. The shops of the Textile District were way behind us now. When we crossed Broadway, I realized we were in the Jewelry District.

Okay, this was weird.

Even though we were only a few blocks from the fashion and textile districts, this area was definitely more upscale. Lots of well-dressed people on the street. BMW, Mercedes, Lexus autos parked at the curbs. The streets were lined almost exclusively with jewelry stores that occupied the ground level of mostly old high-rise buildings.

At the corner of Hill and Seventh sat what looked like a grand movie palace from about a hundred years ago, with lots of stone work, a marquee over the entrance, and a dome on top of the building. According to the lettering on the marquee, the place housed a jewelry store.

Ed pushed his cart past the front of the building and disappeared through a side door.

I stopped at the corner. Why would Ed take bolts of fabric into a jewelry store? Maybe the jeweler wanted it for a display case. Or maybe some crazy old rich lady insisted on buying fabric to match the tiara she wanted for her poodle.

I glanced at the buildings along the street. Most of them were fifteen to twenty floors high. Unlike the buildings in the Fashion District, the windows here were shut tight. Still, I felt exposed standing on the street corner, like anybody anywhere could be watching me.

I crossed the street and went inside a jewelry store on the corner. The huge open space held dozens of small booths where individual merchants sold their bling. Trays of loose, unset precious gems gleamed in the bright light. Diamonds sparkled. Gold and silver glittered.

Should I call Shuman? I wrestled with the question as I stood by the window, my gaze glued to the theater building Ed had gone into. Something nagged at my memory but I couldn't put a mental finger on it.

Maybe it was Ed himself, I realized. Honestly, he didn't look like a criminal. He looked like a businessman, much as Virginia had described him from his days back in Charleston.

Would a criminal walk boldly through downtown Los Angeles, out in the open for everyone to see?

I thought back to the morning Tiffany had been murdered in the Holt's parking lot. Yeah, I'd seen Ed there. No doubt about it. But I hadn't seen him confront Tiffany. I hadn't seen him shoot her, dump her body into the trunk of Ada's Mercedes.

What if he was there for some other reason? What if he'd come to warn Tiffany that someone was after her? What if he'd witnessed her murder?

Maybe the FBI was wrong about Ed killing their undercover agent. I had no idea how much real—if any—evidence they had against him. The newspaper reporter in Charleston that Ben had talked to didn't seem to think there was anything to the story.

Yeah, okay, it looked as if Ed had faked his own death. But what if he'd just done it—with his wife's knowledge—to collect the insurance money? Or what if he'd had enough of Charleston and Tiffany's family, and had simply run out on his wife and kids?

Something weird was going on here. Why would Ed leave his prominent, high-profile life in Charleston to come to the L.A. Textile District to sell fabric? If he'd been selling drugs, like everybody suspected, he sure wouldn't rake in that kind of cash peddling buttons, trim, and material to fashion designers. His lifestyle would take a major hit.

Jeez, Ed must have really hated his life back in Charleston.

Ed came out of the building across the street pushing the cart with the three bolts of fabric still on it. I could see that the black plastic had been ripped open on one of them.

I waited until he'd gotten a little ahead of me, then followed. Ed moved at a steady pace. No looking behind him, no darting from doorway to doorway. Definitely not a man in a hurry or a man who had something to hide.

We took the same route back to the Textile District. Ed wheeled the cart into a shop. I noted the name and address as I walked past.

The guy looked legit to me, so maybe he was. I'd been wrongly accused of murder myself. Not a great feeling. I sure didn't want to do that to Ed—or anybody.

It was kind of weird that he'd taken three bolts of fabric all the way to the Jewelry District for no apparent reason, and only one of them had been opened. But maybe whoever his customer was in that jewelry shop had taken a look at the first roll he'd opened, loved it, and didn't want to look at the others.

Ed probably appreciated the quick decision the jewelry customer had made since, according to Ben, rumor in

Charleston had it that his wife had a thing for diamonds. If Ed had really just run out on his family back there, he probably wanted nothing to do with anything related to them, especially jewelry, which must have cost as much as some of the drugs he was suspected of smuggling.

Hang on a minute.

I spun around and looked back down the block to the shop Ed had disappeared into.

Luke had told me the other day that almost all the merchandise in the districts came in through the Port of Los Angeles in container ships, just a short drive away in Long Beach, and how almost none of it was inspected.

What if the jewelry rumors in Charleston weren't just rumors? What if Ed's wife always dripped in bling because he was smuggling diamonds?

Oh my God. Could it be true?

I pictured the scheme in my head: diamonds arriving in the cargo ships hidden inside bolts of fabric; the bolts transported along with tons of other fabric to Ed's shop; Ed simply wheeling them to the Jewelry District.

Ed stepped out of the shop and stood on the sidewalk. He turned and stared straight at me.

I gasped and took off.

I rounded the corner and ran down Maple, then ducked into Santee Alley. I glanced back.

Oh my God. Was that Ed on the sidewalk behind me? Was he following me? I couldn't tell for sure.

The Alley was packed with shoppers. I wiggled through the crowd, pounded up the stairs, and got my car from the rooftop parking lot. I peeled out onto Maple, cut around a double-parked truck, and headed for the freeway.

I grabbed my cell phone out of my purse and punched in Shuman's number. His voicemail picked up.

Damn. There really is never a cop around when you need one.

As I merged onto the westbound 10, I left Shuman a

message explaining that I'd found Ed Buckley. I gave him the address of the fabric shop on Ninth Street and the jewelry store at Hill and Seventh.

"I think he's smuggling diamonds inside bolts of fabric," I said. "I'm running errands and going to the Queen Mary tonight, so call me as soon as you get this message."

I stared out the windshield at the traffic and wondered if I should do something more.

Since I hadn't connected with Shuman, maybe I should call the FBI agents who'd questioned me at the Federal Building. With one eye on the bumper of the SUV in front of me, I dug through my purse for the business card Special Agent Jordan—or maybe it was Paulson—had given me, but didn't find it. I could have made some calls and tracked them down but, really, I didn't like those guys.

Another minute passed as I drove farther away from downtown. I felt kind of weird about just leaving, knowing a murderer was in a fabric shop on Ninth Street. But I guess Ed wasn't going anywhere. He'd been there for months, apparently, since Virginia spotted him last fall, and even after murdering Tiffany, he'd stayed there. And, really, if he suddenly made a break for the Mexican border, what could I do?

Anyway, I didn't want to be there when the cops showed up. I didn't want Ed to know I was involved with his apprehension. The last thing I needed was another guy out there somewhere with a grudge against me. I'd just gotten clear of Kirk Keegan.

I glanced at my wristwatch. Why hadn't Shuman called me back yet? I felt a little miffed. I mean, jeez, I'd found the guy that the FBI on two coasts was looking for and cracked an international smuggling ring. A simple "thank you" would be nice.

I shook it off. I'd called Shuman with the info I had on Ed's location. I'd done all I could do.

No, wait. I needed to handle one more thing.

I picked up my phone again and punched in Ben Oliver's number. I'd promised him an exclusive on Tiffany's murder. He didn't pick up, so I left him a message much the same as I'd left for Shuman, except for the part about running errands, going to the Queen Mary tonight, and asking him to call me back.

So now I officially had done everything I could do. I had a smoking-hot, kick-ass party to get ready for tonight. I was meeting Marcie at our favorite spa, then we were going to her place to get ready together.

I turned off my phone and tossed it into my purse.

The one cool thing about going to Holt's today was that I wouldn't have to stay and work a shift. I could pick up my paycheck, such as it was, chat with friends, if I wanted, talk on my cell phone on the sales floor, and nobody could say anything about it.

I'd scheduled tonight off when Jay Jax had first texted me the details about the party and nothing—absolutely nothing—would keep me from going. Certainly not the huge mound of blue jeans in the stock room that still needed to be tagged.

I swung into a parking space and hurried into the store. I intended to be in and out in a flash. Marcie and I had appointments in a few minutes for a mani and pedi, and I was getting an updo.

As much as I'd enjoy chatting up friends and talking on my cell on the sales floor—provided Shannon was looking, of course—I decided to keep my head down so nobody would notice me. I needed to get in and out quick. I would be invisible.

"There she is," somebody muttered as I walked through the big glass doors.

All the clerks at the checkout registers glared at me.

Okay, that was weird.

I hurried through the store. Every sales person on the

floor turned and gave me stink-eye as I headed for the rear of the store.

Jeez, what did I do?

"Hey, Grace," I called, as I stopped at the customer service booth.

Sophia from the shoe department was there. She saw me, jerked her chin at me, and walked away.

"What's with everybody?" I asked Grace.

She pulled the accordion file from under the counter where our paychecks were stored and took mine out.

"Things are a little *tense* around here," Grace said.

"Yeah, I got that," I said, as I signed for my check and tucked it into my purse.

Grace glanced around, then leaned closer. "The contest."

I got a yucky feeling in my stomach.

"What about it?" I asked.

"That customer you bitched out at the register yesterday?" she said.

"The jerk who almost made Christy cry?" I asked. "He deserved worse than what I gave him."

"Yeah, well, he was a secret shopper," she said.

The yucky feeling in my stomach got yuckier.

"Thanks a lot, Haley," Shannon barked as she walked up. "Because of you, our customer satisfaction rating is practically nonexistent. We're getting *nothing* in the contest. We're the only store in the Holt's chain to win absolutely *nothing*. All because of *you*."

Not a great feeling.

The Queen Mary had been a permanent fixture in the Long Beach harbor for thirty years or something, since it had been retired after seventy years or something, of hauling the rich and famous across the Atlantic. The ship had done duty during World War II transporting troops to and from Europe. Now it was a hotel and conference center, and a major tourist attraction.

I'd toured the Queen Mary with my fifth grade class, back in the day, and Mom and her ex-beauty pageant cult had hosted a charity event here once; the irony of the whole slightly-past-its-prime, showing-its-years, aging-queen thing seemed lost on all of them.

But I'd never seen the Queen Mary as it looked tonight. Limos rolled up to the red carpet that had been laid out. Paparazzi and fans crowded behind the velvet ropes manned by security guys in expensive suits with earpieces. Cameras flashed. Fans screamed. The never-ending parade of celebrities, musicians, Hollywood insiders, and the rich and powerful exited their limos, smiled and waved, and moved on.

Marcie and I—and lots of other people—entered with far less fanfare and took the elevator up to R Deck.

"Isn't this the coolest thing ever?" Marcie asked.

"*We're* the coolest thing ever," I told her, and we both giggled.

She'd gone sort of retro-eighties tonight wearing a short, white, pink, blue, and green print mini dress, three-inch teal faux snakeskin heels, and pink gloves. With her blond hair down straight around her shoulders, she looked terrific.

I'd picked a brown leather dress embellished with narrow belts across the bodice and around the waist, with a yellow ruffled underskirt that I'd bought at a shop in Piccadilly Circus in London, and fringed, peek-toe ankle boots.

"That Sinful bag would have looked perfect with your outfit," Marcie said.

I'd gone with a Dior clutch, since I'd never found a Sinful, and it looked good. Not as great as the Sinful would have looked, of course, but since I'd searched every store and shop I knew to search in Southern California and come up empty, I figured I could make do with the Dior. I didn't intend to give up on finding a Sinful. One was out there somewhere, and I would find it somehow.

We followed the crowd along the carpeted gangway and

into the ship. The Queen Mary retained its Art Deco décor. Walls were covered in wood paneling. On the left were shiny chrome elevators and the entrance to the ship's swimming pool.

We turned left into the Grand Salon. The huge space was softly lit from the golden rectangular fixtures in the ceiling. Wood panels and artwork covered everything.

At one end of the room, a giant mural depicted the Queen Mary's journey from New York to England. At the other end was a scene of English horsemen riding to the hounds, horse-drawn carriages, pheasants and egrets.

The place was already packed with men and women dressed in hip, funky clothes. A band played at the front of the room. Food stations were set up featuring raw bars, sushi, pastas, meat skewers, desserts. There were four bars. Waiters in white jackets passed trays of fluted champagne glasses through the crowd.

"Haley!"

Jay Jax rushed toward me. We hugged, I introduced her to Marcie, they hugged, we squealed over each other's outfits—where we'd gotten them, how great they looked—all in about twenty seconds.

"This party is fabulous!" I said over the music and the crowd noise.

"The label has the entire ship for the night," Jay Jax said. "Tourists were here all day. Security was still escorting them off the ship an hour before the party started. They caught a couple of girls hiding in a closet."

"Who can blame them for wanting to stay?" Marcie said.

"All the label's artists will be here tonight. Most of them will perform. We'll have music all night," Jay Jax said.

She leaned in and touched my arm, the universal signal that she was about to reveal something terrific. "Mick's supposed to be here, too."

Oh my God. *Oh my God.*

"Mick?" I repeated. "Do you mean *the* Mick?"

"And Eric," Jay Jax said.

I gasped. Marcie's mouth fell open.

Jay Jax leaned in even closer, indicating this was going to be even better news.

"There's a possibility that Cher and Tina might come," Jay Jax said.

Marcie looked like she might faint. I felt light headed.

"No wonder people were hiding on the ship," Marcie said.

"It's super cool of you to invite me," I told Jay Jax.

She waved off my thanks. "I'd have never gotten this job without you, Haley. Got to run. Have fun!"

Jay Jax disappeared into the crowd.

"Maybe she can get you a job at the record company," Marcie said.

"Wouldn't that be cool?" I said. "Maybe I wouldn't have to finish college."

Now *that* would be cool.

A warm hand touched my elbow. I turned and saw Luke Warner.

My heart did a little flip-flop at the sight of him. He looked way hot in a gray silk shirt and charcoal jacket.

I wished my heart hadn't done that, though—and not because he hadn't come through with the Sinful handbag he'd promised. I hadn't seen or heard from him in a couple of days. I already had an official boyfriend who did that.

"You look fantastic," Luke said.

His words—and the look he gave me—sent my heart to flip-flopping again.

I introduced Marcie. She must have remembered him from our conversation in the Holt's breakroom because she gave me a warning look—as a best friend would—then excused herself to go find a drink.

"What are you doing here?" I asked.

Luke gave me his killer grin again, and said, "I come out to these things from time to time."

I hadn't realized his ownership of some downtown buildings put him in the record label orbit. Guess I'd figured wrong.

Luke eased closer. "Let's get out of here. I know a great place we can go."

Leave? With Mick and Eric arriving? Maybe even Cher and Tina?

"No, thanks," I said.

"Come on, it will be a lot more fun than this madhouse," Luke said.

He took my elbow and eased me toward him. I jerked away.

His brows pulled together. "Haley, you really need to come with me. Now."

I didn't know what was up with Luke all of a sudden, but I wanted no part of it.

The last thing I did want, though, was to make a scene. The place was packed with the rich, the beautiful, and the famous. Security would be all over us in a heartbeat. I didn't want to get thrown out, and I didn't want to get Jay Jax in trouble for inviting me. But no way was I going anywhere with Luke.

"Maybe later," I said.

Thanks to my years of clubbing, I had my exit move down pat. I feigned right, then dodged left and darted through the crowd with speed and agility unexpected in four-inch heels. I put some distance between us and started looking for Marcie. I'm a definite believer in the old safety-in-numbers saying. I headed for the bar and ran straight into Ed Buckley.

Chapter 25

My knees shook and my stomach twisted into a knot. Ed Buckley, who'd murdered an undercover FBI agent, faked his death, murdered Tiffany and possibly Virginia and Rita, and run a bicoastal smuggling operation, stood about a foot in front of me.

He hadn't looked like a murderer when I'd seen him in the Textile District this afternoon, and he didn't look like one now. He wore an expensive shirt and jacket—Armani, probably—and appeared relaxed and comfortable among the celebrities and Hollywood insiders.

"I never got your name," Ed said.

Oh my God. Did he really not know who I was? Was he just hitting on me?

"We've never met," I said and turned away.

Ed stepped in front of me.

"I never forget a face," he said. "The parking lot of a department store a couple of weeks ago. Today. Ninth Street. The corner at Hill Street."

Oh my God. Ed remembered me from the morning Tiffany was murdered. He'd seen me following him this afternoon. No wonder I'd had that creepy feeling that I was being watched.

"Still don't remember?" he asked. "Maybe this will jog your memory."

Ed reached into his pants pocket and pulled out a hand-gun. It was small, but I guess size doesn't matter with guns. We stood only a few inches apart. If he shot me at this range, it would do serious damage.

He slid the gun back into his pocket but kept his hand in there, too.

"Let's take a walk," Ed said.

He grabbed my elbow and guided me through the crowd.

I could have started screaming and fighting, but I didn't want to provoke him. I had no way of knowing if the weapon he'd showed me was the only one he had on him. If he started shooting, a lot of innocent people could be hurt.

"How did you know I was here?" I asked.

"I followed you," he said.

Jeez, had everybody on the planet followed me some-where?

And how come nobody was following me now?

Where was Shuman? I'd told him I'd be here tonight. And what about Jack Bishop? He could find me driving down the freeway but didn't think to look for me at a gathering of hundreds of the coolest people on the planet? Never mind that I had an official boyfriend. Where was he in all of this? Luke Warner had showed up trying to get me to leave with him. I don't know what a building owner could possibly do in a situation like this, but jeez, where was he now when I needed him?

Ed and I crossed the room amid the crush of laughing, drinking, talking partygoers, none of whom, apparently, had any idea what was going on. I searched for Marcie's face in the crowd. I didn't want her to get hurt, of course, but she'd know something was wrong if she saw me with this guy. I didn't spot her.

Off to our right, the lights of Long Beach across the harbor shone through the line of portholes as we left the Grand Salon. The party had spilled out into the entryway. Nobody paid any attention to us as Ed pushed the call button for the elevator, the doors opened, and we stepped inside.

"How did you get past security?" I asked, as the elevator rose.

"I'm pretty well thought of in some circles," Ed said with a modest smile. "And it never hurts to be connected to the jewelers to the stars."

Ed must have followed Marcie and me to the Queen Mary, seen what was going on, made a phone call or two, and arranged admittance. Ed did look like he belonged here, and I hadn't seen the security people out front doing a pat-down or running guests through metal detectors.

Or maybe he was full of bull. Maybe he'd slipped onto the ship through the kitchen with the hired help.

"So if you followed me from downtown today, why wait until now?" I asked.

"I prefer privacy for this sort of thing."

"Like with that undercover FBI agent?" I asked.

His gaze lurched to me, then moved away. I figured I had my answer.

And I realized, too, that I'd judged Ed all wrong when I'd first seen him pushing that cart of fabric today. I'd thought he was innocent—of murder, at least—but now I knew I was wrong. I'd been wrong about Tiffany the first time I'd met her, too.

Who else had I been wrong about?

The elevator doors opened. Ed grabbed my arm and pulled me out.

We were on the Promenade Deck. Gift shop windows glowed cheery yellow, displaying hats, T-shirts, cups, books, all sorts of Queen Mary souvenirs. The stores were closed. Not another soul was up here.

Now I was seriously rethinking my don't-scream-don't-make-a-scene decision in the Grand Salon.

Ed pulled me through a set of doors. The enclosed deck had wooden floors and big windows. The lights of Long

Beach sparkled across the harbor. It was dark out here. Nobody was around. I couldn't hear the party noise.

Ed hustled me up a narrow wooden staircase. At the top was a small landing and one of those metal ship doors. He forced it open and I stumbled over the raised threshold. He caught me and pulled me onto the Sun Deck. It was open to the sky.

I remembered the Sun Deck from my grade school tour. I'd seen the lifeboat demonstration there. The white boats topped with bright blue covers hung in their riggings overhead.

We were almost to the top deck of the ship now. I had no idea where he was taking me, but I figured when we ran out of ship, I'd be out of time.

"You must have been pretty shocked when Virginia Foster spotted you," I said.

The ship's three giant smokestacks threw shadows over the deck. Ed moved slower in the darkness, pulling me with him.

"And even more shocked when Tiffany showed up looking for you," I said.

Ed didn't say anything.

"She figured out what you'd done. She asked around, talked to people, figured out you'd killed that FBI agent and faked your death," I said. "Tiffany was sharp, huh? Sharper than you."

Ed jerked me up until my face was close to his. He didn't smell so great. He squeezed my arm harder.

"You know the problem with you women?" he asked. "You all talk too much."

I considered mentioning that Ty yammered on about the stock market after lovemaking—just to try and build a connection, of course—but didn't think Ed was in the mood.

He yanked me forward and up another staircase. We stopped on a landing. The stairs continued up to the Sports

Deck. Ed pushed me against the railing. Behind me a lifeboat hung just a couple of feet away.

The lighting was a little better here. I saw that Ed had pulled the gun from his pocket.

"You women, you're not happy with what you have," Ed said, his voice rising. "It's not enough that you have a beautiful home filled with antiques, a vacation home, a boat, closets stuffed with designer clothes and drawers filled with jewelry. You have to ask where it all comes from, how it's paid for. You want to look at the bank accounts."

I figured Ed was talking about his wife back in Charleston.

"And then when you don't get an answer that suits you," Ed went on, "you go and tattle to your daddy."

I guess it didn't help that his wife's daddy was an attorney.

Ed leaned past me and unfastened the blue cover from the lifeboat, then stepped back and pointed the gun at me.

Oh my God. He intended to shoot me, dump me in the lifeboat, and pull the cover back in place. It could be days before anybody found me there. I had to do something.

"Wait!" I put up both hands. "I have to know something. Did you kill Rita? Because, you know, I never really liked her."

"Haley!" a man called.

I whirled and saw a shadow moving below us along the Sun Deck. A figure appeared out of the darkness at the foot of the stairs. It was Luke.

Oh my God. What was he doing here? He was going to get shot.

Ed circled my waist and pulled me against him, and shoved the gun barrel into my side.

"So this is the deal, huh?" Luke demanded. "You won't hang out with me, but you go off with this guy?"

He started up the steps.

Ed pressed the gun harder into my side.

"No, Luke, stop! Don't come up here!" I shouted.

"Not until I find out what this guy has that I don't have,"
Luke shouted back.

"Not until I find out what this guy has that I don't have,"
Luke shouted back.

He trotted up the stairs.

I felt the gun barrel pull away from my side. I knew Ed
was pointing it at Luke. I had to do *something*.

Jeez, why hadn't I taken a self-defense class at that stupid college I was going to?

I drew back my arm and elbowed Ed in the gut. Luke
exploded up the stairs, grabbed Ed's arm. The gun fired
into the air. I screamed.

"FBI! FBI!"

A half-dozen men in navy blue windbreakers rushed up
the stairs from the Sun Deck and down from the Sports
Deck, pointing guns and rifles.

Luke wrestled Ed onto the landing. Two of the other
men piled on. Someone grabbed Ed's gun. Another snapped
handcuffs on him.

Luke straightened up and turned to me. He pulled back
his jacket and I saw a badge hanging on his belt.

"FBI," he said softly. "Undercover."

Special Agent Jordan—or maybe it was Paulson—escorted me to the ship's security office and put me in an interview room. He gave me coffee and a blanket, for some
reason.

"I want to know what's going on," I told him.

"Just let us wrap up a few things, then somebody will be
in to explain everything to you," he said. He actually
sounded nice—not that I cared.

"I want to see my friend Marcie," I said.

"We're locating her. The party is still going on so it will
take a few minutes," he said, and left, closing the door behind him.

After the FBI guys had taken Ed into custody, Special
Agent Jordan—or Paulson—had brought me here. I'd hardly

had time to take in everything that had happened, let alone process it. I'd gone from scared I'd be killed, to scared Luke would be killed, to relieved that neither of us had been killed, in record time.

But my emotions hadn't stopped there. Not after Luke showed me his FBI badge.

The door opened and Detective Shuman walked in.

"What are you doing here?" I blurted out.

"Making sure you're okay," he said.

For a second I thought he might take me in his arms—he had that look—and hold me, but he didn't.

"I'm . . . confused," I told him. "What's going on? Did you get the message I left for you?"

Shuman nodded. "I went to Buckley's fabric shop on Ninth right away. He was gone already."

"He followed me," I said, then shook my head. "I don't know how he got to his car so fast, how he caught up to me."

"Spotters on bicycles. It's a big network and Buckley was wired in. One phone call from him and everybody down there was on the lookout for you," Shuman said. "When I didn't find Buckley at the fabric shop, I called the FBI."

"Cool," I said and even felt a little grin pull at my lips. "That will show them not to cut you out of a case again."

Shuman grinned a little, too, then put on his cop-face again. "I called you but you didn't answer your phone. I went by the store and your apartment, but couldn't find you. I wanted to warn you that Ed might be coming after you. You told me you were coming here tonight, so . . ."

So Shuman and the FBI had joined forces to bring down Ed here at the party. Luckily, I'd survived their plan.

We were quiet for a few minutes. Shuman's gaze got a little darker, a little deeper.

"Are you sure you're okay?" he asked softly.

No, I wasn't okay. I was mad and scared and shaky.

Shuman glanced at the floor, then up at me again.

"Listen, Haley, I know this probably isn't the best time," he said, "but I need to tell you—"

The door opened again. Luke stuck his head inside.

Now I really wasn't okay.

Luke stepped into the room. He and Shuman murmured to each other, and Shuman left. Luke pushed the door closed.

We stood there looking at each other for a minute and with each second that passed, I got madder and madder.

"You used me," I said.

"I was undercover," Luke said.

At least he had the decency to look contrite, but that just made me angrier.

"Is *Luke* even your real name?" I demanded.

He nodded. "Different last name, though."

"So everything about you—except for your first name— is a lie?" I asked.

I'm pretty sure I shouted that.

"I was undercover, Haley," he said again.

"I guess you're going to tell me that everything you did was in the line of duty?" I asked.

I'm sure I yelled that.

I wasn't finished yelling. "How we *coincidently* met? All that talk about shopping, and you owning buildings, and buying me a Sinful purse? It was all a big, fat lie!"

Luke didn't say anything.

"You used me," I said. "I was just bait in a trap you and your FBI buddies set for Ed Buckley."

That got a rise out of him.

"The first day I saw you in the Fashion District I told you to leave, that you were in over your head. I told you that." Luke pointed toward the wall. "When I saw you at the party, I tried to get you to leave with me. I knew what was going down and I didn't want you to get hurt."

Luke made perfect sense, but I was in no mood to hear it. Not after what I'd been through.

"Yeah? What about the night you came to the store after I was nearly run off the PCH. That was just to make sure your bait was okay, right?"

Luke shook his head. "No, Haley, I was worried about you. I saw the news report. I recognized your car."

"But I never told you where I worked. You found that little bit of info in the FBI folder you have on me somewhere," I said. "You lied to me that night, too."

"Look, Haley," he said softly, "I know we met under bad circumstances. But I really care about you. We'd be good together. I know we would. If you could just give me a chance—"

"No way," I told him.

Luke took a step toward me. He wanted to hug me. I could see it in his face. But if I allowed that, if I felt those strong arms around me, that hard chest against me, and looked into those green eyes, I knew I'd be lost to him.

"I'm out of here," I said.

I yanked the door open and marched into the next room. Special agents Jordan, Paulson, and two others I didn't know saw me. Their eyes widened and they backed up.

Jordan—or maybe Paulson—pointed to the door.

"That's the exit," he said gently.

"I know!" I screamed.

I left, slamming the door so hard behind me that it shook on its hinges.

CHAPTER 26

The Holt's Blue Jeans Blowout sale stopped for no one. Certainly not for me, not even after what I'd been through aboard the Queen Mary last night.

I'd found Marcie outside the ship's security office and she'd driven me home while I sniffled and blubbered and told her everything that had happened. She took my side, of course, as a best friend should.

She told me I should stay home today but I didn't want to be alone. Besides, I still had hundreds of pairs of blue jeans to tag. When I got to the store, Jeanette took one look at me and the dark circles under my eyes and decided Sandy and Bella could help.

"Damn, this is one crappy job," Bella complained, as we all stood around the work table in the stock room. Her saucer phase continued. Today her hair looked like a teacup set.

"I think I'll get my boyfriend some new jeans," Sandy said, holding up a whitewashed pair. "He likes it when I buy him things."

"Dump him," I told her.

Maybe I wasn't the best person to give relationship advice, but Sandy deserved better than her tattoo artist boyfriend who treated her like dirt.

Sandy paused in her work and drew in a breath. "Okay,

Haley, you have to tell me the truth. Are things really over between you and Doug?"

I saw the little twinkle in her eyes.

"Oh my God," I said. "Have you got the hots for Doug?"

"No," she said. "Well, maybe, kind of. When he was in here the other night looking for you, we talked a little and I thought he was nice. But I'd never make a move if you were still interested in him, Haley. I swear, I'd never do that."

"We're done," I told her.

"Really?" she asked.

I didn't want to get into the whole breakup, terrorism-espionage, Kirk-Keegan-setup thing with her, so I said, "When I realized my first name wouldn't sound good with his last name, I knew we'd never have a future."

Sandy nodded thoughtfully. "Okay, right. Gotcha."

"Speaking of things that don't make much sense," Bella said, tossing aside another pair of tagged blue jeans, "did you see that Rita was back to work today?"

Oh my God. I'd forgotten all about Rita and Virginia. I hadn't even asked Shuman or the FBI guys about them last night.

"So where's she been?" Sandy asked.

"She's telling some big-ass story about how she was in protective custody by the FBI or something, because she saw some girl get shot in some parking lot somewhere," Bella said. "Her and some woman from Virginia living in a safe house up in the Hollywood Hills, getting free food, good-looking FBI men all over the place. Claims they just let them leave last night."

She had to be talking about Virginia Foster.

"Was the woman *from* Virginia, or was her *name* Virginia?" I asked.

Bella shrugged. "All I know is that Rita kept complaining that the woman talked funny. She kept calling the balcony *the veranda* and ordering sweet tea, whatever that is."

I heaved a mental sigh of relief that Virginia was alive and well.

"You don't believe Rita's story?" Sandy asked, picking up another pair of jeans.

"All I'm saying is that if that happened to me, no way in hell would I come back to this place," Bella said, sorting through the jeans. "I'd write one of those tell-all books, I'd go on all the talk shows, and I'd get me a movie deal. Then I'd pose for *Playboy*."

The stock room door swung open and Jeanette walked in. Today she had on a tartan plaid pantsuit that could easily frighten small children. I only hoped she wouldn't feel compelled to wear blue jeans during the Blue Jeans Blowout sale.

"Haley, I'd like to speak with you about something," she said, and joined us at the work table.

Since the last conversation I'd had with Jeanette that had started out similar to this one had landed me in this crappy jeans-tagging job, I wasn't all that interested in hearing anything she had to say.

"Sorry, Jeanette," I told her. "I'm kind of busy here."

"This won't take long," she said. "I've been on the phone to Corporate ever since the incident at the checkout register with the customer that you . . . spoke with."

I got a yucky feeling in my stomach.

"Corporate, it seems, agrees with your position," Jeanette reported. "No one should be allowed to come into our store and shout at an employee, disturb our customers, or conduct themselves in a disrespectful manner."

I just looked at her.

"Our vice president of marketing is launching a new publicity campaign featuring the Holt's Customer and Employee Bill of Rights," Jeanette said. "And because you inspired it, Haley, every one of our store's employees will receive a contest prize, after all."

Sandy perked up. "We're getting flat screens?"

"Beach towels," Jeanette said, and left the stock room.

"A beach towel would be cool," Sandy said. "Hey, why don't we all go to the beach together?"

"I'm there," Bella declared.

"Hey, I know," Sandy said, smiling, "let's ask everybody to come. We'll play volleyball and have a fire pit. And we'll all bring our Holt's beach towels."

Yeah, the beach trip did sound good, even though Sarah Covington had stolen my idea and come up with yet another lame publicity campaign that would probably require she glue herself to Ty day and night for the next month.

But maybe that wouldn't matter, anyway, after Ty got home and we had our *talk*.

"Ask that Doug guy to come," Bella said to Sandy.

Her eyes got wide. "Do you think I should?"

"Hell, yeah," Bella told her. "And see if he's got a brother."

The stock room doors swung open.

"Haley?" Grace called. "There's this really hot-looking guy outside who wants to talk to you."

Sandy gasped. "Oh my God. Is it Doug?"

I doubted it was Doug, but it could have been Jack. Or maybe even Shuman. He'd had a weird look in his eye and a strange tone in his voice last night in the ship's security office when he'd tried to tell me something. Looking back, I wondered if I'd missed something.

Luke popped into my head but I pushed him away.

Then Ty bloomed in my thoughts and my stomach got warm and gooey. Of all the hot-looking guys I knew, I wished it was Ty waiting for me outside.

I walked out of the stock room and saw Ben Oliver.

Grace was right. Ben looked kind of hot with his shaggy hair and whiskered chin, wearing rumpled khaki pants and a wrinkled polo shirt. He looked as if he'd been up all night.

Oh my God. He's probably been pounding the keyboard

churning out his big story about finding Ed Buckley in the Textile District yesterday after I'd called him with the tip.

My spirits lifted considerably. Nobody else had thanked me for what I'd done—not Shuman, the FBI, LAPD, or Luke—but Ben had come all the way to Holt's to express his gratitude in person.

"I guess you're the talk of the newspaper office," I said, smiling proudly.

"Oh, yeah," Ben said, nodding. "I sure am."

"Your editor must be thrilled with you," I said.

"Emotions are running high," he said.

"So how did it feel breaking such a big story?" I asked.

"You mean the story about the star-studded, red carpet event aboard a national historic landmark? The story about breaking up an international smuggling operation? The story about bringing down a murderer on the FBI's Ten Most Wanted List? Is that the story you're asking about?"

I started to get a yucky feeling in my stomach.

"I don't really know how it feels," Ben said, "because when all that went down, I was sitting in front of a fabric shop on Ninth Street."

The yucky feeling in my stomach got mega yucky.

"I've got to go," Ben told me. "My editor's assigned me to interview a guy who makes birdhouses out of chewing gum wrappers. Tomorrow I'm covering the opening of a sewage treatment plant. And after that, he's got me covering the cabbage cook-off at a senior center. But I wanted to come by and tell you thanks for the great tip. *Again.*"

Oh, crap.

The blue jeans were all finally tagged—thanks to Sandy and Bella's help—so I left work early. On the drive home, I called the Hyatt and asked to speak with Virginia. The clerk told me she'd checked out already. I figured she was on her way back to Charleston, anxious to sip sweet tea on her veranda again.

I called Marcie to see if she wanted to come over. I promised chocolate and beer but she told me no. She said I needed to rest. Marcie was right. Marcie was almost always right about things.

I went home and fell asleep for hours. When I woke up, I took a shower, pulled on sweats, dried my hair, and headed for my kitchen to find something to eat.

The only food in my house was a package of Oreos— my emergency stash—two slices of cheese, and half a loaf of wheat bread, so I grabbed my cell phone to order a pizza. The screen showed two missed calls and one voicemail. The two missed calls were from Shuman. I played the voicemail as I ripped open the bag of Oreos. It was from Ada.

"Haley, dear, I got a new Lexus—a convertible! Let's go cruising. Call me," she said.

I smiled as I punched in the phone number to Pizza Hut. So Ada wasn't upset with me, after all. Cool. Maybe she'd let me borrow the Lexus when I put my Honda in the shop.

My doorbell rang. Listening to the phone ring in my ear, I put my eye up to the peephole.

Ty.

Oh my God. Ty was here!

I threw the phone on the sofa and yanked the door open. He rushed inside, wrapped me in his arms, and swung me around. Then he kissed me, long and warm.

In the past few days I'd questioned my judgment about Tiffany and Ed—and Kirk, big time—but seeing Ty now, I knew I wasn't wrong about the things I felt for him.

"I missed you so much," he said, holding me tight against him, threading his fingers through my hair.

"I missed you, too," I said, gazing up at him. He looked a little tired, but really sexy in his suit. "This is the best surprise ever."

We kissed again. He pulled away, stepped outside, then came back in with his suitcase and a box.

"You came straight from the airport?" I asked.

He paused. "Is that okay?"

"Sure," I told him. I nodded toward the kitchen. "Are you hungry? I could make you an Oreo and cheese sandwich."

Ty grinned. Ty had a killer grin. My toes curled big time.

He closed the front door and placed his hands on my shoulders, holding me away from him.

"When I called you the other day, I told you I wanted to talk to you about something," he said.

Okay, that was weird. Ty wanted to talk first?

I got a yucky feeling in my stomach.

"So talk," I told him.

"You first," he said.

I must have given him a weird look because he said, "You told me there was something you wanted to talk to me about."

I did?

Oh, yeah, the whole yammering-about-the-economy thing. Honestly, it had bugged me while we were in London and every time that I'd thought about it since I'd gotten home. But seeing Ty now, feeling my toes curl at the sight of him, it didn't seem like such a big deal. Only a little deal.

Still, this was my chance and Ty had asked. I figured I should tell him.

"After we make love, you talk about the stock market and stuff like that," I said.

He frowned. "I do?"

"Yeah," I said. "It kind of bugs me."

His frown deepened. "I do? Really?"

I nodded.

Ty shrugged. "I'll do anything you want after we make love."

"Anything?"

"I'd prefer not to have to sing or dance," he said, "but yes, anything."

I smiled and he smiled, the kind of smile that ignored my toes and curled around my heart instead.

"Okay, your turn," I said.

I couldn't imagine that my worst fear would come true and Ty would tell me that he wanted to break up. Still, I braced myself.

"I want you to move in with me," he said.

I just stared at him.

"London wasn't the same after you left," Ty said. "I missed you so much. I don't like being without you. I want you to move in with me."

Oh my God. I couldn't believe what he was saying.

His cell phone rang. He ignored it. We stood looking at each other, neither of us saying anything. It rang again.

"Go ahead and answer it," I said, grateful for a few minutes to think. "I'll open the present you brought me."

I picked up the box he'd brought in with his suitcase.

Ty pulled his phone out of his jacket pocket to answer it, then said to me, "I didn't bring that. It was outside when I walked up."

My cell phone rang. I placed the box on my coffee table. It was brown cardboard. No shipping label, just my name printed on the top with a black marker. I checked the caller I.D. screen on my phone. It was Shuman.

"I've been trying to reach you for hours," he said, when I answered.

"I'll move to a new place, if you want," Ty said. He was still listening to his cell phone, but talking to me.

"So what's up?" I asked Shuman, as I got a steak knife from the kitchen.

"We can live wherever you want," Ty said.

"I tried to tell you last night but we got interrupted," Shuman said.

I sliced open the tape on the package.

"We'll buy new furniture," Ty said.

"Kirk Keegan," Shuman said.

I pulled back the flaps on the box. Inside was white packing paper.

"What about him?" I asked.

"His SUV was recovered," Shuman said. "He wasn't in it."

"So he's fish food?" I asked.

"The driver's window was down and the seatbelt was unfastened," Shuman said.

My fingers brushed the white packing paper in the box.

"We can keep the place I've got, if you'd like," Ty said, "and still get new furniture."

"So what are you telling me?" I asked Shuman.

"I'm telling you that Kirk Keegan might still be alive."

Slowly, I lifted the packing paper out of the box. Inside was a Sinful handbag. A note lay on top of it. I opened it and read, "Please give me another chance. Luke."

Oh, crap.